From: Delphi@ora⬛⬛⬛

To: C_Evans@athena.edu

Re: news reporter, Shannon Connor

Christine,

You know we've had our troubles with Shannon Connor. From the moment she was expelled from Athena Academy she's been nothing but a thorn in the sides of the students and grads of our beloved school. I've been following her closely for years, and this time she's gone too far.

Turns out, the news reports that made her a superstar were based on leads she received from an anonymous source. That source, I've discovered, was Arachne. Could Shannon have been so devious as to partner with our enemy? I'm not sure, but I intend to find out.

Arachne's death two months ago stopped the flow of information, but it seems it didn't stop her evil. She has at least one protégé who has reestablished contact with Shannon. I have a man shadowing our wily reporter. Whether Shannon knows it or not, she's going to help us finish this thing, once and for all.

D.

Dear Reader,

Every family has its black sheep and outlaws—even those wonderful women of Athena Academy. It's my pleasure to tell Shannon Connor's story, and to finally get all the details straight about everything that happened to her and how she came to attempt framing Josie all those years ago!

As you've seen throughout this series, Shannon is nobody's fool and isn't a pushover. She's been tracking Allison and the Athena women in the field, working the kidnappings and trying to find Marion Gracelyn's archenemy, Arachne. She's closing in on the truth, and this book deals with the price Shannon is prepared to pay to find out what's really going on. Even though she's not usually on Athena's side, Shannon has remained powerful and unwavering in the face of danger—just like all the Athena women she went to school with. Shannon hasn't strayed far from her roots, though she has at times used her powers for not-good!

In *Beneath the Surface*, Shannon meets hunky Rafe Santorini, a former CIA agent and friend to Allison Gracelyn, who's recovering from a year's incarceration behind enemy lines in North Korea. After being betrayed, Rafe isn't ready to give his heart away—but there's nothing as attractive as an Athena woman who has her eyes on the prize! He's never going to know what hit him.

Enjoy,

Meredith Fletcher

Meredith Fletcher

BENEATH THE SURFACE

ATHENA FORCE

Published by Silhouette Books

America's Publisher of Contemporary Romance

MAI 821 2-724

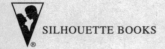

SILHOUETTE BOOKS

ISBN-13: 978-0-373-38981-0
ISBN-10:   0-373-38981-7

BENEATH THE SURFACE

Visit Athena Force at www.eHarlequin.com

Printed in U.S.A.

MEREDITH FLETCHER

maintains a healthy interest in travel and history. She's been to the top of Pikes Peak and to the bottom of Carlsbad Caverns. She's seen the Reversing Falls in St. John, New Brunswick (and eaten purple seaweed) and snorkeled plane crashes in Cozumel.

She comes from a large family and loves sitting at the table while everyone shares their stories. She's also an avid reader and movie enthusiast, enjoying every love story from *Casablanca* to *Spider-Man 3* (which she firmly maintains *is* a love story in spite of all the trappings of superheroes).

This book is dedicated to Alice Clary and Katie McNeil, who have reached for and captured dreams of their own.

And to Natashya Wilson and Stacy Boyd, who made it all happen.

Prologue

Athena Academy
Outside Glendale/Phoenix, Arizona
Fifteen years ago

"Shannon, you need to get up."

"Inaminute," Shannon mumbled automatically. There was something disturbing about the voice. It had a mom quality to it, but it definitely wasn't her mom. *Now isn't that interesting.*

Not that she was getting up. Nope, that wasn't going to happen. This was Saturday. At least she was pretty sure it was Saturday. She always slept late on Saturdays unless the academy had a field day or exercise scheduled.

"Shannon."

Instead of responding, Shannon curled up more tightly into her bed. She reached up and pulled her blanket over her head. The light was on in her room. That bothered her even more than the voice.

Who would turn on the light? Or had she left it on? She wasn't sure. She'd been too excited after her "special mission" last night to go to sleep immediately. Instead she'd stayed on the Internet, shopping for new clothes and a new way to do her hair. Her hair she could deal with, but new clothes were going to be impossible until—

Someone yanked the blanket off Shannon. And that was the last straw. Back home, when she'd been living with her older sister and younger brother, people had learned to give her space.

Usually finding space at home wasn't a problem because she was largely ignored. She wasn't as helpful around the house or as *precious*—whatever that meant, though Shannon had come to believe it meant passive—as her older sister and she wasn't Daddy's only son. They'd gotten all the attention, and Shannon had gotten all the space she'd cared for. In fact, sending her to the Athena Academy after she qualified had seemed an easy way for her parents to get her out from underfoot.

Thoroughly irritated now, Shannon cracked open her eyes. She glanced at the room's only window above her computer desk and saw that it was still dark outside. She might be awake in the middle of the night, but she didn't get up then.

"Hey," she protested. "What gives? This isn't one of those stupid fire drills, is it?"

"No. It's not a fire drill." The voice was losing some of its patient quality. The momness was coming through even stronger.

If Shannon had still been at home, the yelling would have started by now, and her mother would be telling her father how impossible Shannon was to deal with. And she would have been blamed by everyone in the family for whatever went wrong for the rest of the day.

"Get up, Shannon. We need to talk."

That voice—the one so carefully measured it sounded like a

military cadence—finally woke Shannon. That voice said she was in trouble.

Shannon hated being in trouble. Well, *mostly* she hated being in trouble. Sometimes trouble meant that she was getting the only attention she was going to get.

She twisted, shaded her eyes against the light and looked up at Christine Evans, the principal of Athena Academy. Principal Evans was almost fifty years old—at least that's what the rumors around the school claimed—and an ex-Army officer.

She'd lost her left eye in some kind of accident—everyone in school insisted it had happened in a military engagement and Principal Evans had killed a whole platoon of bad guys—and been appointed as principal of the academy by Senator Marion Gracelyn, the founding mother behind the special finishing school for girls. The principal and the senator had been friends for a long time.

Principal Evans was stocky from a lifetime of military work and a dedication to staying in shape rather than staying thin. Her short-cut gray hair offered more testimony to the fact that she didn't try to hide things.

Principal Evans wasn't hiding anything now. She was irritated. Big-time.

Okay. Chill. Buy some time. Shannon levered her legs over the side of the bed to show that she was willing to comply with the request but was too tired to do so immediately. She yawned. She stretched. She rubbed her eyes.

Then she noticed that Tory Patton was standing in the back of the room, near the door. Tory was naturally beautiful. She'd never had to work at it. Gifted with black hair, an olive complexion and green eyes, she turned the heads of boys everywhere she went. And she didn't even seem to care. It was enough to make Shannon gag.

Great. Tory Patton, one of my rivals. In my room. And I have probably the worst case of bed-head since bed-head was invented.

"What's she doing here?" Shannon demanded.

Principal Evans ignored the question. "Get dressed," she ordered. "You've got five minutes. Otherwise you're going in your robe."

"My robe?"

"Five minutes," Principal Evans repeated.

"Going where?"

"Start dressing or we can go now."

Witch, Shannon thought. But that was more a knee-jerk reflex to being awakened in the middle of the night. Normally Shannon got along with Principal Evans all right. Except for a few incidents involving hazing students new to the academy.

She bolted up from bed and dived at her chest of drawers. She wasn't going to be caught walking around the academy halls in a robe. As usual, she'd worn only a football jersey to bed. She'd told everyone her boyfriend had given her the jersey, but she'd actually stolen it from her little brother.

Tory wore boys' pajama pants, an academy T-shirt and was barefooted. Somehow on her it looked like an ensemble and a statement. Even underdressed, Tory still looked beautiful.

It's just not fair, Shannon thought again. Tory hardly had to do anything to look great in the television broadcasting class they were taking together. Shannon, while she was beautiful, still had to work to make it happen.

Arms filled with clothing, Shannon sprinted for the bathroom. Her roommate slept through the whole thing.

Minutes later, dressed in capris, good shoes and a crop top, Shannon walked at Principal Evans's side. Shannon had her arms crossed to show her displeasure but also because it was cold this time of year up in the White Tank Mountains, where the school was located.

Years ago the campus had been a mental-health and rehabilitation facility for movie stars who'd fallen off the wagon or gotten involved in drugs. Wealthy families had stashed their black sheep there.

The girls at the academy even told stories about serial killers and murderers that had been held in the older sections of the school. That made for some exciting walks late at night. Especially for the younger girls who were brought there for the first time. Shannon had enjoyed hazing the newbies with the stories of murderers loose on the grounds.

Many of the first-timers came there at age ten or eleven. The academy recognized potential prospects and sent letters early. The school was so prestigious that hardly anyone ever turned them down. The fact that the tuition was waived made the academy even more enticing.

On Friday and Saturday nights, after the fall semester started, the newbies usually got the full treatment from some of the other girls. Frightened squeals echoed throughout those older sections. Shannon had particularly enjoyed those times. She loved role-play and she was one of the best because she could always tell what would scare a new girl the most. It was almost as though she had a psychic ability to get inside an audience's head.

Principal Evans and her staff turned out to be real buzz-kills. They penalized everyone involved in *hazing* of that nature. Shannon didn't mind. The trade-off—a few days of detention for delicious moments of seeing a newbie totally wigging out—was worth it. The event was all theater, getting the complete, rapt attention of her victims, then being in the eye of the storm that swept out of administration.

"You still haven't told me what's going on," Shannon accused.

"You'll know soon enough," Principal Evans said.

Okay, Shannon thought as they crossed the grounds to the school's administration building, *so you've got me beat when it comes to scary-quiet attitude. That's fine. I'll let you have that one.* There were other ways to deal with adults.

Shannon called tears to her eyes. She could cry on cue. It was one of her best skills, and that little trick had earned her a lot of attention at home until her parents had either figured it out or just stopped caring. She still wasn't sure which it had been.

She swallowed hard, made her voice tremulous and looked at Principal Evans. "It's my parents, isn't it? Something's happened to my parents?"

Shannon was so good that she almost scared herself. Even though she was convinced that her parents didn't much care for her, she still loved them. She didn't want anything to happen to them.

Principal Evans was quiet longer than she would have normally been. Shannon wondered if she'd played the tear card once too often. But Principal Evans went for it anyway.

"No," the woman said. "Nothing's happened to your parents. As far as I know, they're both fine."

Shannon almost grinned in triumph. Not only had she created some sympathy in Principal Evans, but she'd also learned that her parents hadn't been called. Whatever trouble she was in—and she honestly couldn't think of what that trouble might be—it couldn't be that bad.

However, the trouble *was* bad. It had to be bad if Marion Gracelyn was there.

The senator had been waiting in Principal Evans's office. Marion Gracelyn was often at the school, but she'd never been there in the middle of the night, not that Shannon knew.

Marion Gracelyn was a beautiful woman. Her brown hair was shoulder-length and carefully coiffed, and her business suit was immaculate. Her brown eyes were intense, much more scary, actually, than Principal Evans's. Whatever was going on, the senator was taking it way too personally.

In that moment Shannon was pretty sure what the trouble was going to be about. Somehow Principal Evans had found out what Shannon was doing to Josie Lockworth.

Without a word, Principal Evans waved Shannon and Tory into chairs in front of the desk. Then she sat in the big chair on the other side and tapped her computer keyboard.

Senator Marion Gracelyn remained standing.

Seated there in Principal Evans's way-too-neat office and surrounded by proof that the woman had no life outside of what happened at the school, Shannon knew she was in more trouble than she'd ever been in. For the first time in a long time, she was scared.

The three of them—Shannon, Principal Evans, and Tory—watched the computer monitor on the desk. On-screen, Shannon broke into Josie Lockworth's gym locker. Lock-picking, not usually found on a high school curricula, was only one of the specialized skills taught at the academy. Shannon had turned out to be quite good at it.

The personal DVD player was plainly visible in Shannon's hand as she shoved it into Josie's locker. Then Shannon closed the locker and hurried off.

"As you know, Josie has been accused of stealing things around campus," Principal Evans said in her no-nonsense voice.

Shannon did know that. Everything Josie had been accused of stealing, Shannon had actually stolen and put in Josie's locker or room. Those things had been found during subsequent investigations.

Josie Lockworth had been intentionally targeted by Shannon's team the Graces. Upon arrival at the school, each new student was put with a team. Those teams weren't designed to be cliques. They were intended to be a small support system within the school.

The Cassandras—Josie's team—were led by Lorraine Miller. Everyone called her Rainy. She was Allison Gracelyn's strongest competition at the school, and everyone took the competition seriously. Way too seriously, in Shannon's view. But Shannon had gotten attention within Allison's group, the Graces.

"How could you do something so reprehensible?" Marion Gracelyn demanded.

Shannon tried to speak and couldn't at first. She'd never imagined getting caught. Josie had been chosen because she'd been the weakest link among the Cassandras. Her mother had been some kind of engineer for the Air Force. A spy plane she'd designed had failed during a test and killed several men.

Josie lived under that cloud and carried her mother's guilt around with her. Shannon figured that Josie would have cracked under the social stigma of being thought of as a thief. The last week that the "thefts"—Shannon didn't think of her borrowing other people's property as theft because everyone had gotten their things back once it was discovered Josie had them—had taken place, Josie had shown obvious signs of distress. She'd gotten more withdrawn than normal and couldn't seem to concentrate on her work. Not even math and physics, which were two of her most enjoyed subjects.

If you could take away the sheer love of math from Josie Lockworth, Shannon knew she was doing something. Still, part of her had felt bad for Josie. The other girl had never done anything to her. Under different circumstances, if she hadn't been part of Rainy's group and Allison hadn't been so jealous of Rainy, they might even have been friends.

"Who put the video cameras in?" Shannon asked.

"I did," Tory said. Her voice held a note of imperiousness and outrage. She could do a lot with a look and her tone of voice. That was why she got even better scores in the broadcasting classes than Shannon did.

"That was good," Shannon said. "I didn't think about that."

"Josie's my friend," Tory said in a hard voice. "She would have been your friend if you'd given her a chance."

That was probably true, Shannon admitted. But that wasn't how things were. Lines had been drawn and she'd had to choose her allegiances.

"Have you nothing to say in your own defense?" Marion Gracelyn asked.

Shannon remembered then that the senator had once worked in the district attorney's office in Phoenix. She'd had an impressive conviction rate. The pre-law classes at the academy talked about some of her cases.

"It wasn't my idea to frame Josie," Shannon said. She played her trump card. "It was your daughter's."

The Big Announcement—and that was how Shannon had thought of it since she'd first figured out how she was going to respond if she got caught framing Josie—didn't deflect the heat as much as Shannon had hoped. In fact, if anything, the Big Announcement only seemed to turn up the heat.

Marion Gracelyn had become even further outraged at the accusation of her daughter.

Shannon had offered to show them the e-mails that she'd received from Allison. They were all in a file Shannon had set up on her computer in her dorm room.

Everyone knew that Allison was a geek when it came to computers. She did everything on computers. All her free time was spent on them. She organized all the Graces on computers and PDAs, posted their schedules and outlined her expectations in terse, well-written e-mails that came in at all times during the day.

Allison's roommate even complained that Allison used a computer to wake her. Every morning, the roommate told them, Allison's computer would come on and speak like a Borg, one of the cybernetic/human hybrids that were the bad guys on *Star Trek: The Next Generation.*

Allison Gracelyn, Shannon knew, was a complete geek in

her mind, but she had the good looks and body of a runway model. Those were two perfectly good reasons to like her. And to be envious.

As it turned out, Allison was also more clever than Shannon would have believed.

After they'd all tramped back to Shannon's room with the academy coming to life around them, Shannon had logged on to her computer and brought up the file where she'd saved the e-mails from Allison.

The file was empty.

Panic settled into Shannon then. Josie hadn't been the only one who'd gotten set up. Shannon had gotten set up, too.

"I don't understand," Shannon whispered as she looked at the empty folder open on the computer monitor. "They were right here. All of the e-mails Allison sent me about framing Josie for the thefts."

"Why would my daughter do something like that?" Marion Gracelyn asked. She was definitely not happy.

"Because Josie would break," Shannon replied. The tears that rolled down her cheeks now were real. She was in a lot of trouble. She'd never, even in her wildest imaginings, thought she'd *ever* be in this much trouble. "Allison said we should frame Josie because she would crater."

"Why would Allison want that to happen?"

"Because Allison wanted to win the competition against the Cassandras."

Everyone knew about the rivalry between the Graces and the Cassandras. That was a thing of legend at the academy over the last few years. Rainy and Allison had always competed at everything. And everyone knew that Allison carried the competition further than Rainy did. Rainy just wanted to do her best and make everyone else raise the bar. Allison wanted—no, she *needed*—to *be* the best.

Shannon understood and respected that. She felt the same way.

"I can't believe Allison would do something like that," Marion Gracelyn countered.

But Shannon sensed the hesitation in the woman's words. Marion knew about her daughter's strong desire to beat Rainy.

Work with that, Shannon told herself. She tried to ignore the feelings of desperation that ate at her. *You can't get into any more trouble than Allison if you were only following orders. And they're not going to do anything to Allison.*

The problem was, in the end, that Shannon couldn't prove anything.

Allison flatly denied ever sending the e-mails. They'd never talked about the scheme around any of the other Graces. Or even among themselves, Shannon realized only then. Everything had been done through e-mail.

But that was how Allison did everything.

Principal Evans pointed out that the campus server would have created a log and kept track of all the e-mails sent through that server. Athena Academy kept all their computer hardware on-site and managed computer security.

Of course, once a computer interfaced with the World Wide Web, that security could be compromised. They all knew that.

Allison maintained her innocence so strongly and sincerely that Shannon was tempted to believe her, as well. She totally got why Allison didn't confess. Her mother's brainchild—the Athena program—would have been compromised. Millions of dollars in funding would have been at risk.

Shannon had heard all that while sitting outside Principal Evans's office. She knew that things weren't going to go well for her. She also knew there wasn't anything she could do about it.

Waiting outside that office had been hard. Shannon had wanted someone to rescue her. The stares of the other students—all of whom knew what was going on by that time because the grapevine at Athena was incredibly vigorous—were unbearable.

Traitor.

That word came up a lot.

Despite the fact that junior- and high-school-age girls brought with them huge amounts of personal problems and vendettas, everyone agreed that no one would have done what Shannon did.

By lunch Shannon had the same social standing as a plague carrier. She told herself that she could get through this. There had to be a way. No one could hate someone forever.

Could they?

By five o'clock the outcome had been decided. Principal Evans summoned her into the office. Marion Gracelyn stood at the window and looked out at the school. She didn't even turn around to acknowledge Shannon's presence.

"Have a seat, Shannon," Principal Evans said. She pointed to one of the chairs in front of the desk.

Knees weak and trembling, unable to speak, Shannon sat. She held her arms across her chest, but it wasn't out of defiance this time. It was simply to help keep herself together. She was afraid if she let herself go that she would shake to pieces.

"We've talked about this all day," Principal Evans said.

I know, Shannon thought with a trace of rebelliousness. *Who do you think was sitting outside your office, waiting?* But she didn't say anything. She didn't think her voice would work.

"This hasn't been easy." Principal Evans tried a reassuring smile, but it didn't come off very well. She looked more tired than Shannon had ever seen her. "This school is demanding. Of its administration and of its student body. We knew it would be when it was designed. We don't judge a student on her ability to do and understand the work. We trust that the ability and understanding will come in time in an environment like Athena Academy."

Get to it, Shannon wanted to say. Tell me I'm grounded. *Tell me what privileges I'm going to lose and for how long. Then let me get back to my room and disappear till this blows over.*

"What we cannot have here," Principal Evans said, "is anyone who doesn't hold to the higher moral ideals of the academy. What you've done isn't just irresponsible. You framed Josie with malicious intent."

To win a competition that Allison wanted to win, Shannon wanted to point out. But she couldn't.

"I can only hope that in the rest of your academic career you use this experience to make better choices," Principal Evans said.

Shannon almost breathed a sigh of relief. She could make better choices. She would. And one of the first choices she was going to make was to demand to be taken out of Allison's group. If that was how Allison was going to handle loyalty, Shannon didn't want to be around her. No matter how many cool points were involved in hanging with the senator's daughter and the academy's star student.

"Unfortunately," Principal Evans said, "the rest of your academic career isn't going to be at Athena Academy."

It took Shannon a moment to process what Principal Evans had said. "No," she said weakly. "*No.* That's not fair. You can't just kick me out."

"We can." Marion turned then. She was cold and distant. Shannon had never seen the woman like that before. In the past she'd always been understanding and kind. "You're here by invitation, Miss Connor."

Miss Connor? Shannon had never been addressed by Marion like that before.

"An invitation the academy can rescind at any time," Marion went on. "We have rescinded that invitation. Effective immediately. School staff are packing your room for you now. Your parents have been notified. You've already been booked on an evening flight. You'll be back home in Virginia by tonight. Your parents will meet you at the airport."

Shannon wanted to scream. She couldn't imagine going back to her parents or to that small house where it was so cramped she couldn't breathe. She'd been away from there for three years.

That place wasn't home anymore. That family wasn't her family anymore. Didn't anyone understand that?

Even though she wanted to speak and tell them again that she hadn't acted alone, that Allison was as guilty as she was and therefore just as deserving of being kicked out of the academy, Shannon couldn't. Her voice wouldn't work, and her throat hurt so badly that all she could do was cry as silently as she could.

"I'm sorry, Shannon," Principal Evans said.

She sounded so sincere that Shannon believed her. That only made things feel worse.

Chapter 1

Washington, D.C.
Now

The second time Shannon Connor talked with Vincent Drago, the freelance information specialist wrapped a hand around her neck, slammed her against a wall hard enough to drive the air from her lungs, put a gun to her head and told her, "I'm going to blow your head off for setting me up."

The first time she'd talked with him had been over the phone and she'd used an alias. Maybe if she hadn't started everything with a lie, things might have gone more smoothly.

"Wait," Shannon croaked desperately. *Wait? He's pointing a gun at your head, looking like he's going to use it, and the best you can come up with is* wait*?* She really couldn't believe herself. Maybe something was wrong with her survival instinct.

Other reporters—and friends—or what passed as friends,

acquaintances really—had sometimes suspected she had a death wish.

Shannon didn't think that was true. She wanted to live. She glanced around the small room in the back of the bar where Drago had arranged to meet her. Actually, he'd arranged to meet her up front. He'd just yanked her into the back room at the first opportunity.

Then he'd slammed her up against the wall and put the gun to her head. If she'd known he was going to do that, she wouldn't have shown up.

Judging from the low-life clientele the bar catered to and the fact that they were in the Foggy Bottom neighborhood only a few blocks from the Watergate Hotel, Shannon doubted that help would be forthcoming even if she could yell.

"Do you know how much trouble I'm in because of you?" Drago demanded.

"No," Shannon croaked around the vise grip of the man's big hand. "How much?" She'd been trained for years to ask open-ended questions. It was only the politicians that had to be restrained from climbing up on their soapboxes.

Vincent Drago wasn't a politician. He was a private investigator, only he called it "freelance information specialist."

From what Shannon had found out about the man, he had a shady career. Some of Shannon's police contacts had claimed the man sometimes worked for the government on hush-hush jobs. Others claimed that he was a semilegal blackmailer.

One of the people Shannon had talked to had told her that Drago had gone after a blackmailer preying on a presidential hopeful. When he'd gotten the evidence of the candidate's philandering with a young intern, Drago had put himself on the candidate's payroll.

Shannon knew that because she'd broken the story about the intern when the girl had come to her after the affair ended. The intern had come forward so she could claim her fifteen minutes of fame. Everybody wanted that.

Drago was six feet six inches tall and looked like a human bulldozer. The carroty orange hair offered a warning about the dark temper that he possessed. His goatee was a darker red and kept neatly trimmed. He wore good suits and had expensive tastes. He could afford them because he did business with Fortune 500 companies.

According to the information Shannon had gotten, Drago was one of the best computer hackers working the private investigation scene. The man was supposedly an artist when it came to easing through firewalls and cracking encryptions. He was supposed to be more deadly with a computer than he was with a weapon.

Shannon was pretty sure she wouldn't have felt as threatened if Drago had been holding a computer keyboard to her head. Of course, he could have bashed her brains out with it.

She held on to Drago's wrist with both of her hands and tried to reel in her imagination. Thinking about the different ways he could kill her wasn't going to help.

"Somebody found out about me," Drago snarled. Angry red spots mottled his pale face.

"You advertise in the Yellow Pages," Shannon pointed out. "People are supposed to find out about you."

"Somebody got into my computer." Drago looked apoplectic. "*My* computer! Nobody gets into my computer."

"You get into other people's computers. I've heard that's dangerous. That's why I came to you."

"I'm invisible on the Internet," Drago roared. He stuck his big face within an inch of Shannon's. "I'm a frigging stealth ninja."

Shannon couldn't help thinking that *stealth ninja* was pretty redundant. When a ninja killed someone, they weren't supposed to be seen. That was part of what made them a ninja.

"Who are you working for?" Drago slammed her against the wall again.

The back of Shannon's head struck the wall. Black spots danced in her vision. She tried to remember the last time she'd had her life on the line and thought it was during her coverage of the apartment fires that had broken out downtown. Nine people had died in that blaze. She'd very nearly been one of them.

But it hadn't seemed as scary then. She'd been with Todd, her cameraman, and he'd been rolling live footage. Every time the camera was on her, she was fearless.

Unfortunately neither Todd nor a camera were currently present.

Shannon held on to Drago's thick wrist in quiet desperation. Even standing on tiptoes, she could barely draw a breath of air.

"I'm not working for anyone," Shannon said.

"You work for American Broadcasting Systems."

"I told you that. I also told you this wasn't a story I was covering for the news station." That was true. Oddly enough, throughout her years as a reporter Shannon had discovered people believed lies more than truths. They just seemed to *want* to.

"Are you working for the government?" Drago asked.

"No."

"Because the Web sites I tracked the black ICE back to felt like federal government sniffers to me."

That was surprising. Shannon didn't know why the federal government would have been feeding her the information she'd been getting lately. Or before, for that matter.

"I don't work for the government," Shannon insisted. "I don't even know what black ICE is."

"Intrusion Countermeasures Electronics."

"How much do you think someone like me would know about stuff like that?" Shannon pulled her best frightened blonde look. Considering she was suspended and nearly choking to death, she figured she was inspired.

Her mind raced. She knew a physical confrontation with Drago was going to end badly. She was a foot shorter than he was and weighed about half of what he did. The room contained crates and cases of liquor. The single low-wattage bulb in the ceiling barely chased the night out of the room.

There was no help there, and nothing within reach that she could use as a club.

"I've seen you on television," Drago said. "I've seen you lie and wheedle your way into stories that other reporters couldn't get."

Despite being strung up against the wall, Shannon took momentary pride in her accomplishments. Getting recognized for something she'd done felt good. It always had.

"I knew I shouldn't have trusted you," Drago went on. He smiled, but there was no humor or warmth in the effort. "From the start I figured you were out to cross me up. But I bought into that blond hair and doe-brown eyes." He leaned down, a long way down, and sniffed her hair.

Shannon cringed and couldn't help closing her eyes. She hated being manhandled. It had never happened before, but she'd talked to rape and domestic-abuse victims enough to know that she was feeling the same thing they'd gone through. She resisted the urge to scream only because she thought if she did, he might kill her outright to shut her up.

"You sold me, baby," Drago whispered into her ear. "Hook, line and sinker. You had me with that teary-eyed look—"

Shannon didn't use that one often anymore, but she knew it almost guaranteed instant game, set and match when she did. She just didn't like appearing weak.

"And the way you told me you needed help to find a cyber-stalker."

Well, that was almost true.

"Who did you find?" Shannon had to struggle to keep from hiccupping in fear. The need to know what Drago had discovered almost leeched away the power her fear had over her.

"Have I told you this is a really bad part of the city?" Rafe Santorini lay back in the uncomfortable seat of the Ford Taurus he'd picked up to use for the night's surveillance. At six feet two inches tall, he couldn't quite get comfortable in the seat. His bad knee still ached and the gun on his right side kept digging into his hip.

"Yes," Allison Gracelyn replied. "Several times."

"Maybe I just haven't gotten through to you how bad this section is."

"I'm looking at it now."

That caught Rafe's attention. Challenged, he stared around the neighborhood. Since Allison was somewhere at her desk, currently—or so she said—in Fort Meade, Maryland, he knew she had to have some means of electronic surveillance.

Unless she was using satellite coverage. Knowing Allison as he did, Rafe wouldn't have put it past her, but he knew she was wanting to keep this op on the down-low. Whatever business he'd bought into, it was personal to her.

Allison was one of the best ELINT and SIGNIT people he'd ever worked with. Electronic Intelligence and Signals Intelligence were two huge fields in espionage. Usually a person didn't overlap in the job. Allison did.

"Tired of playing Where's Waldo?" Allison asked.

Rafe knew she'd caught him looking. "If I didn't have to watch the bar so closely, I'd find it."

"There's a drugstore on the northwest corner," Allison said.

Rafe squinted against the darkness and didn't look right at the drugstore. Peripheral vision was stronger and clearer at night than direct line of sight. He spotted the familiar rectangular bulk of the camera bolted to the second-floor corner of the building.

"Are you getting my good side?" Rafe asked.

"No. You're sitting on it."

Despite the long hours spent following his target around for the last few days, Rafe had to laugh. He'd met Allison in the flesh twice, but he'd worked with her a couple dozen times over the last five years. He'd been a field agent with the National Security Agency. Allison was tech support—on steroids. There didn't seem to be any computer system she couldn't hack or information packet she couldn't sniff out. She wasn't known for her humor, but—on occasion—he'd seen it.

Rafe turned his attention back to the seedy bar and rolled his watch over to have a look. It was 11:28 p.m. His target had gone inside—

"Seventeen minutes ago," Allison said. Her voice was quiet and controlled coming through the earwig he wore in his left ear.

It was creepy how she did that, but Allison was a queen at multitasking. Agents Rafe had talked to had been blown away by how she could enhance an op and build in rabbit holes when things went south.

"Seventeen minutes is a long time," Rafe said.

"If you're holding your breath, maybe."

"Vincent Drago isn't a nice guy."

"I know. That's why I asked you to look into this when I found out he was involved."

Maybe it would help if you would tell me a little more about what's going on, Rafe thought. But he knew she wouldn't. Agents learned to be careful with the knowledge they had. Information was currency of the realm for a spy, and they never spent it casually, even at home.

In the handful of years that Rafe had worked with Allison, three of them spent before he'd ever gotten a face-to-face with her, she'd never asked for anything. She didn't seem like the type. Her phone call to the rental house in Jacksonville, North

Carolina where he'd been recuperating for the past eight months, had been totally unexpected.

The fact that she was so grudging with the information had hooked him further. He'd known better, but he'd trusted Allison.

And you needed to get out of there, he reminded himself. *Don't forget that. That oceanside rental was becoming as much a prison as the other place.*

For a moment Rafe didn't see the seedy bar. He saw that small underground prison outside Kaesong, North Korea, where he'd been kept for five months. Cinder-block walls had threatened to crush him physically and spiritually every day. The long hours of torture and questions had rolled into one another until they'd become one long, unending nightmare.

The only reason he hadn't told his inquisitors what they'd wanted to know was because he hadn't known. He was certain they'd known that, too.

For a moment fear touched him intimately. It was strange how he'd accepted his death after the first few days of imprisonment yet had been more filled with fear after he'd returned home. Well, not home exactly. After being released from Walter Reed Hospital, he'd tried to go home and ended up renting that summer home in Jacksonville.

He'd gone armed every day. Even though he'd tried to sit in the sun and find that piece of himself that hadn't been shattered by his experiences, he hadn't been able to. He'd been more at home in the night and in the bars.

Come back, he told himself. *You're not there anymore. You're here. You're helping a friend. Stick with the program.*

The gnawing pain in his right knee helped him focus. He absently reached down and massaged it. Kneading the flesh was hard to do through the orthopedic brace he wore.

"Are you doing okay?" Allison asked.

Rafe was embarrassed and irritated at the same time. She'd

caught him. He didn't like dealing with weakness or infirmity. The injuries he'd sustained had kept him out of active duty.

"I'm fine," he said.

"Are you still taking your meds?"

Rafe blew out his breath slowly, aware that she'd be able to pick up the sound over the earwig if he didn't keep it quiet.

"Yes," he lied.

A buzzer rang in his ear.

"Wrong answer," Allison said. "I checked with Medical. You haven't refilled your pain pills. If you were using them the way you should have been, you'd have run out forty-one days ago."

Despite his irritation, Rafe had to grin. Only Allison would know so much. Or would even think she needed to know so much, he amended.

"The pills weren't working very well," Rafe said. But that was a lie. The pills had been working entirely too well. He'd only noticed that problem when he'd started using alcohol with them. When he'd caught himself doing that, he'd poured the pills down the drain and hadn't touched so much as another beer. He'd seen what liquor and pills could do to people.

"Maybe you need something different," Allison suggested.

Maybe I need to work again, Rafe thought angrily. Then he realized that Allison's favor had been a chance to do exactly that. He relaxed a little when he figured out that she wasn't passing judgment on him. She knew exactly what she was doing. More than that, she'd figured him out, too.

"Why are you smiling?" Allison asked.

"Man, that camera is good if you can see that well in the dark."

"I'm running a vision-enhancement-package upgrade on it that I designed. The software takes the available picture, repixelates it based on available light and light sources and reinterprets images."

"Very techie."

"Very techie," she agreed. "The hardest part was collapsing the size of the program so it would run in real time. By the way, you evaded the question."

"Have I told you how much I appreciate you letting me do this?"

"You're doing me the favor."

"Seriously, I think it's the other way around."

"Even if it turns out to be a glorified babysitting job?"

"If you'd thought it was going to be a glorified babysitting job, you wouldn't have asked me to look into this."

Allison sighed. "You're right. So stay sharp out there."

"I think I'm going to recon the bar." Rafe checked the pistol in its holster. When he thumbed the restraint aside, the weapon came free effortlessly. He opened the door and got out. The leg ached, but it moved easily and held his weight just fine. That was encouraging. Of course, that was with the leg brace—and the NSA wouldn't have cleared him for fieldwork while wearing it.

"Getting antsy?" Allison asked.

"It's been twenty-three minutes. Aren't you?"

"Twenty-two minutes. And, yes, I am."

Rafe pulled at the black beanie that covered his dark hair. Gold-lensed wraparound sunglasses covered his eyes. He'd left the semibeard he'd been growing the last few weeks. He wore jeans, boots and a loose gray chambray shirt over a Toby Keith concert T-shirt. Totally suburban ghetto rat. He blended into the neighborhood.

He tucked an expandable Asp baton into the holster on the left side of his belt. Closed, the baton was only seven inches long. Under his shirt it wasn't noticeable.

"Be careful in there," Allison cautioned.

Rafe smiled again as he crossed the street. "You've got my six. How much trouble can I be in?"

"The scary part is, I don't know."

Rafe thought about that. *I don't know* wasn't something often heard from Allison Gracelyn.

Chapter 2

Drago moved his hand up from Shannon's neck and grabbed her chin. He turned her face up to his. She felt his breath hot against her cheeks. He stared into her eyes. Once again she was reminded how lizardlike his green eyes were. They were cold and incredibly clear, like the eyes in a taxidermist's shop.

"You don't have a clue who you sent me after, do you?" Drago asked.

Shannon didn't answer. She hated to admit ignorance. The only reason people with secrets kept talking to her was because they wondered how much she knew of what they were hiding.

"It was somebody big," Drago said. "And they're buried deep within an infrastructure I couldn't even begin to get through. And I'll tell you right now that they don't build firewalls I can't get through. Not until this one."

Excitement escalated within Shannon. Over the last few years her mysterious benefactor had supplied tips regarding political cover-ups, insider trading, blackmail and other problems involving political and economic leaders. Truthfully Shannon owed a big part of her career to whoever that person had been.

Had.

Shannon didn't know why she kept thinking of the person in the past tense. There was nothing to indicate anything had happened to that person except for a months-long silence.

Until June, the contacts had been sporadic, but they'd been there. After weeks of wondering about it, and starved for a juicy story, Shannon had left New York City and taken a meeting with Vincent Drago. She'd hired him to investigate the traffic going on over her ISP. Shannon had covered stories about Internet tracking and the information that could be out there if someone knew how to look.

Vincent Drago was supposedly the best. The downside was his paranoia and violence. Scuttlebutt had it that he'd killed people.

He wasn't the kind of man Shannon would have ordinarily wanted to deal with, but he'd seemed the best for what she'd needed done. Now she found out he hadn't been able to track the messages either.

However, it was interesting that someone from the United States government—if Drago was correct—was involved. Her investigation was getting more fascinating all the time. She could almost see the consumer viewing points piling up. The story was going to be a good one.

If you live long enough to finish it, she told herself.

Drago's eyes raked hers. "You didn't know anything about any of this, did you?"

Shannon decided to go with the truth. "No. What branch of the federal government did you bump into?"

Drago laughed. "You don't know that either? Damn, you're not as intelligent as I thought you were, blondie. And I wasn't thinking you were overly gifted in the intelligence department to begin with."

Thanks for that. Shannon's anger nudged at her fear. She hated being taken for granted, ignored and downplayed because of her hair color. She was smart.

"Look," Shannon said calmly, "you don't have anything to worry about where I'm concerned. I'm not here trying to trap you. I wanted to know where those e-mail messages came from. That's all."

"Why did you come to me?"

"They told me you were the best."

Drago grinned, but again there was no mirth. "I'm flattered to hear that."

"It's not flattery." Shannon knew her throat was going to be bruised for days to come. "I needed the best. I was willing to pay. I did pay."

"You don't have any idea who wrote you those e-mails?"

"No."

Drago shook his head. "There's a lot of juicy information contained in them."

"I know."

"Most of them tie to stories you cracked on the news channel."

Shannon knew that, too. "I wasn't able to prove everything."

"Did any of the people you took down know about these e-mails?"

"No."

"Did you ever stop to wonder where they came from?"

"Yes. All the time. I couldn't get any information."

"But you just kept using the leads."

Shannon shrugged. "They were good. Why shouldn't I? Those people I went after? They needed to be exposed."

"But why?"

"Because the public deserves to know."

Drago snorted derisively. "Save it for the sound byte on the autobiography, blondie. It doesn't wash with me. Those people you took down, they could have paid blackmail for the information you were given. As a matter of fact, I'd be willing to bet my eyeteeth they were."

Shannon had guessed that, too. She really wasn't stupid.

Drago traced a forefinger along Shannon's chin. "Do you know why a blackmailer would give up a cash cow? And most of these people *were* cash cows."

"Because they stopped paying?"

"Very good, blondie. And to make an example for other people that are being blackmailed." Drago smiled. "But there's one other reason."

Like a good captive audience, Shannon waited. *Maybe you can ooh and aah and gush over how smart he is and he'll let you go.* She was prepared to do that if she had to. As to the other reason, she'd already thought of that, too.

"A blackmailer would burn a victim if it somehow netted him more," Drago said. "Did you ever think about looking into what these people had in common?"

Shannon had. She'd looked. There were so many and they were so disparate that she hadn't been able to get a handle on a theory.

"I thought you could just find whoever was giving me the information," she said. "That seemed to be the easiest way." That way had also seemed the most dangerous. That was why she'd exhausted every avenue open to her before she'd gone to a major creep like Drago.

"If the Feds hadn't wanted in on the play, it probably would have been," Drago agreed. "Whoever you're after is good at computers, but I'm better. I would have beaten that firewall."

"I can pay you more," Shannon offered. Greed was always good leverage.

Drago shook his head. "Sorry, blondie. But this looks like the end of a beautiful relationship." His eyes dropped to her cleavage. "Having you around to tie me to this thing isn't my idea of fun."

Shannon's fear crystallized inside her in that moment.

"I've got to tell you," Drago said, "I think it's a damn waste."

A million questions popped into Shannon's head. She'd always experienced that when new situations and people had come her way. That tendency was one of the qualities that had propelled her television career. She wasn't one of those reporters that simply regurgitated scripted questions and punch lines.

How can you just kill me? What makes you think you're going to get away with it? Is it that easy for you to kill someone? How many people have you killed? How did you kill them? Why hasn't someone caught you? How are you planning on killing me? What are you going to do with my body?

When she got to the last two questions, Shannon knew she was thinking *way* too much. She needed to be moving.

"Bye-bye, blondie." Drago smiled and his finger tightened on the trigger.

When Rafe entered the bar, he got the immediate sense that he'd invaded a private party. Every eye in the place turned toward him.

The bartender stood behind the scarred bar on the other side of the room. He had one bar towel slung over a shoulder and used another to dry beer mugs. He was a big, wide guy, an athlete that had gone to seed. The football pictures above the liquor bottles on the wall behind him offered a clue as to which sport he'd played.

"We're closed, mac," the bartender said.

Rafe looked at the other occupants of the room. There were three of them. They were all in their late twenties and early thirties. Their attire wasn't far removed from his. One of them wore a Hispanic kerchief wrapped around his head.

All of them gazed at him with predatory interest.

Shannon Connor was nowhere in sight.

"Door's open," Rafe responded. He pointed to the window. "Sign's still on." He spread his hands. "Look I only want a beer. I just climbed out of one of the warehouses down on the river. My boss nominated me to repack a few shipments going out in the morning. I'm hot. I'm tired. And I'm dry."

"Sorry, mac," the bartender said. "Like I told you, we're—"

"Hey, Tommy," the oldest of the men sitting at the small tables called out. "Man just wants a beer. Ain't nothing. Don't be a chump."

Grudgingly the bartender looked at Rafe. "What kinda beer do you want?"

"Bottle. Domestic. As long as it's cold, I don't care."

The bartender reached below the bar and brought up a longneck. He placed it on the bar without a word.

Rafe looked at the man at the table. "Can I get you something?"

"Thanks. I'm good."

Rafe dug in his pocket and brought out a thin roll of cash. "How much?"

"Four bucks."

"Pretty steep for a working-class neighborhood, ain't it?" Rafe peeled off a five and dropped it on the bar. "Keep the change."

The bartender made the five disappear without a smile. Evidently he wasn't big on repeat business.

"So," the guy at the table said, "you working down at the docks?"

"Yeah." Rafe twisted the top off the bottle and tossed it into a plastic bowl on the bar. He turned his back to the bartender because he could track the man in the reflection of neon-washed glass overlooking the street.

"That's hard work," the man said.

Rafe shrugged and took a long pull on his beer. "I've had worse. Had better pay, too." He grinned.

The man grinned back at him. One of the other guys laughed. "You from the neighborhood?"

Rafe shook his head. He tried to figure where Shannon Connor was and whether she was in any kind of trouble.

"Hanging with a friend for a couple months. Just till I get some cash up. The last girlfriend I had cleaned me out. Packed up my stuff, emptied the bank accounts and took off with my best friend."

"Ouch, dude," one of the other guys said. "Not exactly a happy camper."

"I've had better days," Rafe said. The story was actually true, but it had happened three years ago. He'd learned his lesson. Women and a job that meant long out-of-the-country trips really didn't work out.

He hadn't tried for anything steady since, but he hadn't been completely put off toward women. It wasn't their fault. The job was hard, and he wasn't extremely skilled at relationships.

In the window reflection, the bartender glanced at the clock over the bar. "Maybe you could take that beer for a walk."

Rafe grinned and shook his head at the guy at the table. "Man, I don't understand why Tommy here doesn't play to a full house every night."

The guy at the table laughed. "You're right. But so is he. It'd be better if you finish up that beer."

"Hospitality's about to run dry, I guess." Rafe wondered what was going on.

"Okay," Allison said in his ear, "now I'm definitely getting antsy."

Rafe was, too.

"Don't mean to push you out the door," the man at the table said. "You come around here another night, I'll buy you a beer myself."

"I'll hold you to that." Rafe upended the bottle and drained it. He placed it on the counter as he turned to face the bartender. "Got a men's room around here, Tommy?"

"Got the alley out back," the bartender said. "Just look out you don't hit any bums. They come up swinging sometimes."

"You're a funny guy," Rafe said.

A piercing scream rang out from the back room.

Rafe glanced toward the back of the bar.

"Sure wish you hadn't stuck around long enough to hear that," the guy at the table said. He reached under his jacket and Rafe knew he was going for a pistol.

Chapter 3

Before Drago could pull the trigger on the pistol, Shannon kicked him in the crotch. The big man staggered back and remained standing.

That surprised Shannon. She'd felt certain the kick would have put Drago on the ground. Seeing him still standing wasn't good.

Drago cursed at her and tried to take aim again.

Moving on instinct, Shannon grabbed her opponent's hand in both of hers. She wrapped his thumb with her left hand and wrapped his pinkie with her right. She pulled and twisted, hoping to break either the finger or the thumb.

Despite the hold she had on him, Drago was simply too strong. He curled his hand into a fist again and nearly trapped her hands. The whole time he cursed at her.

Adrenaline slammed into Shannon. She soaked it up, knowing it would help her only momentarily, then leave her weak.

Instead of trying to maintain her grip and lose the battle only a little slower, Shannon kicked Drago in the crotch again. He partially blocked her with a thigh, but she still struck home. Another yelp escaped his bared fangs.

Panicked now as the pistol swung back toward her, Shannon let go with her right hand and raked her nails across Drago's face. Bloody furrows opened up across his right cheek and eye. She thought she might have gotten him *in* the eye, as well.

He screamed and it came out unbelievably high-pitched. But he stumbled back and fired the pistol. The report sounded incredibly loud in the enclosed space. Partially deafened, Shannon turned and fled to the door.

Be open! she thought frantically. She couldn't remember Drago locking the door. Her hand closed around the doorknob. She twisted and yanked. The door came open in a rush.

Another shot banged out and a vibration shivered through the door. A hole opened up only a few inches from Shannon's head. She shoved through the door and stumbled out into the hall.

High-heeled sling-backs are so *not made for running.* Shannon still gave her effort her best, though. Out in the hall, she kicked out of them and ran barefoot. *I can come back for the shoes. Right now I just need to find a cop.*

Gunfire broke out ahead of her.

The bartender went for something under the bar. Rafe pulled the expandable baton from its holster, pressed the release button and felt the weapon chug as it moved instantly from seven inches in length to sixteen.

"Rafe," Allison said. "What's going on?"

"Butt out," Rafe said. "I'm busy." Praying that his knee held together and the brace kept it strong, Rafe twisted around and smashed the baton across the bartender's wrists.

A cut-down double-barreled shotgun dropped from the

bartender's hands. Rafe only caught sight of the weapon for an instant. The bartender tried to back away. With the baton's extended reach, Rafe leaned over the bar only slightly and whipped it against the side of the man's head.

The bartender's eyes rolled up into his head and he sat down hard. Rafe would have been willing to bet that the man was out before his butt hit the floor.

In the mirror, Rafe saw that the man at the table had gotten his gun out.

The man didn't offer a chance for last words or even spend any of his own. He pointed the pistol, not even bothering to aim.

Rafe dived over the bar and hoped it was made of good wood. His leg quivered, and he thought for a moment it was going to buckle under the effort and his weight. His rehab trainer had told him the knee was going to come back slow.

He didn't quite clear the bar, but he managed to get up on top of it. He rolled across as the guy tracked him with the pistol. Bullets missed him by inches. He rolled over the edge and dropped.

More bullets pounded the bar but didn't penetrate. Bottles behind the bar shattered. Alcohol leaked down from the shelves and pooled on the floor. The worst of it was the broken glass. Slivers embedded in Rafe's flesh and raised dots of blood.

He ignored the pain and lunged for the shotgun. His hands curled around it and his finger came to a rest on one of the double triggers. Instead of trying to rise up and become a target, he stayed prone.

The man at the table called out to Rafe. "You still alive back there?"

Rafe didn't answer. *C'mon. Step out here and give me a target.*

"You moved too quick, buddy," the man said. "Tells me you come in here expecting trouble. You ain't no dockworker."

Rafe watched both ends of the bar. He caught a glimpse of movement at the end that fronted the hallway leading back to the bathrooms and storage area. Allison had also uploaded blueprints of the bar to the notebook computer he had in the car.

A quick swivel brought the shotgun muzzle around to cover the spot. He almost pulled the trigger when he spotted the face peering around the corner. Then he caught sight of the blond hair.

Shannon Connor stared at him with fear-rounded eyes.

"Get out of here!" Rafe ordered. "Run!"

She fled at once, and bullets tattooed the corner of the wall where she'd been standing.

Shoe leather scraped the wooden floor at the other end of the bar. Rafe tracked the noise with the shotgun, leveled it with a snap and squeezed the trigger.

The swarm of pellets slammed into the chest of the young man drawing a bead on Rafe. The impact knocked him backward. He continued the fall to the floor without a sound.

An alarm sounded in the back. Rafe assumed Shannon Connor had escaped through the rear door. The alarm was from a panic bar.

The man who'd been sitting at the table cursed. More bullets hammered the bar.

"I'm alive and mobile," Rafe said out loud. He knew Allison would be wondering. He didn't know how she sat on the other end of the connection without saying a word. "Shannon's running for it. Out the back way. See if you can find her for me while I get out of here."

"I will," Allison said.

Rafe found he was more concerned about the woman than he was about himself. He'd been through similar situations in the past. As far as he knew, this was Shannon Connor's first gunfight.

When she'd seen the man lying on the floor with the shotgun so near another man who was dead or unconscious, Shannon's panic had buried the needle and she'd gone on overload. She'd taken martial arts while at Athena Academy and had liked them well enough to keep up her abilities by visiting several dojos in different disciplines. She'd never stayed with any one long enough to get a black belt, but she knew she could take care of herself.

She whirled back from the corner of the wall and heard bullets strike it. By then she was running barefoot for all she was worth. She flew past the opening door where Drago was attempting to stumble out.

As she reached the back door, she swung a hip forward and crashed into the panic bar. The emergency alarm screeched to life immediately. Then she was out in the alley.

The air was muggy and still. Fog off the Potomac River, which had given the neighborhood its name, streaked the night.

She turned to the right, judging that street was closer, and ran. The asphalt lining the alley tore at her feet. She ignored the pain because she knew Drago and the other men would be following. She had no doubt about that.

There in the darkness, Shannon wished she could find a policeman. Or her car. Either would be fine.

Rafe grabbed a bottle of whiskey that had fallen to the floor and miraculously hadn't broken. Still lying on his side, he laid the shotgun over the crook of one arm, grabbed the bottle, opened it, poked a bar towel into the long neck and turned the bottle upside down.

The alcohol poured out and soaked the bar towel. A small pool grew under the upended bottle.

"I think maybe we should talk about this," the man called out.

"I'd be happy to." Rafe fumbled in his pants pocket for the Zippo he carried. He wasn't a smoker. But every good field agent always kept something on his person for starting fires.

"Could be we got off on the wrong foot."

"It's possible. I got two left feet." Rafe knew the man was waiting for Vincent Drago to come from the back. If the man did, they could catch him in a deadly crossfire.

Rafe didn't intend to wait around for that to happen. He flicked the lighter and held the flame to the alcohol-soaked bar towel. A blue-and-yellow flame crawled up the material immediately.

"Are you a cop?" the man asked.

Now we have time for Twenty Questions? Rafe couldn't believe it.

"No." With a quick twist, Rafe lobbed the Molotov cocktail he'd made over the bar and in the general direction of the men.

"Get down!" a man yelled.

Rafe shoved himself to his feet. There was less pain than he'd expected, but it was growing sharper and biting deeper. On the other side of the counter, the whiskey bottle shattered. The alcohol caught fire with a distinctive *bamf.*

During the confusion, Rafe stood and raised the shotgun to his shoulder. As soon as he saw the big man spinning toward him, Rafe blasted the man with the final shotgun round.

The big man sailed backward and dropped bonelessly into the fireball taking hold on the floor. Rafe wiped his prints from the shotgun and scooped the baton from the floor. He assumed Allison would want a clean crime scene. And if he was questioned about his involvement by law enforcement officials later, he had some latitude in the story he'd tell.

A quick rap and a push collapsed the baton. He replaced it on his belt as he drew his pistol and pointed it at the last surviving bar patron.

"Don't shoot! Don't shoot, man!" The third man threw his pistol across the room and laced his hands behind his neck as he hit his knees.

He's got prior knowledge of the position, Rafe thought. He spun and went to the hallway Shannon Connor had come from. He paused at the corner. His leg functioned smoothly enough, but the pain was aggravating.

No one was in the hallway.

Rafe locked his hands in the familiar push-pull grip he'd been trained to use with a semiautomatic pistol and went forward in profile. His steps were smooth and controlled, as if he hadn't been gone from the work for almost two years.

Perspiration trickled down his forehead and into his eyes. Some of it was caused by tension, he knew, but some of it came from the pain in his knee.

He crept up on the storage room door. If Shannon had come from back there, it stood to reason that she wasn't alone. And Vincent Drago hadn't put in an appearance.

When he whirled around the door frame and peered inside, though, the room was empty. He hurried on to the alley and peered in both directions. There was no sign of Shannon or Drago.

Damn it.

"You there?" Rafe asked Allison.

"Yes."

"They're in the wind."

"Get your car." Allison's voice sounded crisp and calm. During the years Rafe had worked with her he'd never seen her lose it.

Rafe hesitated only a second. Was she telling him to get the car because she didn't trust his leg to hold up? Had this been a mercy mission after all?

And if it was, what the hell had gone wrong?

He growled a curse and went back through the bar. The third man was long gone, but that was fine. Loyalty wasn't a big requirement among the crowd Drago ran with.

"Put the fire out," Allison said. "According to the fire code, there's a fire extinguisher behind the bar."

Rafe complied automatically. He'd noted the fire extinguisher himself while he was behind the bar. Allison's thoroughness didn't surprise him. Agents' lives depended on her eye for detail and quick thinking while in the field. He'd been trained that way himself.

"What about the woman?" he asked.

"I'm searching. I'll find her. You'll need transport to get her clear."

"I'm not going to leave her in the lurch."

"Neither am I."

Rafe knelt and felt his knee burn with the effort. He barely kept a cry of pain to himself. This was why Medical wouldn't put him back in the field. And part of the pain was because he avoided putting too much pressure on the leg. He didn't want it to come completely apart on him again.

"What about the local police?" He grabbed the fire extinguisher, pulled the pin, aimed the nozzle at the fire and squeezed.

White foam enveloped the alcohol blaze. The flames went out at once. Only a black scorch mark and a few tendrils of smoke remained.

"The police are on their way," Allison said calmly. "You have no cover for this op."

Rafe figured that from the quiet way Allison had contacted him.

"If you get caught, we both burn for this one," she added.

"So I won't get caught. And if I did, I wouldn't give you up. That's not my way." Rafe felt a little angry. After North Korea, she should have known that.

"I know. I was just mentioning the stakes."

"Find Shannon." Rafe caught his slip too late. He couldn't believe he'd referred to the woman by name. But over the past three weeks of observing her in New York, then following her here, he'd felt as if he'd gotten to know her.

He'd even started wondering what it would be like to talk to her. They had a lot in common. Shannon Connor had her work and didn't invest anything in her social life. She'd had a boyfriend, according to Allison's files, but that evidently wasn't still going on.

Sometimes he'd even fantasized about inviting her to dinner. After all, she wasn't a hardened criminal or a foreign agent. As far as he could tell, Shannon Connor was just a woman in trouble. His impulse was to keep her safe. And he definitely couldn't have told Allison that was going on.

Face it, he told himself. *You may be washed up for fieldwork. Physically you're still a wreck. And you're supposed to keep emotional distance.*

That scared him. He didn't know what he was going to do if he didn't have his work. The last few months had nearly killed him. He didn't like thinking about what might have happened if Allison hadn't called.

After wiping the fire extinguisher down, Rafe jogged through the door toward his car. Sirens screamed into the night. A crowd of people from another bar and a pizza place flooded two street corners under street lamps.

"I'm gonna have to lose the car," Rafe said as he swiveled and slid behind the seat. "There are too many potential witnesses. And cameras."

"The car's not going to be a problem. I can make the car disappear." Allison's voice calmed. "I found your target."

Rafe pulled the transmission into Drive and dropped his foot onto the accelerator.

Chapter 4

Shannon ran down the street. She still didn't remember where her car was. Everything looked different, and she was so scared she couldn't think straight.

During her career as a reporter she'd been in some tough places. She'd seen death up close and personal. Facing that had been hard, and it had touched her more deeply than she would have admitted to anyone. She didn't like being weak.

Memory of the man behind the bar raced through her thoughts. The beanie and the wraparound sunglasses hid most of his face, and she'd been too wigged out to get a good look at him, but she felt certain she didn't know him.

Maybe that didn't have anything to do with you, she thought grimly. *That bar isn't exactly a hub for law-abiding citizens. Especially not if Drago was going to be able to kill you in the back room.*

A yellow cab rounded the corner and came down the street.

Shannon stepped out of the shadows and waved frantically. She was so close to the cab she thought it was going to hit her. Desperate, she stood her ground. Even though she didn't want to, she closed her eyes.

Tires shrieked on the pavement.

Thank God! When she opened her eyes, Shannon found the cab had come to a stop only inches from her.

"Hey, lady," the driver snarled. "What the hell do you think you're doing?" He was an Asian man of indeterminate age, dressed in a short-sleeved khaki shirt. A hula girl danced on the dashboard beneath swinging fuzzy dice.

"I need a ride." Shannon started to go around the front of the cab.

"Yeah, well, I got that. Hasn't anyone ever told you how to hail a cab?"

Ordinarily Shannon wouldn't have let the insult pass. No one got the better of her in an argument. She rounded the corner of the cab and headed for the back.

A line of holes suddenly appeared in the cab's windshield. That appearance was followed almost immediately by the harsh cracks of gunfire.

Though she knew she shouldn't, Shannon couldn't help glancing over her shoulder as she squatted down beside the cab. She'd been in enough combat zones in Iraq and, lately, Kestonia to know gunshots when she heard them.

Evidently the cabdriver had experience, as well. He ducked down behind the steering wheel, shoved the transmission into Reverse and floored the accelerator.

"No!" Shannon couldn't believe it. She tried to hang on to the door handle, but she almost lost her balance and went face-first onto the ground. "No! Don't leave!"

The cabdriver never even looked back. He managed a three-point turn that left the tires smoking.

Shannon got a brief glimpse of the frantically dancing hula girl and the wildly swinging dice, then the cab vanished around the corner. She stayed low and headed for the side of the street.

Drago ran at her. His efforts to reload his pistol only slowed him a little.

A solid line of buildings trapped Shannon out on the street. Bullets chewed at the sidewalk beneath her feet. Sparks flashed at every contact. The whines of the ricochets whined in her ears. She wrapped her hands around her head. Then she ducked into a deep-set door alcove of a cabinetry shop. Her heart hammered in her chest as she listened to Drago's steps close in on her.

She was out of places to run.

Tense and frustrated, fighting to remain calm, Allison Gracelyn sat in the ergonomic chair at her desk and watched the action playing out on the three computer monitors in front of her. This was one of those times when it was hard to remember that she was in a position to help.

Allison hadn't slept in thirty-seven hours. A scrunchie held her brunette hair back. Her brown eyes burned with the effort of watching the computer screens. She was slim and athletic despite years spent in front of a computer. She was disciplined enough to keep her physical health as sharp as her mental faculties.

She'd learned that at Athena Academy all those years ago and maintained the practice. She wore yesterday's business suit, but the jacket lay on the couch at the back of the office where she sometimes caught naps on ops that ran long.

All three monitor feeds came from street cams she'd "borrowed." One monitor showed Shannon hiding in the doorway. Another showed Drago from behind. The third showed Rafe Santorini desperately weaving through traffic.

"Left at the next block," Allison directed.

"You've still got her?"

"I do."

On the screen, Rafe made the turn. He was going too fast to make the turn cleanly. The tires broke traction and the vehicle drifted a few feet.

"I thought I heard gunshots," Rafe said.

"You did. She's all right. I have her on-screen. But you need to hurry." Allison cursed herself for that. Rafe knew he had to hurry. Her frenzy was unprofessional.

But you put them both in harm's way, didn't you? Allison had to acknowledge the guilt and shelve it for later. *You knew going in that Drago was going to kill Shannon.*

Allison had intercepted the e-mail when Drago had received it yesterday. There had been plenty of time to warn Shannon Connor.

But you chose not to do that, didn't you?

Even right now, as she watched the tragedy that was about to unfold, Allison didn't know if Shannon was about to become a victim because of the residual animosity that remained from all those years ago at Athena Academy or because Allison had been too confident.

Allison tapped the keyboard, dropping the camera as Rafe headed out of view. She picked him up with the next. Even though she couldn't see his features on the other side of the darkened windshield, she knew he had his mad face on.

Get there, Allison said silently.

"Ahead. On the left."

Rafe recognized the metallic tightness of panic hovering in Allison's voice. Unaccustomed as it was, her tension put him a little on edge. He breathed out and raked the street with his gaze.

"Do you see her?" Allison asked.

With all the neon lights, pedestrians and cars on the street,

Rafe had a hard time spotting Drago and Shannon Connor. It got a little easier when he noticed the cars and pedestrians gave the left side of the street wide berth.

"Got Drago," he said.

Drago jogged toward a doorway.

"Where's Shannon?"

"She's in the shop doorway. It's recessed."

Rafe knew he didn't have time to get out of the car to intercept the man. Besides that, with the way his knee was hurting, he wasn't sure how much mobility he'd have. It already felt as if it was swelling.

Instead he switched off the headlights and aimed the car at Drago. He hoped that Shannon didn't step out of the doorway at the wrong time.

Even driving far too fast for street conditions, Rafe barely arrived in time. Drago had reached the doorway and was raising the pistol. He was so intent on his prey that he didn't hear the car bearing down on him.

Rafe hit the horn. The strident noise rang out and drew Drago's attention. At that moment Rafe switched the lights back on. He hoped they would stun Drago and present a warning to Shannon to stay put.

Drago knew he couldn't run, but he was a predator. He didn't give up. He turned the pistol in the direction of the car and fired. Two shots tore through the windshield. One of them ripped the passenger seat headrest into a flurry of padding that filled the car's interior.

Rafe stayed on track. He put the car in close to the wall. His side mirror disappeared in an explosion of twisted metal and shattered glass. Then the whole side of the car turned into a stream of rushing sparks that bounced off the window and trailed behind him.

At the last minute Drago tried to break and run. He didn't even get turned before the car struck him.

The air bag exploded into Rafe's face at the same time. The gunshot of propellant setting off temporarily deafened him. His face stung from the impact and he was blinded.

Shut it down, shut it down, he told himself. He put his foot over the brake and shoved. The antilock braking system kept the tires from locking up as he slewed around. He hit another object and felt certain from the weight and mass involved that it was a car. He remembered there'd been a line of them.

There was a sickening moment of not knowing what was going on, then the car came to a stop. The smoky haze left by the air bag deploying burned his nose and mouth, then his lungs. The gunpowder taste was all too familiar.

His face and chest felt as though he'd gone rounds with a heavyweight. He had no doubt that bruising would show in a few days.

"Are you there?" Allison asked.

"Yeah." Rafe reached into his jeans and took out a small lock-back knife. A quick flick of his thumb deployed the blade. He pierced the air bag and it deflated in a rush. By the time he got out of the car, he had his pistol in hand.

Drawn from her hiding place, Shannon watched the maniac driver force the door of his vehicle open. It screeched as it yawned wide.

At first Shannon had thought her salvation had been luck. In this part of Washington, D.C., there were plenty of bars. It would have been easy to believe a drunken driver had come along fortuitously.

Not that Shannon's luck ever really ran that way. She wasn't the lucky one in any group. She'd had to work for everything she'd gotten. Whatever luck she'd had had gone away while she was at Athena Academy.

Then, when she recognized the man stepping out of the car as the man from Drago's bar, she knew her luck was running true to form. She held her position even though every nerve in her screamed, *Run!*

The man limped a little, but he moved quickly and efficiently. He kept the pistol in his hand close to his side as he surveyed the street.

Several curious pedestrians hovered along the sidewalk. Three young men hurried over to Vincent Drago's body lying a hundred feet from where the car had hit him.

"Get away from him," the man ordered.

"He's hurt," one of the onlookers yelled back.

The man lifted the pistol as he stepped into the headlights of his car. "Get away from him. *Now!*"

"Dude, that guy's got a gun," one of the other pedestrians said. He grabbed his friend's arm and pulled him back.

Go, Shannon told herself. *Get out of here while you can.* But she couldn't move. The story hadn't finished. Her reporter's instincts and curiosity refused to let her budge.

The man walked to Drago and pointed the pistol at the prone man. For a moment Shannon thought the stranger was going to shoot Drago on top of hitting him with the car. She couldn't help wondering what the man had against Drago.

Then the man knelt and quickly ran his free hand through Drago's clothing. He took out a wallet and a PDA, a few papers and anything else he could find. He removed his beanie and tucked everything he'd collected inside the hat. Then he stood.

It didn't make any sense to Shannon. Robbers didn't commit their crimes by taking out victims with cars.

More than that, why had the man left the bar looking for Drago? Shannon's curiosity was in full bloom.

The man returned to the car long enough to stash the beanie in the backseat while police sirens filled the air. Flashes from brave onlookers using the camera function on their phones flickered along the sidewalk.

Ignoring the fact that he was getting his picture taken, the man turned his attention to Shannon. He walked toward her. The pistol was still naked in his fist.

Shannon pushed out of the alcove and started to run. She didn't know how far she'd get before a bullet punched through her back.

"Shannon!" the man called. "Don't run!"

She kept waiting for the "or I'll shoot" addendum. It didn't come.

"Please."

That was even more surprising.

"If you run," the man said, "they might get you."

They?

"I can help you."

The sirens sounded closer. Shannon looked around the street. Only then did she realize how much trouble she could be in. The police would want to know what she was doing there. If she told them she'd employed Drago, which might be something they learned anyway, she was going to be buried in legal difficulties.

She didn't know enough about what was going on to feel safe. Not only that, but Drago had been convinced that the federal government was interested in the inquiries she'd asked him to make.

It wasn't a good position to be in. There would be a lot of questions, and she wasn't liked by many in the police departments or political offices. In fact, she'd covered a story for ABS three years ago concerning politically motivated murders that had involved a particularly offensive cover-up.

The District of Columbia Police Department and the Hill had gone ballistic when she'd broken the story without their approval. She'd barely escaped town one step ahead of the lynch mob. Only the news station's lawyers had kept her from being brought back and charged.

The man made no move to pursue her. He didn't put the gun away.

If he really wanted to hurt you, he'd have shot you by now, Shannon told herself. *And if you run, you're never going to know what's going on. Or who he is.*

She took a deep breath and walked back to him.

"Get in," he growled.

Evidently politeness wasn't his forte. Or maybe he had an issue with cops. Tall, dark and mysterious, he definitely looked like the type who would have a chronic problem with law enforcement.

Dirt streaked his hard, angular face, but Shannon could still make out the small scars on his right cheek and his neck. Another small scar stood out at the outside of his right eye.

He wasn't a stranger to violence.

She became fully aware of the broad chest and lean hips encased in denim. He smelled like an outdoorsman, not like the metrosexuals of the broadcasting studio. His dark hair was longer than the norm. She wished she could see his eyes, but she was willing to bet they were dark. Dark brown or dark hazel would suit him perfectly.

"Get in," he repeated.

"Are you in a hurry?" Shannon asked.

Without a word, the man climbed into the car and slid behind the steering wheel. He keyed the ignition and pulled the transmission into gear.

Only then did Shannon fully realize he intended to leave her standing there.

Chapter 5

Shannon ran around to the other side of the car and found it locked. She rapped on the window, which was somehow miraculously still intact.

The man looked at her for a moment, then spoke as if talking to himself. Maybe he was cursing whatever impulse persuaded him to get involved with her.

Shannon rapped again. She didn't want whatever story he represented to just ride off into the night. Not only that, he obviously knew Vincent Drago. It was also possible that he knew why Drago had decided to kill her.

"Open the door," Shannon ordered.

The man just looked at her. The sirens screamed more loudly and sounded closer.

Shannon took a page from his book. Mirroring the way someone treated her in an interview—a noncombative one, at least—often bought some trust and generosity. The wrap-around sunglasses didn't look inviting at all, though.

"Please," she said in the same no-nonsense tone he'd used when he'd asked her.

This time the man leaned over and unlocked the door.

"Thank you." Shannon slid inside the car. She glanced distastefully at the exploded headrest. The cottony fuzz was going to make a mess of her hair.

"Belt up," the man ordered as he got the car under way.

"Are you always this friendly when you meet someone?" Shannon asked before she could stop herself. She reached for the seat belt and put it on.

The man's voice was ice and his face was carved granite. "I don't normally have to kill three people to get to know someone."

"Did you go to the bar to meet Vincent Drago?" Shannon asked.

The man drove quickly. From the way he made the turns through the streets, Shannon figured he was a native to the city.

"No," he said.

"It didn't take you long to decide you didn't like him."

The man turned to her and grinned, but the effort was mirthless. "It didn't take him long to decide he didn't like you. Do you normally have that effect on people?"

Shannon frowned. "Drago and I had already met."

"So how long did it take him to decide to kill you?"

"Are you always such a charming conversationalist?"

"I'm a charming guy." He turned back to face forward as the stoplight turned green.

"Why were you there?"

"Why were you?"

Shannon studied him and tried to find all the things about him that made him unique. "Drago was a private investigator."

The man nodded. "He specialized in electronic information and data management."

"You knew that about Drago, but you'd never met him? I find that interesting. And how did you know my name?"

"I've seen you on television."

"You're a fan?"

"You might say that."

Shannon didn't believe that. He didn't seem like the type to spend his life rooted in front of a television. He looked like more of a hunter or a fisherman.

"Then how did you just happen to be there at that bar tonight?" she asked.

The man checked the rearview mirror and the one remaining side mirror. "Why don't you give me a few minutes before you keep hammering me with questions?"

"Sure." Shannon debated retrieving her iPhone and taking his picture. She was fairly certain he wouldn't like the idea. She also knew she was going to have a hard time holding the questions back.

"Head downtown," Allison said.

Without responding, knowing Shannon Connor would be listening to every word he said, Rafe followed the directions Allison gave him. He'd worked in Washington before, so the city wasn't entirely unfamiliar to him.

"I know you can't talk," Allison went on, "so I'll try to hold up both ends of the conversation for you."

Rafe didn't reply. He didn't want Shannon to know he was connected to someone else. He concentrated on driving. D.C. was a city trapped between disparate economies. Citizens drove new cars as well as beaters. He fit in. The only problem was that his beater was newer than most of the others around him.

Gradually Allison gave him directions that took him to a

public pay lot near the late-night action on U Street. It was shortly after midnight and the Washington, D.C., club scene had come to life.

The bars and taverns would stay filled with political and military aides and employees until the small hours of the morning. The city's nightlife was one of the most active in the country. Newspapers, magazines and Web sites were dedicated to the topic in an effort to keep everyone up to date regarding entertainment.

"Half a block up on the right," Allison said. "The lot there has a lockbox, not a human operator."

That was good. No one on duty meant no eyewitnesses later. Rafe didn't worry about being identified himself, but Shannon Connor was way too high-profile.

"I'll have the car taken care of," Allison went on. "After you walk away from it, someone will pick it up. That car will never be seen again."

Rafe was impressed.

"I have a lot of friends," Allison said.

And it was spooky how she seemed to read his mind. He wondered if she knew how irritated he was at being left so far in the dark.

"I'll tell you more as soon as I get you in a safe spot," Allison went on.

Rafe almost laughed, but he figured that Shannon would think she'd crawled into the car with a crazy man. That wasn't exactly the impression he wanted to make.

"I'm going to need you to sit with her a little longer," Allison said.

"Where are we going?" Shannon asked.

"To get rid of the car." Rafe signaled and made the turn onto the lot. "Unless you want investigators to find your fingerprints in here and come ask you a lot of questions." He glanced at her.

"No," she replied.

During the last few minutes he'd found looking at her easier and easier to do. Shannon Connor was one of the most beautiful women he'd ever met. Her long blond hair was currently a tangled mess, but it gave her a wild, untamed look that threatened to take his breath away. Her blue eyes seemed to drink him in every time she looked at him. Even wearing disheveled clothing, her figure was striking.

Keep your mind on the job, he told himself. But he was acutely aware of how long it had been since he'd met a woman who intrigued him.

In Jacksonville there had been a steady buffet of women with which to lose hours, evenings and even whole weekends. All of them had been fun to be around, and many of them had possessed personalities that were interesting.

But when he'd first laid eyes on Shannon Connor, Rafe had been aware of a deepening interest that normally didn't seize him just from looking at someone of the opposite sex. Having Allison hold back information about the woman had made Shannon even more intriguing.

The fact that she hadn't continued running, that she'd come back when he'd asked, had created even more curiosity.

Unfortunately he'd bought further into the idea of taking responsibility for her, as well. That had been a drawback in his work performance that more than one supervisor had noted. And ultimately it had been that trait—becoming a little more involved than he should have—that had gotten him caught in North Korea.

This situation was starting to feel uncomfortably close to that business.

"This lot is full," Shannon said.

Rafe had to agree that things looked pretty hopeless. The bars and nightclubs got slammed on most nights, and tonight was Friday.

"There's a parking space two rows ahead and on the right," Allison said.

Rafe glanced around and spotted the camera at the back of the large lot. That could be a problem.

"Don't worry about the camera," Allison said. "I've already got that under control. It's going to experience technical difficulties that will wipe the night's digital recording starting one hour ago."

Rafe smiled at that.

"What's so funny?" Shannon asked.

Rafe pointed at the parking space. "We got lucky." He pulled into the space and started to get out.

Shannon unfastened her seat belt and started to get out, as well.

"Give me a minute, okay?" Rafe asked.

Suspicion darkened Shannon's features. "Why?"

"I've got to make a call."

"To whom?"

"Someone who wants to know that you're safe."

"I generally know all of those people."

Rafe ran a hand over his face. His whiskers felt rough. "Please."

"Being polite doesn't always get you what you want."

In spite of his best efforts, Rafe let a little of his anger show. The pain in his knee had increased and showed definite signs of staying around for a while. "Saying *please* beats the hell out of getting a roll of duct tape out of the back of the car and restraining you." He smiled when he said that.

Shannon blinked at him in surprise. "You'd do that?"

"At this point, yes."

She folded her arms. "What happened to the knight in shining armor who saved me and asked me to get in the car?"

"Rescuing you is turning out to be a lot harder than I thought it was going to be."

"I didn't know I needed to be rescued."

Rafe snorted and shook his head. "You're a television reporter, lady. Not exactly in league with guys like Vincent Drago."

"I've interviewed serial killers and terrorists," Shannon argued.

"While they were pointing a gun at you?" Rafe struggled to remain polite. He couldn't believe she could be so pushy after nearly getting killed. Most women would be basket cases.

But that's one of the reasons you find her so…interesting, he told himself. *And you definitely have no business being interested.*

"Not exactly," she admitted.

"Well, that's exactly the kind of thing that's going on here."

"Drago's dead. You killed him."

Rafe sighed. He didn't know how she'd made saving her suddenly sound like a crime against society. But she had. "Yes, I did. But he might not be the only person involved."

"Do you know that for certain?"

"Look," Rafe said sharply, "I don't know what your business with Drago was. The person I'm doing a favor for hasn't told me much more than you have." He meant that for Allison. "I'm working at a deficit here and I'm not happy about it. But I'm really, really trying to make the best of it. Okay?" He tried the smile again.

Shannon didn't look convinced. "All right," she replied grudgingly. "You just want me to stay in the car?"

"That would be great. In fact, if we get out of this alive, I'll buy you dinner." Rafe slid out of the car. He needed answers and he was going to have to put pressure on Allison to get them.

Chapter 6

Did he just ask me out? Shannon couldn't believe it. She couldn't believe that he would have said what he did—and she couldn't believe she'd be thinking about taking him seriously.

She stared through the cracked driver's-side window at the man's retreating back. He walked straight for the metal payment boxes. She had to admit that it was a hell of a sexy walk. The limp just added more flavor.

Thinking about sitting down to dinner with him consumed Shannon's thoughts for a moment. Then she got angry because he obviously didn't think she was safe on her own.

Or maybe that was just an act to scare her or lull her into a false sense of security. Once she got to thinking in that direction, it took no time at all to turn her suspicions into paranoia, because she had to admit that she *didn't* know if she was safe.

But would he really take his time about killing her if that was what he meant to do?

*Get that thought out of your mind. Focus. You're a reporter.
An uncoverer of truth. And—even if you're at the eye of the
storm—this is an incredible story.*

She couldn't help wondering if the man had been brought to
Drago because of business of his own or if it had been her
business that had brought him there. Creating a timeline of
events usually provided the backbone of the story.

The man's arrival at the bar could have been circumstan-
tial—as well as fortuitous. Except that he knew her name. That
hadn't been by lucky coincidence.

The question was whether the man had been at the bar
because of her or because of Drago.

Shannon looked through the bullet-pocked windshield at her
rescuer. There was a pay phone by the payment center. The man
lifted the handset and stood so that he was between her and sight
of the keypad.

Careful, aren't you?

While he was occupied with his *secret* phone call, Shannon
decided to do some snooping. She took her iPhone from her
pocket and brought up the camera function. The screen pulsed
brightly, but a quick glance at the man at the phone assured her
he was still occupied.

The screen showed the image of the floor and her feet. She
noticed how dirty her feet were, and that only reminded her of
the Christian Louboutin glitter sling-backs she'd left in the bar.
Those shoes had cost seven hundred dollars.

They'd been her birthday present to herself when she'd turned
thirty, two years ago. She'd just broken up with Perry Jacobs,
who had—at one time—been Tory Patton's boyfriend. Shannon
hadn't really been after Perry, but she hadn't wanted Tory to be
happy after what Tory had done to her at Athena Academy.

Of course, now Tory was currently married to Bennington
Forsythe, of *the* Forsythes, who had been one of the most eligible

bachelors in the history of eligible bachelors. She'd even secured her place among that family by delivering the first grandchild back in March.

That was another example of the bad luck that had plagued Shannon. Not that she would have ended up with Ben Forsythe, but that she had cleared the runway for that relationship by deep-sixing Tory's relationship with Perry Jacobs.

Some days, life sucked.

Shannon opened the glove compartment and took out the documents inside. As she'd hoped, rental papers lay neatly folded inside. She took them out and started taking pictures.

As soon as she had a picture taken, she e-mailed it to one of the data dumps she used to keep story research. Then she moved on to the next.

Rafe leaned a hip on the metal security boxes where he was supposed to pay. He didn't pay, though. There would have been fingerprints on the bill. He held the handset of the pay phone.

"You with me?" he asked as he kept himself between the pay phone and Shannon's line of sight.

"Yes," Allison replied over the earwig. The phone was only a cover.

"You're going to have to level with me. I can't keep operating in the dark here. You're going to get Shannon—or me or both of us—killed. Either tell me what's going on or I'm going to walk away from this." *Limp away,* Rafe corrected himself. He tried to find a comfortable position for his knee.

"You wouldn't do that."

"Try me." Rafe attempted to sound as if he would really do that.

"That's not how you do things," Allison told him. "The reason I asked you to do this favor was because I knew you'd stick. No matter how bad it got."

She had him there. Rafe blew out his breath. "Look, you wanted me to be there tonight to lend a hand if it came to that. I did. I lent considerably more than a hand. I may have left what remains of my career scattered over that street back there. I just want to know enough to know that she's going to be safe."

Allison was quiet for a moment.

Rafe thought maybe he'd lost the connection or that she'd hung up on him. Thinking that way wasn't pleasant. It raised the abandonment issues he'd gone through during his stay in the North Korean prison.

Finally, in a subdued voice, Allison said, "I don't know what all is involved."

Rafe shifted again, striving in vain to get comfortable. He wished he'd brought the pain pills now. He hadn't expected—he hadn't known *what* to expect with regard to the physical demands of the job.

He also wanted a drink to wash the stink of fresh death out of his system. It had been over three years since he'd had to kill a man.

"Tell me what you know." Rafe shifted around till he caught the reflection of the Taurus.

Shannon kept moving around. Occasionally a light flashed inside the car. Even though he knew it meant she was taking pictures of the false identification Allison had arranged for him to use while he was in Washington, D.C., he had to grin. Even scared out of her wits and in over her head, the woman was definitely a schemer.

"Some of this is personal," Allison said.

"I knew it was personal when you called me a few days ago," Rafe said.

Allison hesitated.

"C'mon," Rafe coaxed. "You've run ops before. You've worked with me before. You know I don't tell everything I know and you know I don't ask for info I don't need."

"I know." Allison took a deep breath. "Do you remember anything about the kidnappings that took place at an all-girls school called Athena Academy? It's located outside of Phoenix."

Rafe vaguely did, but he listened as Allison told him an edited version of what had happened. Both of them knew he wasn't getting all of the truth.

Allison had been involved in the investigation into the kidnappings, but on a tangential level. Rafe hadn't known how dangerous things had become in Kestonia at the time. But the girls had been safely returned.

"Shannon Connor was involved with that," Rafe said. He'd seen Shannon before, but the story and the possible conflict with Kestonia had been so big that he'd paid attention all those months ago. He'd known the NSA—and Allison—had been all over it. He just hadn't known Allison would be doubly interested.

"Shannon was there," Allison agreed. "But I wondered how she got the information she had."

"Was there any reason to be suspicious of her presence? It was a big story. There were a lot of reporters there. I followed the story on all the major networks." Rafe had figured he'd have surely been cleared through Medical at that time. But it hadn't happened.

"There was no reason then, but Shannon's continued to pop up while this thing has played out."

"What thing?"

Allison hesitated. Rafe could almost hear her thoughts bumping into each other. He watched the reflection of Shannon still taking pictures.

"When we dug into the Kestonia thing," Allison said, "other information surfaced."

"What information?"

"About my mother's murder. There was more to it than we thought."

* * *

When she'd finished taking pictures of all the rental car's documentation, Shannon put everything back in the glove compartment. Guilt stung her. She didn't feel completely comfortable about invading the man's privacy.

He invaded yours, she told herself. *He knew you were in danger.* She sighed. *So what? He's guilty for coming to save you?*

Hi. My name is Robert—at least, according to the rental agreement, that was his name—*and I'll be your rescuer this evening.*

To which she could only counter, *Hi. I'm Shannon Connor. I'm going to snoop into your life and expose you to the world. All because you seem totally at ease killing bad guys and driving away from a confrontation with the police. Oh, and you have a thing for rescuing damsels in distress.*

Not that she was a damsel in distress.

Her role didn't feel as good as the one of rescuer. But reporting was what paid her bills. She glanced at him, still talking at the phone. She couldn't help wondering what could be taking so long.

An idea popped into her head. She looked at the steering wheel. As she'd thought, dark smudges showed on the wheel. If there hadn't been a lot of ambient light from the nearby bars and clubs, she wouldn't have been able to see them.

She opened the glove compartment again. In addition to a road flare and a city map, there was also a Scotch tape dispenser. That had to have been from a previous renter. Or maybe *Robert* had a thing for tape. After all, he claimed to have duct tape in the car's trunk.

Over the years Shannon had interviewed a lot of people. Some of them hated her and some of them loved her, but she'd always paid attention to the stories that she'd covered. The best ones had always touched her emotionally and taught her something.

Only a few weeks ago she'd interviewed one of the New York City Police Department's crime-scene investigators. They'd done a special on how a crime scene could be processed in times of emergency with household items. Shannon couldn't remember all of it.

Thankfully she didn't have to. This was easy. She reached into the glove compartment and removed the Scotch tape. After a quick glance to check on Mr. Tall, Dark, and Mysterious, she pulled off a two-inch piece of tape.

She studied the steering wheel and found the clearest fingerprint on the surface that she could find. Delicately she laid the tape over the fingerprint. It was only wide enough to cover about half of the print. She cut off another strip and laid it partially over the first, then pressed it into place over the print. It took a third strip to completely cover the loops and whorls.

Then she took three more strips and crosshatched them over the first three, thickening the "lifting" medium, which was what the crime-scene investigator had called it. After another quick glance, she peeled the lifting medium from the steering wheel. She laid it on its back on the dash. Meticulously she laid three tape strips over the fingerprint to seal it, then three more to reinforce it.

When she picked up the lifted print and examined it, she felt satisfied. There, trapped between the layers of tape, was the fingerprint.

Okay, Mr. Tall, Dark, and Mysterious—or Robert or whoever you are—I'll be willing to bet I know who you really are by morning.

That was one of the perks of working for ABS. American Broadcasting Studios had inroads to information all over the world.

Shannon slid the lifted fingerprint into a storage compartment in her iPhone's protective case. For the first time in days she felt as if she was about to deal with the truth she'd been looking for in Kestonia, Puerto Isla and Cape Town, South Africa.

When she had it, she knew she was finally going to be able to unveil all the secrets that had been hidden for so long at Athena Academy. If those secrets tied into genetic research, as her mysterious information broker had intimated on several occasions, the school would finally be destroyed once and for all.

Nothing the other Athena grads—like Allison Gracelyn and Tory Patton Forsythe—or Principal Christina Evans could do would stop it.

At last, after fifteen years of pain and frustration, Shannon would finally have her revenge.

Chapter 7

Out of respect, Rafe waited for Allison to continue, even though the story had definitely taken on even more intriguing aspects. He knew about Senator Marion Gracelyn's murder. The nation had learned about it and mourned the loss of a great woman.

"I thought that had been solved," Rafe said gently.

"It had. But there were…extenuating circumstances." Allison's voice carried a lot of emotion, but it never wavered. That was Allison, though. She never broke down or became too emotional to do her job.

Rafe waited. He knew it was hard. Allison had been close to her mother.

"I can't go into all of it," Allison said. "Not yet. But I will someday. I'll owe you lunch and a dinner, because it'll take that long to tell it." She sighed. "And that's only if this thing ever comes to an end. We followed the trail that turned up as a result of Kestonia to Puerto Isla. That was a difficult op to put together. You know what it's like down there."

Rafe did know. He'd conducted missions in Puerto Isla on a handful of occasions. On each one he'd barely escaped with his life, and he bore scars from two of them.

"I do," he said.

"We were successful down there. After a fashion."

"Who's *we?*"

"My friends and I."

Ah. That was interesting. *Friends* meant that whatever op Allison had finessed hadn't been through the NSA.

"If you didn't do this through the organization," he said, referring to the NSA, "then you must have some amazingly talented friends."

"I do," Allison stated quietly. "That's why I called you."

"Point taken." Rafe grinned and noticed in the phone's reflective metal plate that Shannon had stopped taking pictures. "So Shannon showed up down in Puerto Isla."

"She did. And when the trail led to Cape Town, South Africa, she turned up there, too."

"How?"

"I don't know. No one does. But she was there and she almost got in the way."

"I don't suppose anyone tried asking Shannon how she happened to be there."

"Do you realize that you use her first name with increasing ease?"

"No," Rafe responded.

"You do."

"Maybe you want to suggest a code name."

Allison did. It wasn't ladylike.

"Potty mouth," Rafe said. "Animosity much?"

"There's a lot of history where Shannon is concerned," Allison said.

"How did you get to know her?"

"She went to Athena Academy for a while. She's the only student that was ever kicked out. What she did was reprehensible, but to make matters worse, she tried to take me down with her."

Rafe understood how that could be the kiss of death. Allison didn't hold grudges, exactly, but she definitely knew who her friends and who her enemies were. Those balance sheets were always up to date.

"What did you find out that put you onto her?" Rafe deliberately didn't use Shannon's name.

"After Cape Town, I peeked into her electronic records. Phone. Internet. At home and at work."

Rafe didn't say anything about the illegality of such a thing. There were rules, and there were rules. After 9/11 a lot of those rules had changed or weren't as strictly enforced. When it came to getting an op done, an agent did whatever was necessary.

He glanced back at Shannon, who was sitting patiently in the car. He sighed tiredly as he thought about the way he'd thought about being her champion.

You're thirty-three, brother. Way too old to believe in that kind of nonsense.

But it was precisely that kind of thinking that had drawn him into the NSA after he'd pulled eight years with the Army Rangers. As soon as he'd turned eighteen, he'd signed in and finished his GED while in the service.

If Homeland Security and the other alphabet agencies hadn't gone trolling for guys with military experience who weren't overly educated, he'd have stayed in and done his full bit. But the NSA had come along when he was twenty-six. He'd pulled five good years filled with excitement and danger till he'd gotten tripped up in North Korea.

* * *

Shannon punched a speed-dial number on her iPhone. The phone rang twice before it was answered.

"Yo." The voice was youthful and peppy. Laser beams and electronically enhanced radio commands sounded in the background.

"Gary, it's Shannon."

"Hey, Shannon. What do you know?"

Shannon strained to hear over the sounds of warfare.

"Dude," another guy's voice crowed, "he just blew you up *so* bad!" Maniacal laughter echoed over the phone. "Look! There's pieces of you splattered all across the screen! That is *so* messed up! This game is *totally* sick."

"I was on the phone," Gary said. "It's work."

"Yeah, the other four-letter word."

"I'm gonna get blown up a little while I'm on the phone," Gary protested. Then he turned his attention to Shannon. "What d'you need, boss lady?"

Ignoring the irritating noises, knowing that Gary was at one of his interminable video games, Shannon said, "I need you to do some deep research for me."

"Hang on just a sec."

Shannon stared at her "rescuer." Something had gone on. Bad news, probably. She could tell it by his posture, the way he looked as if the weight of the world had been dropped on his shoulders. She felt bad for him.

That's stupid, she told herself. *For all you know, he's just been told where to dump your body.*

The war noises quieted.

"Had to get out here where I could hear myself think," Gary said. "He can kill me the rest of the night and he won't catch up to me." The sound of a refrigerator door opening carried over the phone.

Shannon imagined Gary as he prowled restlessly through

his refrigerator. Twenty-six years old, he was red headed, pale and skinny, with a penchant for black concert tees and khaki shorts. He lived in a small walk-up apartment in Brooklyn, but he worked part-time for ABS as a researcher, fact-checker and computer tech support. He was also a great copywriter/editor for breaking stories and he was receiving writing credits.

"Ah," Gary chortled. "Last bottle of apple juice. The gods of war must really be smiling down on me."

"Focus," Shannon told him. "I just e-mailed some pictures to you. I need the guy in them identified and his background checked."

"What kind of background?"

"As deep as you can go."

"Want to give me a clue about what direction to look in? The closer you can get me, the more time you cut off the search window."

Shannon thought for a moment. "Try looking in the military first." From the way he'd seemed to move and how quickly he'd acted, she felt as though that was a good match for him. "As I learn more, I'll let you know."

"Sure. How soon do you need this?"

"Yesterday."

Gary laughed. "You always say that."

"Let's put it this way—if you can get the info back to me in a couple hours, I'll talk Mike into letting me cover the next big video-game show. And I'll have him okay you as an assistant for it."

"Seriously?"

Shannon thought about it. Video games weren't her thing, but she was aware they were attracting larger and larger audiences. Even making the agreement, she wouldn't be entirely losing out.

"Yes," she said.

"Sweet! I'll call you in a couple of hours. Are you going to be at this number?"

"If I'm not, give the pictures I sent you to the D.C. Police Department and tell them to start looking for me."

"Seriously?"

Shannon looked at the man near the pay phone. "Seriously."

"So she's a bad guy," Rafe said, looking at Shannon Connor.

"I haven't been able to track her records all the way back," Allison said, "but it looks that way. She's been getting heavily encrypted communiqués from China—from Shanghai, in particular—for years."

"Tips on the stories she broke?"

"Not all of them, but enough. Every one she's gotten from Shanghai has been huge. Career changers. Political upheaval. Big."

Rafe's heart hardened a little toward the pretty blonde. "I wish you'd let me know that before you got me in this deep." He would have turned down the job. One of the primary reasons he'd bought in on the op was to protect the woman.

"I needed you," Allison said. "If I'd told you what I suspected, you wouldn't have come."

"You don't know that."

"Yes, I do."

Rafe had to admit that Allison was right. If he'd known the woman wasn't an innocent or possibly didn't deserve protection, he wouldn't have come. He'd have stayed on that damn beach and remained a hermit. Hermits had simpler lives.

"Why haven't you taken her down?" Rafe asked. He didn't bother to take the displeasure out of his words. Even if he had, Allison knew him well enough to read between the lines.

"I don't have anything I can prove. I can't even prove it to you."

"I know you. You don't have anything to prove to me. If you get a bad vibe on her, then she's got to be bad."

There was a slightly uncomfortable silence, then Allison said, "I'm sorry."

"For what?"

"For pulling you into this. If everything had gone right, I would have had you shadow her back to New York and let her go. I needed someone who was off the books. Someone that wouldn't connect up anywhere in case this op turned high-profile."

Well, it had certainly done that.

"And I wanted someone good enough to save her if things went badly at that end." Allison paused. "I wanted you for this. I just didn't know that you would…get involved on a personal level."

"I'm not," Rafe said automatically. But he was sure they both knew he was lying. After everything that had happened to him, after all those boring months in Jacksonville, he'd gotten vulnerable. He'd wanted to believe in good things.

Rafe had guessed that he would have been expected to follow Shannon back to New York after the night's foray. He'd already been fantasizing about spending a few days in New York and *accidentally* bumping into Shannon at some point. Probably nothing would have happened, but it would have been fun to see.

At the very least, it would have been a good change from that lonely expanse of beach.

"That's water under the bridge," he said. "What do you want me to do with her?" Personally, he was ready to walk away.

"I need you to take care of her for a little while longer," Allison said. "Just till I can make some other arrangements. It won't take long."

Rafe took in a deep breath and let it out. "I'm not entirely happy with that. And the longer that takes, the less happy I'm going to be."

"I know. But she's not going to trust anyone else."

"She doesn't trust me."

"She trusts you more than anyone else I could get down there to take over for you."

"All right. But I want out of this. Soon."

"You will be."

"What do you want me to do with the assets we've used tonight?"

"Just leave the car and the weapons there. I'll have them taken care of."

"Sure. And you may want to double back the ID you used to lease the car."

"Why?"

"Because she's gotten to it and she's been on the telephone."

"It's covered," Allison said. "Shannon always was high-maintenance and a lot of trouble." She paused. "Keep the ear-piece, but we're going off this frequency for the time being."

Rafe understood that. Allison was probably "borrowing" the satellite communications relays involved, as well. The longer she "borrowed" them, the greater the chance of discovery.

"I've got your cell phone information," she said.

Rafe knew that she should have. After all, Allison had arranged for the cell phone and had it waiting for him in the car.

"All right," he said.

"If you need me, let me know."

"I will." Rafe said goodbye, stripped the earwig from his ear, shoved it into his pocket and walked back to the car.

"Did you get everything worked out?" Shannon asked when the man opened the door.

"Yeah." His response was nearly noncommittal as he opened the trunk, stripped the holster and gun off his hip and threw them inside. He added extra magazines. "Get out of the car."

Anger stirred within Shannon. "Stay in the car. Get out of the car. I'm not five years old." She didn't budge.

"I get that," he said. "I can't make you stay in the car. I can't make you get out of the car. You're not five years old." He didn't

even look at her. "Stay in the car if you want. It's your choice."
He turned and walked away.

In disbelief, Shannon watched him walk away. "Hey."

He didn't respond.

"Hey," she repeated, louder.

Without a word, he kept walking.

"You can't just walk away like that."

But he could. He proved it when he did. He kept taking one
step after another. His back was straight, militarily erect.

Shannon was tempted to let him walk away, but she wouldn't
have gotten to know what his story was if she did. Not only that,
but she was in a bad part of the city. *With no shoes,* she lamented.

Frustrated, she got out of the car and trotted across the
parking area asphalt to catch up to him. "You know, for someone
who seemed to have come a long way to prevent something bad
from happening to me tonight, you sure don't act all that happy."

He looked at her. His gaze behind the wraparound sunglasses
was impenetrable.

"I'm not," he said flatly. "If I'd known what I know now, I
wouldn't have been here tonight."

His anger, so palpable, hit Shannon like a slap in the face. She
didn't know how to respond. There wasn't enough information
to launch an attack of her own that wouldn't have sounded
stupid.

He swung his attention away from her, and that—apparently—
was the end of the conversation.

Shannon struggled to keep up and ignore the pain in her feet
from walking shoeless on the sidewalk. Neither one was easy.

Chapter 8

"You could slow down, you know."

Rafe did know that, and despite his irritation at being with the woman, he did slow down. From the corner of his eye, he watched her stumble across the pavement in her bare feet.

"We could take a cab," Shannon grumbled.

"We take a cab, we could also get remembered," he said. "Cabdrivers have a real tendency to call the police when they realize they've just given fugitives a lift somewhere. I'd rather not start my morning out in jail."

And there was no guarantee that the morning would be the end of it. He'd killed three men and fled the scene. If staying wouldn't have compromised Allison—and, at that time, Shannon—he would have remained on-site and worked things through with the local police.

"Is that prejudice developed from past experience of starting out mornings in jail?" Shannon asked.

Despite his dislike for the woman, Rafe couldn't help but respect her acerbic wit.

"Yeah," he said. "But the mornings on Death Row were the loneliest. Still, you can't buy that kind of quiet anywhere."

Shannon glared at him. It was obvious that neither one of them cared very much for the other. He told himself that he was fine with that, but he knew her reaction was based on his sudden change of behavior.

Then she stumbled and would have fallen if he hadn't caught her by the arm.

"Don't," she said. "I can do this. Just leave me alone."

Rafe released her, but she wobbled and favored her foot.

She cursed as she tried to walk. Dark smudges stained the pavement. For a moment Rafe was mesmerized by the feel of soft flesh under his callused hands.

When he realized she was bleeding, Rafe took more of her weight across his shoulders. His knee throbbed in protest.

"Hold up," he said.

"Why?"

"Let me see your foot."

"I'm okay," she protested.

"You're bleeding."

Shannon glared at him. "Do you really care? Because it seems like you don't. You acted like you were plenty willing to leave me in the car back there."

Allison, you'd better put a damn rush order on my relief.

"Let me see your foot." Rafe intentionally spoke more slowly.

With obvious reluctance, Shannon leaned into him and lifted her foot.

Rafe was all too aware of the feminine flesh pressed against him. Despite his best intentions, it was having an effect. He tried to focus on her foot. He caught it and turned it up to get a better look. But that contact turned sensuous, too. His response, uncontrollable and understandable though it was, grated on his nerves.

The streetlight only a short distance away provided enough illumination for Rafe to see the damage that had been done. The cut was small, but the sidewalk had been hard on the bottoms of her feet. Most of the skin was torn and abraded. Going barefoot wasn't something she often did.

"You should have said something," Rafe growled.

"Why? You haven't been exactly Mr. Free and Friendly the past twenty minutes."

"You can't keep walking."

"Are you just going to shoot me because I've pulled up lame?"

Rafe glared back at her. "I don't have my gun anymore."

"You could probably kill me with a tongue depressor. I mean, you've been trained to do stuff like that, right?"

Rafe made himself breathe out. "I don't have a tongue depressor either."

"I have to say, I'm surprised. I figured any man who packed duct tape for tying people up would probably carry tongue depressors for assassinating people, too."

"I'm not an assassin." At least Rafe wasn't most of the time.

"You could have fooled me."

"I figured that. Vincent Drago didn't seem to have any problem in that regard."

Pain flashed in those blue eyes. Rafe felt guilty and didn't care for the feeling much. She was the enemy. He didn't feel apologetic for the way he treated the enemy. He didn't feel bad for running over Vincent Drago.

"Give me back my foot," she ordered. She pulled, but he didn't let go. For a moment she looked as though she was going to hit him.

That early defiance that he'd liked so much was beginning to wear thin.

"Hitting me would be a mistake," Rafe said. "You're giving away seventy pounds at least. And I hit back."

Shannon glared at him some more. "Okay, then what do you propose we do?"

A cab out on the street passed. For a moment Rafe considered calling out to it in spite of Allison's cab embargo.

Without a word, he bent down and took Shannon into his arms.

"What are you doing?" Her arms slid naturally around his neck to keep herself from falling backward.

"I don't want you to get hurt," he answered. For the first time in a long time, he realized what he'd been missing while not committing to a relationship. She lay in his arms.

"Carrying me is stupid. Your leg is already bothering you."

She'd noticed that? Rafe was impressed. But he had to wonder if she'd noted the hesitation in his step out of concern or while looking for weakness.

"I'll manage," he said

"I could manage, too."

"Enjoy this while you're getting it. It might not last long." The way his knee felt, it probably wouldn't. But he was stubborn, too.

Thankfully, his cell phone vibrated before he'd gone three blocks. The knee was acting up something fierce, but the distraction caused by Shannon's soft body bumping against him held narcotic properties of its own.

Holding on to Shannon with one arm, he fished the phone out of his pocket. Only one person would have that number.

"Yeah," he growled.

"Are you okay?"

"Peachy. Tell me you've got a replacement."

"Not yet. But I do have a car. Leave the phone on while I track the GPS and get it to you."

Rafe walked to the nearest building and stood in the shadows. A cool breeze whispered through downtown D.C. The flashing neon of the bar scene and the traffic interrupted the darkness. A news copter *whop-whop-whopped* by overhead.

"Do you know how long I'm going to be stuck with this?" Rafe asked.

"Thanks," Shannon said.

Rafe ignored her response.

"I'm working on it," Allison said.

Shannon shifted against Rafe. He guessed that being held wasn't much more fun for her than it was for him to hold her. In fact, judging from his own treacherous response to her proximity and the hormones flashing through his brain that carried endorphins and pain suppressors, she was probably in a worse condition.

Her shifting wasn't helping. Her blouse gapped open and revealed the lacy edge of a nude bra and the rounded fullness of her breast. Breathing became a little difficult.

"Are you all right?" Shannon asked. She looked up at him innocently.

Rafe had the distinct impression she knew exactly what she was doing. She shifted again and the blouse shifted, offering a greater expanse for his perusal.

"I'm fine," Rafe growled.

"What's going on?" Allison asked. "It sounds like she's standing on top of you."

"She lost her shoes back at the bar. Her feet are cut up. If you could get shoes for her, that would be great."

"Size seven and a half," Shannon said. "Preferably something with a heel."

"I don't care if they're clown shoes," Rafe said. "Carrying her isn't easy."

Shannon punched him in the chest and tried to shove out of

his arm. He let her go because he was too tired to fight her and his leg felt as if it were on fire. For a moment he wondered if she was going to run.

Instead she stood at his side with her arms crossed. The delectable cleavage had been covered over.

"I've got clothing and toiletries for both of you at the hotel," Allison said.

"What hotel?" Rafe grew more agitated. "Nobody said anything about a hotel."

"You haven't seen the news, have you?"

"We've been a little busy."

"Shannon's wanted for murder."

"What?" Shannon yelped.

Allison sighed. "She can hear me?"

"Evidently. She must have ears like a bat."

"Terrific."

"What about me?"

"At this point, you're in the clear. Everyone knows that a man was there, but he—you—haven't yet been identified."

"Yet?" Panic thundered at Rafe's temples. If he got arrested, he didn't know how he was going to react to being locked up. The nightmares of North Korea suddenly seemed to surround him.

"There was a security camera in the bar that I couldn't access. The police have pictures of you. So far I'm blocking your files, but I don't know how much longer I can do that. The police are using facial-characteristic software, so that's going to take time."

There was just no telling how much time.

"I'm sorry," Allison said. "I didn't expect this to turn out to be so big."

"We need to go to the police," Shannon said. "I can't be wanted for murder."

"Tell her that turning herself in isn't a good idea," Allison said.

"Why not?" Shannon demanded. "I didn't kill anyone. He did."

"I have to tell you," Rafe said sarcastically, "I find your show of loyalty really impressive." He meant that for both women.

"Drago received orders from someone to kill Shannon," Allison said.

"Who?"

"The e-mail was in Drago's personal computer. Whoever contacted him told him that Shannon was setting him up. Your arrival reinforced that idea."

"*You're* the government hacker he was so angry about?" Shannon demanded. She pinned Rafe with her gaze. "Who are you people?"

Rafe ignored her. "Personally, I'm ready at this point to gift wrap her and deliver her to the police. She's becoming a pain in the ass."

Shannon glared at him.

"We can't do that," Allison said.

"*We?* It's not *we*. It's *me*. And I can do that."

"You don't know that Drago is the only one that was assigned to kill her. If the information network that Shannon's been part of is shutting down, whoever's behind it may want to burn every bridge that leads to that network."

"You said Shannon doesn't know anything."

"I don't think she does. That doesn't mean that whoever set up Drago to kill her believes that. If Shannon turns herself over to the police, she might be making herself an easier target for anyone trying to kill her. Not only that, but going to the police is going to increase the paranoia of whoever wants her dead."

Rafe looked at Shannon to make sure she'd heard that. When he saw the uncertainty and fear in her eyes, he knew that she had. But even as he saw those things, she glared at him again and looked competent and determined.

Good. At least she wasn't going to break down or do something stupid.

"For the time being it makes more sense to stash the two of you until I see if I can leverage any information," Allison said.

"I'm not going to be her jailer," Rafe said.

"Think of it as protective parent," Allison responded.

"I heard that," Shannon said icily.

"By the way," Allison said, "your car is there."

Rafe had been tracking the sedan since it had made the corner at the end of the street. "Toyota SUV?"

"Yes. The clothes are at the hotel. The driver has your room key card."

"Room?"

"It's hard to play bodyguard if you're booked into separate rooms," Allison pointed out.

Rafe had to admit that was true. He noticed that Shannon's immediate response was also muted.

"I'll be in touch if I find out anything," Allison said. "If you need me, you know where I'll be."

Rafe said goodbye and closed the phone. He looked at Shannon. "I meant what I said. I'm not going to be your jailer."

"You offered to take me prisoner earlier."

The pain in Rafe's knee continued unabated. He really didn't feel like arguing the point with Shannon or with Allison.

"That was in the heat of the moment," Rafe said. "You were stuck there like a deer in headlights."

"I wasn't—"

"I don't have the time or the inclination to debate this with you. The way I see it, I'm safer without you, so if you want to stay behind, that's fine with me." Rafe took off walking for the SUV.

The driver got out, and he saw at once that it was a young woman. She had chin-length bronze hair and looked petite. She also wore a pistol somewhere on her person that was concealed by a nondescript dark hoodie over her slim-fit capris. Rafe knew about the weapon from her stance, but only because he'd been trained to look for such things. She looked like Jill College, but she obviously wasn't.

"Hi," the young woman said in greeting.

Rafe guessed that she was in her early twenties only because he knew Allison would never risk someone so young. She looked considerably younger.

"Hey," Rafe said.

The young woman nodded to the SUV. "The keys are inside. You've got a package under the seat."

Rafe nodded. "Drop you anywhere?"

The young woman shook her head. "I've got a party to get back to. Got some bad guys to bust before dawn. This was just a breather."

A breather? Over the years Rafe had met some of the women Allison called in on ops. They were all impressive and skilled. *Where the hell does she get these women?*

"Thanks," Rafe said.

The young woman shrugged. "No big deal. Make sure you stay safe out there. Heard you've already had an exciting night."

"Yeah."

Without another word, the young woman turned and walked up the street she'd just driven down.

When he glanced back, Rafe saw Shannon limping toward the SUV. He opened the passenger door for her. She climbed in without a word.

Okay. The silent treatment. Now that's a punishment I can live with. Rafe walked around the vehicle and clambered in. *Too bad it won't last.* He knew that as soon as she figured out silence wasn't upsetting him, she'd try a new tactic.

He glanced around the street, saw that no one was in view and reached under the seat. The package was a box that reeked of gun oil. When he opened it, he found a Glock pistol chambered in .45 ACP. Two extra magazines, one loose round and a paddle holster lay in a side compartment.

A small plastic bag held an electronic key card and an address written in a neat feminine hand. The hotel wasn't far from where they were.

A quick pull of the slide revealed that the pistol had a full magazine. He let the slide snap forward and strip the first round from the magazine. Then he popped the magazine free long enough to insert the loose round and slid the safety on before holstering the weapon. He loosened his belt long enough to loop the holster through.

Then he put the SUV in gear and pulled into the light traffic.

Chapter 9

The hotel was a surprise. It provided five-star accommodations near Dulles Airport and was often hard to get into.

Shannon had expected a roach-infested hole-in-the-wall. But that was judging by the blue-collar mentality her mystery man exuded.

And when—exactly—did you start thinking of him as yours? She got irritated at herself.

The whole trip to the hotel had been silent. She guessed that surprised him. He'd looked at her a couple of times as if expecting her to say something. Not *wanting* her to say anything but expecting it.

Truthfully, there was a lot Shannon had to say. The thing was that she knew none of it mattered. Whoever he was, he had more questions than she did.

It was interesting that the woman—whoever she was, nefarious government agent, maybe—knew about Shannon's contact.

Shannon hadn't known that the e-mails had been from Shanghai. Or even from China.

She didn't know anyone in China.

Not really. She still had a few contacts from stories she'd covered over the years, but they weren't people who'd be sending the kind of information she'd received.

Melton Flowers would still be CEO of Solar Life, the alternative fuel R & D corporation, if it hadn't been for the information Shannon had received and then used in her broadcast. Thomas Burke would have still been a strong contender for mayor of New York City. Paula Crenshaw would have still been head of one of the most influential public relations offices in California. Bob Hooker, whose last name ended up being fairly prophetic, would still have been a favorite son in Texas.

Thinking back over the years of her career, there were a lot of people who had reason to hate her. So why had the China contact given her the information she'd been given?

She'd thought about it before, but not as hard as she was thinking about now.

Shannon felt awkward walking through the elegant hotel lobby without shoes. Thankfully, at that time of night there weren't many people around.

And people tended to stay away from the man she was with. He guided her to an elevator, gave a look to three young twenty-something guys who were half in the bag and wanted on the elevator but decided against it and tapped the button for the eighth floor.

The worst part was the elevator mirror. Shannon wanted to die. Her blond hair was a mess and her clothing was rumpled. Mascara streaked her eyes. She looked as if she'd been on a month long bender.

Looking at her reflection hurt. In the television news business, appearance was everything. The way she looked had meant a lot to Shannon even when she'd been growing up.

At least by not looking like herself there was less likelihood of her getting picked up by the police. That wasn't much, but it was something.

"You okay?" he asked.

"I'm fine," she said in a cold tone that made it crystal clear she wasn't going to discuss the matter.

"What about your feet?"

"My feet are fine." Shannon looked at the floor indicator. What could possibly be taking so long?

He leaned a hip against the wall and kept his arms folded over his chest. His face, especially with the wraparound sunglasses, looked implacable. Under the artificial lighting, the scars stood out a little more. They still carried a hint of pinkness that indicated they weren't all that old.

"How's your leg?" she asked, knowing he was standing like that because he was in pain.

"My leg's fine."

So they were both natural liars.

The elevator doors opened.

Shannon started forward, but he grabbed her elbow and held her back.

"Wait." He moved forward and peered out into the hallway.

Anxiety rattled around inside Shannon. After tonight, she wanted to feel safe. At least for a little while.

"Okay." He released her and stepped out into the hallway.

"Don't trust your friend?" Shannon taunted.

"I trust my friend," he responded. "But I also know that friends don't know everything. Her systems could be compromised."

"She's not as infallible as you seem to want to believe she is?"

He turned to her and gave her that sugary-sweet grin again.

"My friend's systems have been prowling through yours. She's probably aware that she could have picked up some trash while she was slumming."

Shannon didn't say anything.

He sighed. "That was uncalled for. You should have cried foul on that one."

"It's all right," Shannon told him. "I was trying to punch your buttons for freezing me out on the way over here."

"As I recall, you weren't talking to me," he said.

"You didn't want me to talk to you."

"No."

"So the decision to talk or not to talk, ultimately, was yours. You chose not to talk."

"There's nothing to talk about."

"There's a *lot* to talk about."

"Okay," he admitted as he stepped in front of a door, "there's a lot we're *not* going to talk about."

Shannon got the room number—817—and committed it to memory.

He took the key card from his pants pocket and swiped it through the reader. "Step away from the door. Wait till I ask you to come in." He waved her to the side in front of him, then slipped his hand under his shirt to rest on the pistol.

Watching him was interesting, Shannon discovered. When he went on point, it was almost as though he channeled some predatory animal. Or maybe he flipped the script and pulled on a civilized mask when he was in polite society.

He went through the door and it closed behind him.

For a moment Shannon thought about just walking away. Doors opened at the elevator bank. She was fast enough to catch it before the doors closed. By the time he figured out what she'd done, she'd be long gone.

But where would you go?

Another moment passed, just enough time for Shannon to start getting worried about him. Then he opened the door.

"Okay," he said.

The room was done in quietly understated luxury. If she'd been visiting Washington, D.C., she'd have been content to stay there.

However, the fact that the room had only one bed was glaring.

"Are you going to get them to bring up a bed?" she asked.

"No."

"If I'm the prisoner, I get the bed."

"Fine." He started inspecting the room.

"Just so you're clear on this, you're not sleeping in the bed," Shannon said in case he didn't understand.

"Don't want to sleep in the bed." He started unscrewing the phone's base.

Shannon didn't know if she'd been insulted or not. "Then where are you going to sleep?"

"The couch."

She glanced at the couch and saw that it was covered over with bags and boxes. Curious, she walked over to them. "The couch doesn't look all that comfortable."

"I'll sleep like a baby."

"What are you doing with the phone?"

"I'm going to call room service as soon as I find the number." He picked up a pad and pen from the desk. He wrote quickly. "Are you hungry?"

When he showed her the pad, it read, Room's bugged.

The announcement took a moment to sink in to Shannon's understanding. She picked up a tablet from the nightstand and wrote quickly while she said, "I could eat. What are you hungry for?"

She wrote: Who would bug the room?

I don't know.

"Looks like room service is shut down. We should be able to get pizza."

"Pizza sounds good."

Your friend? she wrote.

No.

"I'll call and get a pizza," he said.

"While you're doing that, I'll take a bath." Shannon wrote again.

Didn't your friend check the room?

How?

When she reserved it.

I don't know. I'll ask.

"While you're taking a bath, I'm going to pick up a paper."

"All right."

Shannon wrote: Audio or video?

Only audio. If video, I wouldn't write.

Doh. Shannon felt stupid.

"There are clothes in those boxes." He pointed at the couch. "You should find something in there to wear. I'll call in the pizza, then be back in a few minutes. Will you be all right?"

"Yes." Shannon crossed her arms as a chill thrilled through her. Her life seemed as though it was completely out of control. She wanted out of that room, but she knew that she probably wouldn't be any safer on the streets. At the very least, she wanted a pair of shoes she could wear.

True to his word, he called for pizza.

"What do you want?" he asked.

"Anything," Shannon said. She was surprised to discover how hungry she was.

When he finished, he hung up the phone. "I'll be back in a few minutes."

"All right."

As she watched him go, Shannon couldn't help wondering if

he was going to come back. The thing that was most confusing was that she didn't know for sure how she'd feel if he didn't.

Down in the lobby, Rafe reconned. Walking the perimeter to look for familiar—or threatening—faces was a reflex at this point.

When he didn't find anything that set his inner alarms off, he retreated to one of the pay phone areas and called Allison.

"I thought you'd be tucked in by now," Allison said.

"The room's bugged," Rafe announced flatly.

Allison was quiet for a moment. "That's Washington. A lot of rooms get bugged. Maybe it was left over from someone who was in the room before you."

"Want to check on that?"

"Give me a minute."

Rafe watched the lobby traffic and wondered if Shannon Connor would be in the hotel room when he got back. He thought about her out there on the streets alone and didn't like the idea of it.

"I checked back through the last six months of reservations," Allison said when she returned. "They were all real people with real histories."

"There's always the chance the room was bugged because of someone they were meeting," Rafe said. "This doesn't have to be about her."

"You and I both know we're not going to play it that way."

"No. What about this phone connection?"

"I traced it while I was looking into the room. It's clean."

That was something, then.

"If that room is bugged," Allison went on, "that means someone has pierced my firewalls. I'm not even going to begin to tell you how impossible that is."

"Not impossible," Rafe said. "You're outside the NSA channels."

"My personal systems have as much security on them as

anything the NSA has. I designed a lot of what the NSA is working with."

"Just means that the caliber of whoever we're up against is impressive."

"In the stratosphere of impressive," Allison agreed.

Rafe smiled at that. Allison never doubted her computer abilities. Neither did he.

"The fact that they bugged the room tells us something else," Allison said. "Either whoever is behind it doesn't have all the information they want—"

"Or their position isn't strong enough to simply come by and take us," Rafe said. He'd been thinking along the same lines.

"Right."

"The question is—what are we going to do about it?"

"For the moment stay there. It'll help if they think you're stationary."

"I can't begin to tell you how dissatisfied I am with that answer."

"I've hacked into the hotel security system. I'll be watching. All night. I'll also have a team standing by. If someone makes a move on the two of you, I'll know soon enough to warn you."

Rafe paced even though the effort made his knee hurt. "I don't like playing the stalking horse. You know that."

"I know that. That's why if you decide to take her and get out of there, I'll understand."

Rafe breathed into the silence she left for him.

"But the truth of the matter is that if the two of you go into motion before I'm ready, I don't know how much I can help. Tonight has proven that this is larger than I thought it was."

That was an understatement. But Rafe was too tactful to point that out.

"This might be the only chance I get to shut the door on this," Allison went on. "And you've seen some of the people that have been targeted. Politicians. Military personnel. This is a national threat that no one knows about yet."

"Have you told the president?" Rafe asked.

Allison had a personal tie to President of the United States Gabe Monihan. Her father Adam had been an Arizona state senator and a mover and shaker in Washington before accepting a position as an Arizona Supreme Court Justice. Her brother David was the U.S. Attorney General.

Allison hesitated. "Yes. But that's off the record. He trusted me to get this investigation done quietly."

"Understood." Rafe felt better knowing the president was in the loop. His whole adult life had been spent observing a chain of command. Even when he stepped outside the lines, as he had tonight, it was better to know that what he was doing was to benefit his country.

"And by telling you that, I'm trusting you."

"You knew you could do that when you placed the first phone call a couple weeks ago."

"I know. I'm getting paranoid. I hate when I can't trust my own systems." Fatigue resonated in her voice.

"When's the last time you slept?"

"It's been a while."

"You might want to think about it."

"I'll take that under advisement. And if you're insinuating that I might go to sleep while I'm keeping watch over you tonight, I'm not alone."

Some of the tension uncoiled inside Rafe. That had been a concern, but he'd been reluctant to voice it.

"Provided we make it through tonight," Rafe said, "what do you have for a game plan in the morning?"

"I'm hoping to have more information on the China connection. I've got data miners and sniffer packets thrown all through the Internet around those servers. I promise you, whoever's behind this isn't going to stay invisible for long. Computers are my kung fu."

Rafe knew that. Every op she'd assisted had come down to the wire in one place or another and had depended on her cyber expertise. He'd never met another person who was as detail-oriented, driven or cool under pressure as Allison Gracelyn.

She'd trusted him—even after North Korea—to help out in an op that was eyes only for the president. How could he do any less?

"All right," he said. "We'll do it your way. I'll be the cheese. You just make sure I have a fair chance at any rats that might come calling tonight."

Chapter 10

I don't know who you are, Shannon thought as she went through the packages the mysterious woman had arranged to be delivered to the hotel room, *but you've got good taste.*

The packages contained quality clothing. And shoes. Nothing like the sling-backs she'd lost at the bar while facing Drago but good shoes nonetheless. Even if Shannon couldn't be friends with the woman, they could definitely shop together.

As she unpacked the clothing and hung it in the closet, she listened to the news channel on television. She'd turned it to ABS first and had been mortified to learn that she was the object of a large manhunt throughout Washington, D.C.

Her phone had started blowing up, too. As she'd watched the screen, pictures of her producer, her boss and then *his* boss had shown up.

Everyone was trying to get in touch with her.

It felt good being that popular—but creepy at the same time.

She also felt as if she was in the middle of the story she'd been chasing for five months. Ever since the students had been kidnapped from Athena Academy and ended up in Kestonia, and the other business had taken place down in Puerto Isla, then the diamond mine rebellion outside of Cape Town, she'd felt as though there was another story—a bigger story—lying right there beneath the surface.

She just hadn't been able to get down to it.

Seeing the young woman who'd delivered the SUV had reminded Shannon of Athena Academy. The women turned out there just walked through life with a different kind of confidence. That was especially true of the ones who ended up going into military, espionage or law enforcement. As the instructors had taught at the academy, those fields took a remarkable kind of woman.

They didn't put one woman above the other, though. Artists, musicians and even the one stand-up comedienne Athena had turned out had all received the adoration of the staff upon their graduation and subsequent successes.

Shannon was the only one who hadn't—and still didn't— receive those accolades. In her own way, she was every bit as successful as Tory Patton Forsythe. She'd even received one more journalism award than Tory had.

But Tory was one of the golden girls.

Don't go there, she told herself. *You'll only be unhappy.*

Even fifteen years later, her expulsion from Athena still left its mark. That embarrassment was one of the reasons she'd pushed herself out of her parents' home and away from the constant infighting that went on there to find her own life.

Despite those successes, it was hard not to think of the academy. In fact, when she'd first heard the woman on the phone, Shannon had thought the voice sounded familiar.

However, that was foolishness. Other than Tory, Shannon didn't see anyone from the academy.

But Stefan Blackman hooked up with that FBI agent, Katie Rush, after the kidnappings, didn't he? Shannon knew they must have just missed each other on that investigation. Katie Rush, as Shannon had found out from Gary's background material, had been an Athena graduate.

Then there was Sasha Bracciali. Shannon had met that Athena grad while in Kestonia covering the return of the kidnapping victims.

Coincidence?

You're a reporter, Shannon chided herself. *There's no such thing as coincidence.*

Then she remembered Jessica Whittaker. Also an Athena grad. She'd been down in Puerto Isla when all the confusion down there had taken place.

Shannon picked up her notepad, flipped the page and started making notes for herself. Now, in the middle of her own problems, she started connecting the dots on those other instances.

Something was definitely going on. She had to wonder how big it was.

But she'd gotten the biggest piece of the puzzle while down in Cape Town, South Africa. While down there, Shannon had crossed paths with Lucy Cannon, the mercenary who'd been involved in the fallout of the diamond mine uproar.

While in Cape Town, Shannon had also gotten a tip from her unknown source that Allison Gracelyn was an agent for the National Security Agency and was responsible for the unrest involving the diamond mine.

Even though Shannon had wanted that particular story to be true, she hadn't been able to find any proof of the claim and Lucy had denied it. Shortly after the uprising at the diamond mine, the voice that had given Shannon so many hot leads over the years had gone silent.

For almost two months Shannon had wondered what had caused the silence. She'd also had to wonder if that disappearance had anything to do with her inability to tie the troubles at the diamond mine to Allison Gracelyn.

During the last two months Shannon had increased her investigation into Allison. The two women hadn't spoken since that night in the academy when Allison had denied her involvement in the prank on Josie.

Before she knew it, Shannon was trapped once more in the memory of her frustrating inability to save herself. If Allison had spoken up that night, simply owned up to her culpability and the fact that she'd put Shannon up to it, Shannon knew her whole life would have been different.

Different maybe, Shannon told herself, *but that doesn't mean anything would have been better. Who was it that had said living well was the best revenge?* She couldn't remember.

That was what she was doing, though. She had a good life.

Except for the whole getting-killed-by-Drago thing.

That hadn't gone the way she thought it might.

Shannon pushed the thoughts out of her mind and concentrated on putting away the clothing. She also thought about the man and wondered if he was actually coming back.

She felt an unaccustomed twinge at that thought that he was gone for good. Although they'd been together intensely for the last few hours, she gotten to feel as though she knew him. She'd also realized there was a lot about him that she didn't know.

Like where he'd gotten those scars.

One of the boxes revealed an unexpected surprise that almost made Shannon groan in delight. And wouldn't that have sounded great to whoever was listening in on the bugging devices?

The makeup kit in the box was *exactly* like the one she'd purchased for home use four months ago. That realization was uncomfortable. It meant someone had either broken into her house and found out what makeup she used or they'd gone through her charge cards with a fine-toothed comb.

Either one of those options left her feeling violated.

I'm going to find out who you are, Shannon promised, *and you're going to feel just as violated after I get through with you.*

She grabbed fresh panties, raided one of the male T-shirts from the His boxes, picked up the iPod that was included in her things and the terry-cloth robe and headed for the bathroom.

Rafe entered the hotel room and looked for Shannon. When he didn't see her immediately, he figured she must have bolted as soon as the chance had presented itself. There were two other exits in addition to the main entrance.

Then he noticed the clothes hanging in the closet. It didn't make sense that she would take time to hang up the clothes and then run.

Where is she?

The bathroom door was closed, but he heard the sound of running water. He stood outside the door and called her name.

There was no response.

He called again, louder this time.

Still no response, and the water kept gurgling.

Slightly alarmed, he slipped the pistol from his hip and slid the safety off. He tried the door and discovered it was locked.

He called her name one more time, then rapped on the door.

When there was still no answer, he took the fake driver's license from his wallet and loided the lock. Images of Shannon Connor with her throat cut flooded his mind. They hurt in ways he didn't expect.

He'd spent days thinking about her while shadowing her in New York. He knew how her hair fell across her face when she was caught up in an interesting interview and how her lip curled slightly when she knew she was being lied to and treated like a ditzy blonde. A congressman and a movie producer had both learned the error of their ways in the last couple weeks.

Rafe couldn't have put a name to what the woman had that had caught him so completely. She was interesting, but he'd met several interesting women. Allison Gracelyn was one of the most interesting women he'd ever met, and he hadn't thought about her as much as he had Shannon Connor.

He thought maybe part of the appeal was the possibility that she was in danger. Saving people mattered, and when he helped save people, Rafe knew *he* mattered. That felt good. He liked feeling good.

He hadn't felt good like that since before North Korea. In fact, until Allison had made that phone call, he'd thought he wasn't ever going to feel that way again.

That was before Allison had told him that Shannon Connor wasn't one of the good guys. Now the possibility to save an innocent was gone.

The door was open, but he paused even though he wanted to know if she was alive or dead.

"Shannon," he called in a loud voice.

Only silence answered him.

Fearfully, not knowing how he was going to handle it if the woman had ended up dead on his watch after all, Rafe pushed the door open.

Then fear melted and turned to anger.

Shannon lay soaking in the large bathtub. The air was thick with heat and soap that smelled faintly of lemon and lilac. Foam covered only part of her beautiful body. The generous curve of her breasts and the flaring of her hips was visible. Her wet hair was combed back and left her delicate features uncovered.

She had her head back on the bathtub and her eyes closed.

Earbuds from her iPod were in her ears. She rocked her head in time with whatever she was listening to. The delicate motion created eddies that were echoed by her breasts.

Rafe stood there, taking her in. He couldn't help it. Seeing her naked took him back to the time when he was twelve years old and had discovered his uncle Pete's *Playboy* stash. He'd been living with his parents in upstate New York then. He'd had a dog and a tree house and had been utterly innocent in so many ways.

He'd flipped through that magazine and promised himself when he got old enough he'd have a girlfriend who looked just like Miss May.

Then he'd grown up and discovered that women were more complicated than pinups. There were a lot of beautiful women in the world. He'd shared drinks and dinner and beds with several of them.

But none of them left him feeling the way he did now. Lying there in that bathtub with the soap only partially covering her, Shannon Connor could have been a pinup just like the ones he'd grown up with. There still remained that sense of innocence and fun about her.

Most women merely got naked.

Shannon was…unearthly.

It was the most amazing thing Rafe had ever seen.

Then her eyes opened and she looked at him. She screamed and slapped a torrent of water over him.

Chapter 11

Rafe didn't have time to escape the waterfall thrown in his direction. In a heartbeat he was drenched. He stood there in the doorway, the pistol at his side, and refused to give up the territory he'd claimed. He dripped onto the floor.

"What are you doing in here?" Shannon exploded. "Get out!"

The illusion of unearthly beauty faded in a heartbeat.

Shannon reached for a nearby towel and dragged it into the water in an attempt to cover her body. Since the material floated, the effort was only partially successful.

"Knocking," she said loudly. "Have you ever tried it?"

Irritated and embarrassed because he wasn't in the habit of walking in on naked women unless by invitation, Rafe banged his knuckles on the door. Shannon still had the earbuds in place. She couldn't hear him.

Shannon's harsh gaze softened a little. Sheepishly she reached up for the earbuds. "You did knock."

"Three times." Rafe turned his back to her. "When I didn't hear you, I got worried."

"Oh."

"Now that I know you're okay, I'm going to leave." Rafe started to pull the door closed behind him. The water-soaked clothing was already turning cold under the room's air-conditioning.

"Hey," she called.

"Yeah."

"Thanks for coming to check on me."

"You're welcome."

"But there's something you need to know."

He waited, but he didn't turn around.

"If someone does come after me, you'll be able to tell."

"I'll keep that in mind." Rafe pulled the door closed behind him. He looked down at his drenched clothing and blew out an angry breath. *Allison, after this, you owe me big-time.*

While Rafe was going through the boxes of clothes looking for a dry shirt, someone knocked on the door. Drawing his weapon, he stepped into the closet beside the door rather than stand behind the door. If someone wanted to surprise him by shooting through the door before they broke in, they'd be even more surprised not to find him there.

"Who is it?" he asked.

"I got a pizza delivery."

Rafe slid the pistol back into the holster and asked how much the order was. When he got the quote, he slid the money and tip under the door.

"Just leave the pizza. I'll get it when I get dressed."

"Okay. Thanks."

After a moment, Rafe looked through the peephole. No one was in the hallway. He opened the door and brought the pizza inside. He left the food on the table by the balcony, then walked down to the vending area, bought three Diet Cokes and three waters, put them in the room's ice bucket and filled the bucket the rest of the way with ice.

When he got back to the room, Shannon was out of the bath and dressed in a terry-cloth robe that accentuated her figure in ways it wasn't intended to. The effect was especially noticeable as she bent over the table to divvy the pizza onto paper napkins. Rafe forgot about being mad.

"Want a piece?" Shannon asked.

It was about then that Rafe realized he'd forgotten he knew the language. The terry-cloth material had left little to the imagination.

Shannon turned, holding a piece of pizza in her hand. "Pepperoni or sausage?"

Rafe tried to speak and couldn't. He had to clear his throat to get his voice working again. "Sure."

"Which?"

"One of each."

Shannon placed the pizza on a napkin. "We don't have any plates."

"My fault. I forgot to ask for any."

"Plates would have made everything simpler."

Rafe bit back a reply about how if she hadn't gotten involved with Vincent Drago, everything would have been peachy. He set the ice bucket of drinks on the table, scooped up the pizza and walked to the balcony. He peered through the window, wondering if Allison had her people in place.

"Expecting company?" Shannon asked.

"The police are looking for you. Anything can happen." Rafe turned to her and pointed at the lamp to remind her about the bug.

Shannon mouthed the words, *I know.* Then aloud she said, "I was watching the news."

"Learn anything?"

She shook her head. "Not yet."

Rafe looked at the television, then used the remote control he found on the bed to turn up the audio. Unable to talk about what was really on their minds because the room was bugged and because apparently neither of them was in the mood for small talk, they watched television and ate in silence.

Things didn't look promising. The bar's camera clearly showed Shannon when she'd entered the bar and joined Vincent Drago. They also had some really bad pictures of him that he felt certain they couldn't use to identify him.

When he finished eating, Rafe sat and flicked through the various news stations. He knew channel-hopping was probably driving Shannon crazy, but he didn't care.

"Why don't you go soak your leg?" Shannon asked.

It was only then that Rafe realized he was massaging his knee the way he had in the weeks shortly after the surgery, before the pain had turned into something he found tolerable. Tonight the aches had teeth.

"The tub has a whirlpool function," Shannon said. "Maybe it'll help."

Rafe was going to refuse the suggestion on general grounds of cussedness. *That would be really stupid. You're going to need your knee in shape when you walk off this assignment tomorrow.* He wasn't holding out any hope for tonight. *Go soak the knee and keep it loose.*

"All right." Rafe stood and drained the last of his Diet Coke. "While I'm in there, you might want to keep the television down low and not use the earbuds. It's just a suggestion."

Shannon's eyes narrowed and her jaw locked, but she didn't say anything.

Rafe took a change of clothes and headed to the bathroom.

What an arrogant butthead! Shannon sat on the bed and painted her toenails. Whenever she was majorly stressed—and being on the run from the police after nearly being killed counted as major stress—she could work on either stories or nails.

She didn't have a handle on the story that was breaking loose around her. So it was nails. Either toenails or fingernails would work. As tired as she was, she didn't trust her fine motor skills to deal with fingernails.

She also noticed that *he*—she thought of other names to call him but settled for the gender-specific at the moment—had left the bathroom door slightly ajar. Doubtless that was because he didn't trust her to be alert. With the door open, he could hear everything that happened in the room.

What he didn't realize was that the positioning of the mirrors in the room allowed her to watch him as he undressed.

At first Shannon wasn't going to watch. She didn't like thinking that watching some Neanderthal remove his trappings of civilization was of any interest to her. But when he'd pulled his shirt off and revealed a broad chest and rock-hard abs, she'd been mesmerized.

She felt a little guilt at watching.

It's only fair, she told herself. *He saw you starkers.*

Finished with her toenails, at least for the moment, she capped the polish and set it aside.

The water in the tub was so hot it filled the room with steam that partially obscured her view. That was aggravating, but there was enough clarity that she didn't have to guess at much.

What there was turned out to be impressive. She wouldn't have guessed *that* much. An anticipatory quiver peaked in her stomach and her loins. She lay back on the bed and stared into the bathroom.

His body was a tapestry of scars. Most of them were old, but there were a lot of new ones, as well. He was muscular and defined. He'd been working out and it showed. He sat on the edge of the tub with his feet in the water as if gathering his nerve to crawl in.

Shannon took in the sight of his naked back, his wide shoulders and that firm butt that was so white against his bronzed skin. Wherever he'd been, he'd stayed outside most of the summer. That kind of tan didn't come out of a bottle or a tanning booth.

Before Shannon knew it, her hand had drifted down past her stomach and was threatening to continue on farther south where her body demanded release. Reluctantly, definitely aware that she would have had enough time before he finished his bath, she curled her fingers into a fist and drew it away. Frustration on several levels bit into her.

You need to think about something else. She even managed to turn her head away from the open gap presented by the bathroom door. How she could even think of something like that after the events of the evening was beyond her.

She concentrated on the television news, but it was already becoming repetitive. Her iPhone vibrated on the bed beside her. She checked the screen and saw Gary's picture there.

"Hello?" Shannon answered.

"Hey. I got lucky on your man of mystery. That advice about the military connection was *mucho* solid."

Conscious of the bug in the room, Shannon watched what she said. She sat up on the bed.

"All right," she said.

"His name's Rafe—short for Raphael—Santorini, but he's still mysterious. At least for the moment. My cyber minions are pursuing him even now. Whatever secrets he's got, he's not going to get to keep them."

A picture floated to the surface on the iPhone's view screen. It was of the man, but it had been taken before he'd gotten the scars on his face and neck.

"Give me the *TV Guide* version for the moment," Shannon instructed. "Then e-mail me whatever you get."

Gary sounded disappointed. "All right. I just put a lot of hard work into gathering this quickly."

"It'll still be appreciated later. When I'm digging into the file for myself."

"Okay. I've pulled up his military record. He was in the United States Army Rangers for eight years. From what I can tell—and some of this information hasn't yet been released for public consumption—most of those eight years were spent in combat."

That explains the scars, Shannon thought. "That background doesn't tell me what he's doing here now."

"Six and a half years ago, he left the military. The feeling I get is that he turned spook."

Spook as in government agent, Shannon thought.

"During the last year of his military career he remained constantly on loan to the CIA, the DEA and other agencies of that ilk. What he did there is still beyond my reach at the moment, but I think we can safely think what he was doing was bloody and violent. When he mustered out, even though the Army had been willing to keep him around, he left. He files tax forms that list him as a partner in a New York private investigations firm, but I checked with people who've used that firm. Santorini's name is on the door, but he's hardly ever there. Kind of a silent partner. I don't know about you, but that sounds like government agent to me."

Shannon silently agreed. She'd been on the fringe of operations she wasn't supposed to know enough about to know what she was supposed to know and what she wasn't. Some of those stories had been painful to let go when she couldn't get corroboration.

Thinking of the man—of *Rafe,* she amended—as a soldier helped. Most of them didn't think for themselves. They just followed the commands of God and President. He was there doing what the woman told him to do.

"What is this craziness you're involved in?" Gary asked.

"You're in the nation's capital with a bona fide hero who might also be a hit man for the federal government—and you're wanted for murder."

"That wasn't me," she insisted. "I never killed anyone."

She glanced back at the bathroom. Rafe had finally crawled into the tub. Everything might have now been hidden, but she could still see his face—sans sunglasses, even—and his shoulders. Either of those would have been acceptable to her.

Except that he was potentially the enemy.

"I believe you," Gary said. "But they're trying you in the media."

She knew that, too. Unfortunately, there was nothing she could do about that at the moment.

"E-mail me those files," she told Gary. "And keep digging. It would help if I knew which government agency he's working for."

"I will. You just stay safe."

Shannon said she would, but she felt paranoid when she did. What if someone out there tracked the call? They could do that now. She'd done stories covering that technology.

She broke the connection and started to lay the iPhone aside. It vibrated again. She guessed that it was Gary again. He called often when he was researching a story because he didn't want to make mistakes. For all his computer guruism, he was still occasionally insecure.

But it wasn't Gary. The view screen was completely blank except for the declaration: *Your life is in danger.*

Chapter 12

Shaken, Shannon glanced at the bathroom. He—*Rafe,* she reminded herself—was still in the tub. The wispy hot water fog eddied around the bathroom and blurred him as he sat in the whirlpool.

She opened the iPhone to the miniature keyboard. Shaking a little, she typed rapidly with her thumbs.

Who are you?

A friend.

All my friends have names.

I am Kwan-Sook.

The name looked Chinese to Shannon. She wasn't an expert, but it definitely fit the bill.

I don't know anyone by that name.

We've never met. I've worked with you for years, giving you little snippets of information here and whispers of secrets there.

Shannon's heart beat faster. She didn't know if it was the person she'd been working with for so long. In fact, she didn't know if the name Kwan-Sook belonged to a male or a female. It might have been the name of a species of lizard or lotus.

Where have you been? I haven't heard anything from you in months. I thought something had happened to you.

Things have been very difficult for me. We share an enemy that is very crafty. I've been forced to become more crafty. Contacting you now is not without risk.

How can I trust you?

How can you not? Your whole life has changed tonight. You don't have the luxury of staying still at this time. If you're going to keep on living, you've got to take control of your fate.

Shannon didn't have an argument for that.

Being in charge of what's happening to me sounds fantastic.

Good.

Except that I've not got a whole lot of experience eluding the police.

I can help you. I will help you.

For a moment Shannon just concentrated on her breathing. She glanced at the bathroom and saw that Rafe seemed to be asleep in the tub, his head tilted back. The dark bulk of the pistol sat on a small table he'd pulled closer. The weapon was within easy reach.

The view screen pulsed with the arrival of a new message.

I need you to escape that room.

Even if I did, where would I go?

Come here.

Where?

To Hong Kong.

Shannon stared at the iPhone's view screen in disbelief. Hadn't Rafe's woman contact mentioned Shanghai? Not Hong Kong? She wasn't sure. She was tired and she knew her mind might be playing tricks on her.

I can't get there. I'm wanted in a murder investigation. My passport and identification are going to be flagged in airport computers everywhere. I won't be able to get out of the country.

If you'll allow me, I can get you out.

Why?

Because I can't tell the story that needs to be told without you. I need you to be free to find out things I can't. When you do, I need you to tell the world.

What's the story?

Do you know the man you're with?

Shannon typed, *No* because she'd learned a long time ago never to give up more information than she got. Furthermore, it would be a test of "Kwan-Sooks'" knowledge.

His name is Rafe Santorini. He's an agent for your country's National Security Agency.

Okay, Shannon thought, *you know some things. And that fits with what Gary was thinking.*

I also know that Rafe Santorini works for Allison Gracelyn.

Suddenly Shannon was halfway across the United States in principal Christine Evans's office as Marion Gracelyn passed judgment on her and banned her from the academy.

Allison? Allison is behind this? Shannon calmed herself, but it was hard. All that old anger and the feelings of betrayal surfaced within her. She knew she didn't trust Allison. Especially not after the way she'd acted like Little Miss Innocence after Tory Patton had caught Shannon red-handed.

Allison had let Shannon hang by herself fifteen years ago. If she was involved with what was going on now, there was no way Shannon wanted to trust her.

Can you prove that?

There was no answer for a moment, then an image floated to the top of the screen. It was an identification card. Even though she hadn't seen her in years, Shannon recognized Allison at once.

Don't believe the first thing you're shown, Shannon reminded herself. That was one of the rules given to her by her first supervisor. Anything that was shown freely the first time out was only the tip of the iceberg for what could be gotten.

Almost immediately a Web link floated onto the screen. Shannon clicked on it.

Pictures and files filled the screen. All of them focused on Allison Gracelyn at a nondescript office building. Military guys managed the security gates. It was exactly the kind of place where a clandestine government agency might set up operations.

The Web page vanished.

I can show you more at a later time if you'd like. We don't have much time.

Shannon knew that was true.

Did you bug the hotel room?

Is the room under electronic surveillance?

That's what I was told.

Then you're in more danger than I believed.

What danger?

Allison Gracelyn isn't the only enemy we face.

And isn't that just perfectly mysterious? Shannon stared at the statement and tried to figure out the implications behind it.

Hello?

I'm here.

You need to decide what you're going to do. If you don't trust me, I can't help you. And you're not going to be able to help yourself at this point.

Shannon stared at the blinking cursor. Given what had happened with Vincent Drago, she was inclined to agree with the blunt assessment. Of course, she still didn't care for it.

She took a deep breath and let it out. Okay, so which was it? Did she trust or did she sit still and hope everything worked out? And if she sat still, wasn't she trusting Rafe Santorini and Allison—who had, by the way, already betrayed her.

Not a big fan of waiting for everything to work out, she told herself. Very few things in her life ever had.

Okay. I'm in.

Good! ☺ Then we need to get you out of there.

I don't know if I can get past Rafe. He's good, and he acts quickly.

Go to the desk. Pull out the middle drawer. There, taped underneath, is a small envelope containing a pre-measured amount of powder. Put it in something he's eating or drinking.

You should have told me before now, Shannon thought, remembering all the pizza and water he'd inhaled.

She went to the desk and found the packet exactly where she'd been told to look. The packet was glassine. The white powder was clearly visible.

Then a sobering thought hit her. She retreated to the iPhone.

What does the powder do? I don't want him hurt.

It'll only make him sleep for a short time. Nothing more. You'll have to make the most of the time the drug gives you. The D.C. police are only searching for you as a person of interest. If Raphael Santorini turns up dead in a hotel room where only you were known to have been with him, they will search even harder for you.

Allison is tapped into this room somehow.

Shannon was certain of that. Otherwise Rafe wouldn't have stayed there with her.

She's inside the hotel's security system. So am I. When the time comes, she'll never see you leaving.

The announcement impressed Shannon. It was kind of intimidating trusting people who had that kind of power. She knew systems could be hacked. They were all the time. She'd talked to people who did that. However, her life had never been hanging in the balance.

Who are you?

I can't tell you any more at this time. But you've got to move soon. Our other enemy is probably closing in on your location right now.

Right. The other enemy. Shannon took a deep breath and calmed herself. Mentally she went through the clothes that Allison had provided for her and picked out the evening's attire. It was important to be organized.

I'll be here waiting when you need me.

Shannon stared at the words, then turned the screen off. Through the gap in the bathroom doorway, she watched Rafe Santorini push up from the tub. He looked just as interesting coming out as he did going in.

Then she remembered she had an escape to arrange. She picked up the glassine packet and emptied it into one of the water bottles. Quietly, feeling as if her nerves were crawling inside her, she watched Rafe dress.

The soak helped Rafe's knee. By the time he clambered out of the tub, with more difficulty than he'd had in months, it felt looser. It was markedly swollen, though. There was even a hint of bruising.

He dressed a little awkwardly, but he pulled on the Dockers over the knee brace. Normally at night he didn't wear the brace and allowed his leg time to air out. With him acting as the cheese in a trap tonight, though, that wasn't going to happen.

He ran the belt through the Dockers and the holster, then slid the pistol into place. He slid into a beige collarless pullover, used deodorant and cologne and walked into the room.

Shannon sat cross-legged on the bed. That surprised him.

"I figured you'd be asleep by now," he said.

"Can't," she said. "I tried."

Rafe studied her. Her casual, almost friendly tone surprised him, too. His warning radar came up and started sweeping.

"Look," she said, "I want to apologize for throwing water on you."

Rafe didn't say anything. He tried to figure out where she was coming from.

"I shouldn't have had the earbuds in," she went on. "I wasn't thinking. I just wanted to relax. When I bathe, I listen to music. Evidently your *friend* knew that. She's the one who sent the bath oil beads and the iPod. Loaded with some of my favorite music, I might add."

At that, Rafe grinned. That was typical Allison. Always superthorough and detail-oriented.

"Your friend is very nosy," Shannon said.

"She prefers to think of herself as well-informed."

"I'm not going to be happy thinking about her raiding my home."

Rafe had to admit that he wouldn't be either. In fact, he wasn't any too happy about being manipulated into the present situation.

"I've been thinking," Shannon said.

Rafe waited.

"I've realized that I haven't been trained to keep myself alive the way you have," she said. "With that being the case, as long as it's known that I don't agree with what's going on, I think we should declare a truce."

"What kind of truce?"

"I'm not going to interfere with how you handle things anymore."

Rafe didn't know if he believed that and he supposed his reticence showed on his face.

"That doesn't mean I'm not going to have questions," Shannon said. "Or reservations." She shook her head. "Especially reservations. And I'm not going to let the being-spied-on thing just fade away."

"Catching my friend is like reaching out for a fistful of smoke," Rafe said.

"Maybe you just haven't managed to catch her."

Rafe grinned. "Some of the best people in the world have tried to catch her. They haven't."

"I'll concede that she's a challenge." Shannon got up from the bed and walked to the table. "In the meantime, I'm willing to declare a truce. If you are." She took two bottles of water from the ice bucket.

Rafe crossed his arms and leaned against the wall to ease the weight off his knee. "I could live with a truce." *Because as soon as morning comes, I'm out of here.*

Shannon loosened the cap on one of the water bottles and handed it to him. "Good. Then a truce it is." She smiled as she opened her own bottle, then toasted him. "What is it you military types say? Hydrate or die?"

A grin pulled at Rafe's lips. "Something like that." He touched her bottle with his and drank deeply.

"There's still some pizza," she offered.

Rafe shook his head. The hot water from the bath had left him parched. "I couldn't eat any more." He nodded at the television. "Anything new?"

"They're retreading the story." Shannon resumed her seat on the bed. "Folding in extra details. They've got a better bio of me, but a lot of the pictures are still weak. They don't have my good side."

Personally, Rafe didn't think she could take a bad picture. He took another pull on the bottle. "You stood up to Vincent Drago tonight. That was pretty intense."

Shannon pulled her knees up to her chin and wrapped her arms around her legs. "I haven't been that scared in a long time."

"Me, neither."

She looked at him. "You weren't scared."

"I was. After things got crazy in the bar, I didn't think I was going to find you in time."

"But you did."

He nodded. "I did."

"He could have killed you when he shot into the car."

"It was a close thing. It wasn't from lack of trying." Rafe drank more water. A wave of weakness rattled through him. His head suddenly felt heavy, and he thought it was going to tip him over.

"Are you okay?" Shannon's voice sounded as if it was coming from the bottom of a cave.

Rafe knew something was wrong, but by that time his face was closing in on the carpeted floor like an out-of-control express train.

Chapter 13

When Shannon saw how fast the drug took Rafe under its control, she was afraid it had done more than put him to sleep. She hurried over to him and put two fingers against the carotid artery in his throat.

His pulse was slow and faint, but it was there.

Thank God.

Relief flooded through her. She looked at his lips and saw they held their normal coloration. If they'd been blue, it would have meant he was cyanotic and not getting enough oxygen.

His breathing was shallow but regular. It also looked deep enough to clear the carbon dioxide from his lungs. That was one of the problems postoperative patients faced after coming back from heavy sedation. People breathing too shallowly while anesthetized could actually "drown" in carbon dioxide.

She rolled him over onto his back, which wasn't easy because he was big and dead weight. Then she took a pillow from the bed and put it under his neck to tilt his head back and open his breathing passages normally. In that position he'd be able to breathe more easily.

Then she went to the closet and pulled out the jeans, light sweater and shoes she'd chosen. She skimmed into panty hose while she opened her iPhone.

One-handed she typed,

HELLO?

I'm here.

He's asleep.

Good. When you get out into the hallway, call me. Texting isn't going to be beneficial at this point.

Okay.

Shannon finished dressing, decided she could live without makeup for the moment, ran a brush through her hair, then swiped all the cash in Rafe's wallet. He had a lot of it. A quick count revealed almost three thousand dollars.

Nobody innocent carried that kind of money.

Cash ensured no paper trail.

She paused at the door and looked back at Rafe, comatose and helpless on the floor. If she hadn't known he worked for Allison, she might have felt guilty. And maybe—just a little—she still did.

She walked through the door and left the guilt behind. She had no choice if she wanted to get to the bottom of the story that had been building for years.

And maybe, just maybe, she was going to find out what was being hidden at Athena Academy.

* * *

In the hallway Shannon dialed the number that showed on her iPhone's screen.

The area code was three-one-oh, which should have made it a Los Angeles number. However, since phone customers could now take their phone numbers with them, that didn't necessarily mean anything.

She plugged her earbuds in as she listened to the phone ring. Once.

"Hello," a mellow woman's voice answered in a proper British accent.

"Hi."

"Go to the elevators."

Shannon hesitated as she looked at the security cameras in the hallway. "If Allison is tapped into the building's security systems, she's seen me by now."

"I've guaranteed that she hasn't. What she's looking at now is a loop of an image that I've prepared for just this instance. But we must hurry. In my dealings with her I've discovered that she's very competent."

That hasn't changed, Shannon thought.

"Take an elevator down to the second floor. I'll walk you through the rest of your escape."

Shannon did as she was told, but the whole time she was afraid she was going to get caught.

"Allison has a sentry on duty in the lobby," Kwan-Sook said. "We'll dodge him."

"How did you get the powder into my room?"

"I employ various agents in a number of countries."

"'Agents'? Are you part of the Chinese government?" The possibility that she was doing something potentially treasonous hadn't occurred to Shannon until that moment.

"It's just an expression. You would call them employees. I'm not a member of the Chinese government, nor do I represent them. I do, however, act on behalf of several businessmen whose interests are presently being menaced by American involvement."

When the elevator doors dinged, Shannon got out on the second floor.

"Walk to the end of the hallway. There's a fire hose station hanging on the wall."

Shannon walked to the end of the hall and found the glass case containing the neatly folded fire hose.

"Leave your iPhone here and use the one inside the case."

Further inspection revealed an iPhone that was identical to the one Shannon carried.

"Why am I changing phones?"

"Yours has a GPS transponder in it. Allison would be able to follow you."

We definitely wouldn't want that. Shannon lifted out the other iPhone.

"Do you know how to change SIM cards? If you don't, I can provide instruction."

"No, thanks. I know how." Shannon made it a habit to manipulate her own SIM card anytime she bought a new phone. She had too many private phone numbers and information on hers to risk anyone getting access to it.

"I'll call you in a few minutes," Kwan-Sook said. "While you're waiting, make your way to the emergency escape at this end of the hotel. It lets out onto a side street."

The phone went dead.

Shannon quickly changed out the SIM card. When she turned the phone on, she saw the battery was fully charged. She hooked the earbuds in and clipped the iPhone to her waistband to leave her hands free.

She headed for the fire escape.

* * *

Minutes later, Shannon stepped from the hotel. Streetlights lit the back area parking lot. She gazed around, but the few people making their way through the parking lot didn't seem interested in her.

Her phone rang and she answered.

"Yes."

"Good. You're in the parking lot."

Shannon glanced around. "You can see me?"

"Through the security cameras outside the hotel, yes. Three rows up, on your left, four spaces over, you'll find a gray Honda Civic."

Shannon strode across the silent parking lot and found the vehicle exactly where she'd been told it would be. She tried the door.

"It's locked," she said.

"One moment, please."

Only a moment later, the door lock lifted with a snick.

Calmly, as if she had every right to be there, Shannon opened the door and slid behind the wheel. She looked around for keys but didn't find any. She was about to say something when the car started all by itself.

"Ah," Kwan-Sook said, "you have to appreciate the car manufacturers' way of making everything electronic. So many things are easier these days through the telematics systems they build into the cars."

"I suppose," Shannon said. She wasn't all that enamored of car services, not even ones that seemed as if they came right out of *Blade Runner.* New York wasn't a driver-friendly city.

But she knew how to drive. She put the car into gear and rolled through the parking lot.

"Where am I going?"

"To Dulles International Airport."

"I don't know how to drive there." Shannon had always taken taxis.

Abruptly the navigation system on the dash came to life. A city map spread across the screen. A heartbeat later, a driving route limned in red snaked through the streets.

"You do now," Kwan-Sook said.

Shannon had to smile at the sound of exultation in the woman's voice. At the insistence of the soothing baritone voice provided by the navigator system, she turned right onto the street beside the parking lot and pulled into the early-morning traffic.

Despite the clandestine nature of the meeting and the double-oh-seven technology being used, Shannon hadn't lost sight of the fact that Vincent Drago had tried to kill her and Allison Gracelyn was leveraging the vast, unknowable resources of the National Security Agency against whatever Shannon was trying to find out.

She drove automatically, but she found herself distracted by thoughts of Rafe Santorini. He worked for the NSA. She wondered how much trouble he was going to be in.

"All right," she said calmly, "I need to know what this story is about."

"This is the greatest story of all those I've given you," Kwan-Sook said.

That's a hard promise to deliver, Shannon thought. Over the years she'd gotten some truly stellar news scoops.

"You're aware that the Athena Academy is privately funded to a large extent?" Kwan-Sook asked.

Shannon did know that.

"Have you heard of Dr. Aldritch Peters?"

The name struck a chord within Shannon's memory. She thought as she drove and followed the directions. Just when she felt certain she wasn't going to remember, it came to her.

"He's a geneticist," Shannon said. "One of the pioneers on the human genome research."

"That's correct. You've got a very good mind, Ms. Connor."

"Just call me Shannon."

"Thank you."

"I—*we*—did a story on one of Dr. Peters's students who has set up an egg clinic in Dallas, Texas."

That had been an interesting story. Prepackaged fertilized eggs from select donors were sold to childless couples who had trouble conceiving for one reason or another. Peters's name and work had come up several times in the interview.

The strange thing was that Peters himself seemed to have disappeared and didn't have as much research published as the student had believed he did.

"Dr. Peters was involved with an entity known as Lab 33," Kwan-Sook said.

Lab 33 was easy to remember. It had existed only a short distance from the Athena Academy. In fact, some of the personnel at that lab had taught at the academy as well as maintained research centers on school premises.

A few years ago there had been a fire in Lab 33 that had destroyed nearly everything. Shannon had been surprised that the story wasn't given more coverage, but it had quietly faded away from public view.

"I've heard of Lab 33," Shannon replied.

"What you don't know is that Lab 33, under Dr. Peters, was heavily involved with genetic experimentation."

A tidal wave of pure adrenaline washed over Shannon. She oversteered on the next turn and nearly sideswiped a car parked at the side of the street. She recovered—the car and herself—and kept driving.

"What kind of genetic experimentation?" Shannon asked.

"On human test subjects."

Shannon couldn't believe it. Her heart thumped to renewed life. Illegal gene research was a *huge* story. If it was tied to the Athena Academy, with the political and military connections the school maintained, it was even bigger.

"Did Marion Gracelyn and the other academy heads know about Lab 33?" Shannon asked.

"Yes."

Shannon smiled. *Score!* There was no way the Athena Academy or Marion Gracelyn's sainted memory was going to survive something like that. They'd torpedoed themselves.

"The girls who were kidnapped from Athena were some of the results of that genetic manipulation," Kwan-Sook went on.

"Why were they taken to Kestonia?"

"They were going to be sold to the highest bidder as research subjects. The young women who've been experimented on tend to end up with fantastic abilities."

Just when Shannon didn't think her heart could beat any faster, it did.

Athena Academy, one of the United States' most prestigious schools for girls, is secretly a Nazi-inspired experiment to create a female master race.

Shannon wasn't content with the wording, but the idea behind it was pure dynamite. The story was going to shatter Athena Academy and all those associated with it.

"This is the story you want me to break?" Shannon asked.

"Yes."

"I'll have to get the police to drop their interest in me first," Shannon said, already making a mental punch list.

"In time. First you'll need to gather more of the story."

"More?" Shannon couldn't believe what she was hearing. "You don't need anything more than that. That's enough to bring a government investigation into Athena that will rip them to shreds. We're talking massively illegal human gene research."

"You need proof to release a story like that," Kwan-Sook said.

Unfortunately, that was true.

"You don't have proof?" Shannon was disappointed.

"No. Most of the proof about Lab 33 was lost in the fire. However, I want to introduce you to a man in Hong Kong that will have more information about the story."

"Who is he?"

"A man who at one time worked with Dr. Peters."

"What's his name?"

"Patience, Shannon. I've had to do a lot of things, manipulate many events, to get tonight to happen. Meeting with this man is going to take some finesse. I haven't gotten all the details worked out yet."

Shannon made herself breathe out. "You can get me to Hong Kong without getting arrested?"

Kwan-Sook laughed. "That is the plan."

"It's a great plan." Shannon wasn't looking forward to the long trip, but the story was going to remake her career and put her up for several journalism awards.

Not only that, but she was going to be instrumental in bringing down Athena Academy.

"Control, this is Cerberus Four. We may have a problem." The woman's voice was calm and confident. Like the other women on-site there, she was an Athena grad that Allison had called in to work site security.

Tired and frustrated, Allison glanced away from the monitor she was currently working on to the monitor that tied her in to the security systems at the hotel where Rafe and Shannon were staying.

The touch-sensitive monitor allowed her to bring up any of the camera views she wanted. Nothing looked amiss.

"I don't see anything."

"Four Asian men just entered the lobby. They were over-dressed for the weather and they didn't stop at the desk."

Allison glanced at the screens. She didn't see any of the individuals in question.

"I'm not seeing them," she said.

"They just got on the elevator."

Allison pulled the wireless keyboard over to her as she turned to face the fifty-inch screen to her left. She hit keystrokes to freshen and cycle through the camera views.

All of the views locked up at the same time.

Chill fear crystallized inside Allison. Her system had been hacked. She was blind. If Cerberus Four had spotted a group, it was probable that it wasn't the only group.

"Everyone get up there," Allison said. She hit the keys to reboot her hack into the hotel's security system and got kicked out completely. She didn't even have access now.

A stick figure of a soldier took shape on the monitor. Words printed beside it.

If you hurry, you'll get to witness Captain Rafe Santorini's death. Thanks for playing.

It was signed with a spider icon.

Chapter 14

Dulles International Airport was enjoying a lull when Shannon arrived. She was met at the passenger boarding area by a slim, young Chinese man.

He walked to the rear of the car, stood patiently as the trunk released, then reached inside for a slim valise and a carry-on. He closed the trunk, then handed the valise to Shannon. He waved to a skycap and tipped the young man.

"Please escort her to the Air China gates," the young Chinese man said. "She is a very important guest."

The skycap nodded and took up the carry-on.

Air China? Shannon was impressed.

"You will have other baggage at your disposal when you arrive in Hong Kong, miss," the Chinese man said to Shannon. "Your computer and notes are in the valise. You have an e-ticket waiting for you at the desk."

"Thank you," Shannon said. She felt more than a little overwhelmed at how fast everything was happening.

"Please enjoy your trip. We will be watching over you."

Before Shannon could ask him about that, he turned and slid behind the steering wheel of the car. She didn't know if she should feel protected or threatened.

"Miss," the skycap said. "If you're going to make your flight, we've got to hurry."

Shannon nodded.

Inside the terminal, the skycap waved down a cart and put Shannon aboard. Within less than a minute she was speeding through the terminal. The driver used his warning horn liberally. Insolent stares followed in their wake.

The iPhone rang.

Shannon picked up after checking the view screen.

"Hello."

"I'm sorry everything is so abrupt, but it appears Allison Gracelyn is a much more worthy opponent than I had believed."

"Why?"

"She's already discovered the subterfuge at the hotel. Unfortunately for your recent jailer, this might not be soon enough to save him."

Shannon's breath stilled in her lungs. "What do you mean?"

"I told you we had other enemies afoot tonight," Kwan-Sook said. "They have apparently tracked you to that hotel. They just don't know that you're already gone. Your decision to trust me may have just saved your life."

But it may have gotten Rafe killed. Shannon thought about the shape he'd been in when she'd left the hotel room. He'd been unconscious. He wouldn't be able to defend himself.

Sickness twisted her stomach.

* * *

A warning klaxon strobed Rafe Santorini's brain. He felt as if it had shattered into a million jagged pieces and none of them would ever fit together again.

He blinked open his eyes. They felt thick and stiff. His mouth was dry as a desert. The room was dark except for the bathroom light. He moved his head and the room swam unevenly.

Damn! He felt as if he'd gotten slammed by an eighteen-wheeler. The only good thing out of the woozy feeling that filled him was that the pain in his knee was gone. Then he thought about Shannon.

He rolled over onto his stomach and saw the pillow his head had been resting on. The pillow hadn't been on the floor before. Someone had put it there.

Damn it!

Although he knew better than to expect Shannon to be there, he looked anyway. The hotel room was empty. He felt that as much as he saw it. The lights and television had been turned off.

Rafe cursed and focused on shrugging off the effects of whatever he'd been given. He knew he'd been drugged. During his imprisonment in North Korea he'd been given drugs to break down his resistance and make him physically ill.

He knew drugs. He also knew pain and betrayal. This felt a whole hell of a lot like all three.

Desperate, he tried to remember the last thing he could. All he remembered was talking to Shannon.

Go slow, he told himself. *Don't panic. How much time have you lost?*

He glanced at his watch. It was a few minutes after two in the morning. He hadn't lost any time. Couldn't have been out for more than a few minutes after he'd climbed from the tub.

And bought into the little Miss Let's Be Friends act. You knew she was the bad guy. Allison told you that.

Rafe sighed in exasperation. The whole op wasn't even three hours old, and he'd already managed to lose Shannon Connor.

Allison is going to be seriously pissed.

Rafe ran a hand through his hair. It made his head hurt. He still felt off from whatever Shannon had given him.

His phone shrilled for attention.

He slid the instrument from his pocket, checked the Caller ID and saw that it was Allison's number. *Terrific.* He punched the talk button and held it to his face.

"We have a problem," Rafe started.

"Stop," Allison commanded.

Rafe did. His hand automatically slid down for the pistol.

"Someone hacked my computer and looped my access to the hotel's cameras. A four-man team is headed your way. All Asian. I've picked them up now. They're getting off the elevator on your floor."

Adrenaline pumped through Rafe's system and leveraged free the remnants of the drug in his system. He started for the door.

"Get Shannon out of there," Allison said. "I've got an intercept team on the premises. They should be able to help you—"

"Shannon's not here." Rafe opened the door and stepped out. He pulled his shirttail out over the holster as he stepped out into the hall. He kept the pistol in his hand. There was nothing in the room that he couldn't leave behind.

"What?"

Rafe strode down the hallway. If he got trapped in the hotel room, he knew he was a dead man.

"She's gone," he said.

"What happened?"

"I don't know. I think she slipped me something."

The four Asian men Allison had to have been referring to rounded the corner of the hallway. They remained focused, looking straight ahead. They definitely knew where they were headed.

Rafe kept the pistol out of sight behind his back as he walked past them. He felt the men's eyes on him, but there was no sign of recognition. Maybe Allison was overreacting.

Almost immediately he retracted that. Allison *never* over-reacted. The fact that Shannon disappeared at the same time the four Asian men decided to show up couldn't be a coincidence.

In two more strides he was by the men. He resisted the urge to turn around and watch to see if they headed straight to his hotel room. If they did, how did they know where he was staying?

"Do you have access to the cameras back?" Rafe asked.

"Yes."

Rafe relaxed a little at that. Allison would be watching for him. Still, his back remained tense as he expected a hailstorm of bullets to cut him down at any time.

"Watch my six," he said.

"I've got you," Allison responded as she watched Rafe walk through the hallway. What he'd done had been gutsy. It was a play not a lot of agents would have thought to do, much less have the courage to implement.

If the four Asian men were there for him—and Allison was inclined to believe they were—walking straight at them would be the last thing they'd expect.

Allison's eyes roved the monitors in front of her. With all the concentration on the hotel room, she had most of the available monitors focused on that area.

Coverage came from both ends of the hallway so that she was able to watch Rafe or the Asians approach her while they walked away from each other. Other views showed the two women closing on the scene from either end of the hallway. Two more were in the elevator.

The women—all Athena grads that Allison worked with and

had called in for double coverage on Shannon—were going to arrive just a moment too late.

"Cerberus Team," Allison said calmly, "be advised that your target and the suspect force have crossed paths in the hallway."

"He walked past them?" one of the women in the elevator asked.

"Affirmative," Allison said. "Cerberus Two, you're going to have our friendly immediately in your sights when you step out of that fire escape. Be careful."

"Acknowledged, Control." The woman raced through the stairwell, taking steps two and three at a time. "I'll contain the friendly—"

"Negative," Allison said. She thought of all the time Rafe had spent in the North Korean prison. If someone attempted to take him into custody, there were going to be nasty repercussions. "Be advised that I want these men alive for questioning if there's any way possible."

Even as she said that, Allison knew she was running the risk of breaking cover on her private operation. The four Athena grads could keep quiet, and work with her. Rafe would keep quiet too.

But if the conflict was about to turn as bloody as she thought it was going to…

One of the Asian men lifted his left arm. He slid his sleeve back.

Although Allison couldn't see what was there, she knew what it was. Special Ops members used wrist-mounted photo viewers to help find target suspects.

The man studied his arm for a moment, then drew a pistol from under his jacket and whipped around. He yelled orders to the other men with him. They unlimbered weapons and came around, as well.

"Rafe," Allison said, fearing that she was going to be too late. "They made you."

On-screen, Rafe spun and brought his pistol up in a two-handed grip. He didn't try to find cover. In the hallway cover was practically nonexistent.

Allison couldn't believe he stood there in profile, left hand supporting the right. Since he already had his weapon in hand, it gave him a slight edge.

Despite the hardship of being imprisoned in North Korea and working his way through rehab, Rafe slid easily into position. He profiled in the hallway, standing close and tight so he provided as small a target as possible.

At that moment Allison knew there was no way to stem the violence about to erupt. Automatically she opened her headset microphone and put a call through to one of the guys on the D.C. Police Department who owed her.

With the amount of work and kind of work she did, a lot of people owed her. But a favor like this was heavy and expensive to call in.

On-screen, Rafe started firing. Since there were no audio pickups in the hallway, Allison couldn't hear any of the pistol reports, but she knew they were there.

"Chief Ginsberg," a sleepy voice answered.

"Forgive the late call, Chief," Allison began. "This is Special Agent Allison Gracelyn." She watched the action breaking loose in the hallway and hoped she hadn't sent any of her people to their deaths.

And where the hell had Shannon Connor gotten off to?

Chapter 15

Bladed, focused and as calm as he could be under the circumstances, Rafe pointed his pistol at the face of the man who had most turned to face him. He didn't aim. That hadn't been the way he'd been trained. Gunfights took place instantly, and usually the first person to start triggering rounds won.

With a tight grip on the pistol, his hands wrapped, the left hand on front and pulling back against the pistol butt as his right hand shoved the weapon forward because a relaxed grip could cause the pistol to jam, Rafe fired immediately. Brass flipped and spun in the air as the action spat the fired shells out.

The first man caught at least two rounds in the face. Dead or dying, he fell back into the man behind him. The four Asians had stayed bunched in together too tightly. Now that proximity caused them to bump into each other and become much easier targets.

Bullets whipped by Rafe's left ear, and he knew he'd

narrowly missed becoming a casualty himself. He shifted targets, moving to the man on the right. After bringing the pistol into line, Rafe fired again.

Part of him was afraid as he faced the men. He'd have had to have been brain-dead not to be afraid. For all intents and purposes, he was naked out in the hallway.

The second man went down, twisting sideways and cork-screwing into the floor.

The other two men split up, each taking a different side of the hallway.

Rafe went to ground, dropping low into a crouching position as he tried to track the men.

"You've got friendlies in the field," Allison told him.

With all the thunder breaking loose in the hallway, Rafe could barely hear her. But he understood other people were going to be in the hallway.

The first one he saw was the slight young woman who'd brought him the SUV. She held a pistol and used it with grim efficiency.

Then she spoke in Mandarin Chinese. Rafe followed her in the language. His earliest career at NSA had involved China, so he'd learned that language as well as Cantonese.

"Put your weapons down," the young woman said.

By that time, three other women were in the hallway. Two of them went forward and kicked the weapons away from the men Rafe had shot.

Where is Allison getting these women? Rafe wondered.

"Are you all right, Special Agent Santorini?" one of the women asked.

"Yeah." With the adrenaline hitting his system and screwing with whatever was left of the drugs he'd been given, Rafe felt light-headed.

"Good. You handled yourself very well."

Rafe watched in disbelief as one of the women put the surviving Asian man in a come-along hold and expertly bent him
down face-first into the carpeted floor. She took a pair of dis-
posable cuffs from the back of her waistband and zipped the
man's wrists together.

"Thanks. You, too." Rafe looked at the young woman
standing beside him and guessed that she was ten years younger
than he was, barely old enough to walk into a bar and order a
drink. "You do this kind of thing very often?"

The woman looked up and smiled. "Not often enough. I'm
usually stuck behind a desk." She nodded to the gunmen. "This
is the kind of work I love to do. Catching the bad guy. Being
face-to-face with something that could go incredibly wrong."

Rafe shook his head. "You're too young to be thinking
thoughts like that."

She raised an eyebrow at him. "This coming from the man
who joined the Army at eighteen and went straight into battle?"

Rafe grinned. "Okay."

"But thank you for the thought. It was very sweet." With a
practiced flourish, the young woman holstered her weapon.

Rafe reloaded his weapon with a fresh magazine. That was
a habit started in the military and continued through his time
at the NSA.

Once the surviving Asian man had his hands secured, two
of the women yanked him to his feet. The third woman calmly
and carefully went through the dead men's clothing. She
dumped the wallets, watches and personal effects into a
plastic bag.

Only then did Rafe realize the fourth woman was actually
acting as lookout.

A few curious hotel guests stuck their heads out of hotel rooms.

"Please stay in your rooms," the young woman said. She held

up an ID case. "We're with the Department of Justice, United States Marshal's Office. Everything is fine here. You're all safe."

A moment later, hotel security arrived. Two big men in suits almost filled the corridor.

"Are you there?" Rafe asked over the cell phone.

"Yes."

"I don't know if you see this, but—"

"Everything has been taken care of," Allison said. "Just stay quiet. Don't talk. And follow the lead of those women there."

"All right. Where's Shannon?"

"I'm looking. Whoever got into my system did a number on it. They also had enough foresight to send an encryption code to the off-site storage facility that handles the streaming video dump coming from the hotel cameras."

"You don't have a record of what happened here tonight?"

"The hotel doesn't," Allison said. "I didn't say I didn't. I twinned the outgoing video stream to an off-site dump I used. I'm accessing that now."

"Hotel security," one of the men arriving on scene bellowed as they took up positions around the edge of the corridor.

"We're with the Department of Justice," the young woman said in the tone of a jaded veteran. "United States Marshal's Office. This is a Homeland Security matter. We've got this situation under control. Please stay back."

"Lady," one of the men said, "I don't know who you think—"

The young woman's voice turned to ice. "If you want to stay out of jail tonight, I'd suggest you do as I ask. Do you understand?"

After a long moment, the two men nodded. They didn't give up their positions and they didn't put their weapons away.

"How much trouble are we in here?" Rafe asked Allison.

"None. You're going to be able to walk out of that hotel in a few minutes."

Rafe couldn't believe that. "How did you manage that?"

"I've helped a lot of people while I've had this career. Some of them remember they owe me a favor. I'm calling them in."

"What about the Agency?"

"There are people in the Agency who owe me favors, as well."

Seated in first class, awaiting takeoff, Shannon scanned the breaking news on the *Washington Post* Web site with her iPhone. When she found the story about the gunfight at the hotel where she'd stayed with Rafe, she nearly got sick to her stomach.

There weren't enough details, but she knew there had been fatalities. The thought of Rafe getting hurt was almost more than she could take.

He'd protected her and come after her while risking his own life. Shannon hadn't known many men who would do something like that.

Especially not for someone he thought was the enemy.

Shannon knew that Allison had turned Rafe against her. When they'd first parked in that lot, he'd been open and protective of her. After his phone call off by himself, he'd come back more defensive.

Maybe if they'd met at another time, under different circumstances—

Don't play that game, Shannon told herself. *Thinking like that only gets you in trouble. Stick with the story you're after.*

The story made her feel good. After fifteen years of being treated like an evil stepchild, Shannon was going to get to fight back.

She couldn't wait.

In between refreshing the Web browser on the iPhone, she tried to call Kwan-Sook. But she got no answer.

A short time later one of the flight attendants got on the public-address system and asked everyone to shut off all electronics. Reluctantly Shannon did, reminding herself it would only be until the plane took off and leveled out.

She took out a small legal tablet she'd bought at one of the stores in the terminal and started taking notes on questions she had about the genetic experimentation. When they were able to use their electronics again, she intended to make use of the slim-line notebook computer and mini satellite relay she'd been given to do as much research as she could.

"You don't have to be here, you know."

Frustrated and tired, Rafe entered the office where Allison sat at her computer array. True to her word, he'd been able to walk out of the hotel within minutes. No one had tried to stop him because the District's top cop had been on the job.

"I know." Rafe blew on the foam cup of coffee he'd gotten from the downstairs kitchen. He sipped, then peered over Allison's shoulder at the computer monitors. "D.C.'s police chief ran interference for us at the hotel."

"I know."

"If you can pull him out of bed in the middle of the night to come down and clean up my mess, that's pretty impressive."

Allison sighed and looked back over her shoulder at him. "It wasn't your mess. It was mine. I underestimated what I was dealing with." She paused and her voice softened. "I was damn lucky I didn't get you killed."

"I can take care of myself." Rafe sipped coffee again. It was still too hot.

"I should have told you more about what you were dealing with."

"I'll agree with that."

Allison kept pounding the keyboard. The monitors shifted constantly, cycling through information and images. "This thing is personal, Rafe."

"You think that this connects to your mom?"

"I know it does." Allison paused and looked up at him. "I owe you, Rafe, and I know that."

"It's not—"

"No," she interrupted. "I *do*. And I hate owing people."

"We're friends. Calling me in like this is probably the best thing I've had happen in a long time."

Allison smiled and shook her head. "You almost get killed and it's the best thing that's happened to you. You have got to seriously reevaluate your priorities."

Rafe smiled. "I think we both believe in what we do. That's why we're here."

"I know. That's why I'm going to tell you what I'm about to tell you. But you can't talk to anyone else about this. It's not just my secret. It's also a matter of national secrecy."

"All right."

Allison turned back to the keyboard and typed, then pointed at one of the screens. It showed a picture of a dark-haired, dark-eyed woman. "That was my mother's mortal enemy—and the deadliest woman I've ever seen."

Chapter 16

Rafe studied the woman's face. There were several pictures of her at different angles. She had hard, unforgiving eyes. "Who is she?"

"*Was* she," Allison corrected. "Her name was Jackie Cavanaugh."

More documents spilled across the array of monitors. There were also a few pictures. Some of them were of the woman in urban landscapes, but others were taken in the middle of a jungle.

"She grew up in Boston," Allison said. "Her family was poor, Irish working-class. Her brother ran guns for the IRA. Her father cooked books for criminal business enterprises."

"With a pedigree like that, I'm sure you couldn't have anything but the best of hopes."

Allison gave him a thin grin. "A lot of kids don't ever get out of an environment like that. But Cavanaugh was smart. She went to college and signed on with the CIA back in the 1960s."

Rafe stared at the photographs and tried to imagine what that must have been like back then for a woman to do such a thing. "Women were getting popular with law enforcement and espionage agencies back in those days."

"While with the CIA," Allison went on, "she became a sniper for the Phoenix Program."

Rafe had heard of the Phoenix Program. The clandestine war effort was legendary. The CIA-driven operation had existed in one form or another before and after it had been set up in Vietnam.

"They were supposed to neutralize high-ranking North Vietnamese officers," Rafe said. "But they ended up being primarily assassination teams. The South Vietnamese handed over four hundred targets that were marked for death. They worked in penetration teams. I've talked with some of those guys. Very hard-core."

"That's right. But while she was out killing CIA-designated targets, Jackie Cavanaugh met and fell in love with one of the assassins the CIA used. What she didn't know about killing before joining up with Evaristo—a Cuban national who'd fled Cuba after Castro came to power—she learned from him."

Another picture flashed onto the monitor. Rafe studied the hard, cruel face. "Doesn't look like the kind of guy you'd want to meet in a back alley."

"Unless you were really good, it would be the last time you met anybody," Allison said. "Evaristo was good at his chosen occupation. He enjoyed the killing."

"If Cavanaugh was an international assassin, how did she meet your mom?" Rafe noted the pain on Allison's beautiful features and felt badly for her. His own relationship with his parents hadn't been nearly that close.

"Mom was a new assistant district attorney in Phoenix," Allison said. "Cavanaugh came to Phoenix to do a contract hit and hung around to murder a man named Tom Marker, who was a retired ex-Army colonel and Vietnam War hero. Mom prosecuted the case. Although it was never proven, Mom always thought the CIA had used Cavanaugh as bait in a trap for Evaristo. During the jailbreak, Evaristo was killed, but Cavanaugh escaped. She'd been pregnant, but she lost the baby."

"Why did Cavanaugh murder Marker?"

"While Cavanaugh was working in Vietnam, the CIA decided to get rid of her. Marker was the one who set her up to be killed."

"I take it Cavanaugh wasn't exactly thrilled with that."

"Marker was a frequent visitor at the home of Bryan Ellis's family in Phoenix."

The name brought up an immediate memory for Rafe. After getting out of North Korea, he hadn't paid much attention to news. But Bryan Ellis's story had been big enough that it had penetrated even the pain and confusion he'd carried out of prison with him.

"*The* Congressman Bryan Ellis? The one whose father hired the stand-in in Vietnam that got killed?"

Allison nodded. "Marker was the leader of the team that supposedly pulled Bryan Ellis and those other men out of the prison camp over there."

"Cover-up much?"

"Yes. We're not dealing with nice people in this. They're not weak, either, Rafe. From what I've been able to find out, they are very powerful."

"And this is what Shannon Connor is part of?"

Allison nodded. "It is now. I didn't know that for certain before this evening."

"What changed?"

Allison tapped another key. "This."

As Rafe watched, the e-mail with the spider at the bottom filled one of the computer monitors. Reading the news of his impending death sent a chill through him.

"Glad that didn't turn out to be prophetic," he said, trying to make a joke of it. But inside he was seething. He'd risked his life to save Shannon Connor and she'd left him drugged and marked for execution. If he'd drunk more of the drug or it had hit him more slowly so that he'd gotten more of it in him, he might not have made it out of that hotel room alive.

"Me, too."

"What's the significance of the note?"

"It's not the note. It's the icon."

"The spider?"

"Yes. That spider became Cavanaugh's signature." Allison tapped the keyboard and the image lit up. "She dropped her identity. She became an international blackmailer. An arms dealer. A contract killer clearinghouse. If it was illegal and made money, she tried to own a part of it. She called herself Arachne."

Rafe was impressed that Allison was impressed. In the time that he'd known her Rafe had never heard that mixture of awe and dread in Allison's voice.

"From what I've been able to find out," Allison went on, "Arachne's database was incredible. She had dirt on heads of state and CEOs and she used her power to steadily build an empire down in Cape Town that you can't imagine."

"So Cavanaugh sent you this?"

Allison shook her head. "That's not possible."

"Why?"

"Because Jackie Cavanaugh is dead. I sent in the team that terminated her."

Rafe took that in without comment. As an NSA handler, Allison was sometimes called upon to make decisions or recommendations that resulted in the deaths of others. That, Rafe had always thought, was infinitely harder than being in the field and getting menaced by someone gunning for him. In the hallway, against those men, there'd been no choice.

"You're sure she's dead?" he asked quietly.

"Yes. There's no way she was left alive."

Rafe stared at the spider. "Then someone's borrowing her identity."

"I know."

"Gotta be a short list."

"At the time of her death, Arachne—Cavanaugh—sent out three information packets. I tried to intercept them, then track them, but I lost them. All I know for sure is that one went to Shanghai, China. One went to Nairobi, Kenya. And the third went to Jammu and Kashmir, India." Allison paused. "When it came to computer systems, Arachne was about the best I've ever seen."

"Like the person that got around your systems watching over the hotel."

"Exactly like that."

"You're sure Cavanaugh is dead?"

"There's no question about that."

"Then you've got to ask yourself where those three packets of information went," Rafe said. "And whether Arachne had an apprentice."

"I've been asking myself that for two months."

While Allison continued working on her own avenues of investigation, Rafe turned his attention to Shannon Connor. No matter how things had turned out at the hotel, he had trouble believing Shannon had meant to kill him.

He flipped through the huge dossier Allison had assembled on Shannon. The study was so deep and complete that it felt invasive. Guilt worried at Rafe the whole time he read through the file.

The dismissal at Athena Academy had colored much of Shannon's life. She just hadn't gotten over it and moved on with her life.

Vindictive? Rafe wondered. *Or something else?*

Guilty people proclaimed their innocence, too. But after a while, unless they were incarcerated and such proclamations might eventually lead to their freedom, they stopped fighting the system.

Shannon hadn't lain down and quit. She'd fought back with Athena. Her primary rival had been Tory Patton—now Tory Forsythe—who had been a reporter for United Broadcasting Studios. Their rivalry had attracted attention in the news world.

Allison had also flagged many of the stories Shannon had covered. In all of those stories Allison had noted other background she had uncovered: rumors, conflicting stories and investigations she'd conducted of financial assets that showed a steady stream of outgoing capital. All of them had been noted as possible blackmail.

Some people stopped paying and were summarily broken in the news. Once the cash deliveries had stopped, whatever secret the person had been hiding had been pushed into the public eye.

But that wasn't the only reason the victims had been exposed. Sometimes heads of state or CEOs were brought down to undermine their standing. New people had been brought in, and those people had also been blackmailed. If what Allison thought was true, Arachne had propelled people into greater positions and success just so she could leech more from them.

Rafe was awed and sickened by what he read, both fact and conjecture on Allison's part. He'd never imagined anyone like Arachne, so malign and so manipulative. The woman had had forty years to build one of the largest criminal empires Rafe had ever heard of.

But the more he read, the more unsettled Rafe became. There were basic issues that were missing regarding Shannon Connor's guilt.

* * *

Rafe waited till Allison leaned back in the ergonomic chair, then he asked, "Why?"

Allison turned to him. She looked confused. "Why?"

Nodding solemnly, Rafe said, "Why?"

"You're going to have to do better than that."

"Why was Shannon Connor involved in this? Why was she taking the information you say Arachne was giving her? Why was she using it?"

"Arachne wanted someone to break the stories in the media."

"It could have been any other reporter. Or reporters, for that matter."

"Because Shannon is conniving and selfish. And because she's power-hungry."

Rafe folded his arms over his chest. "You don't like her. I get that. But as intelligent as you are—and I do know you're intelligent, Allison—I think you're letting yourself be blinded by your own dislike of Shannon."

"Shannon's betrayal at Athena was unforgivable."

"Tell me about that."

Allison hesitated for a time, then she did tell him.

"So you have a vested interest, too," Rafe said when she finished. "Shannon tried to blame you for her actions."

"Damn right."

"Let's look past the problem of all of you being way into the competition at the time—and the fact that you were sixteen years old as well as not necessarily of age to make decisions that are going to be forever. I can remember the cheerleader wars at high school. Not a pretty sight. And it got bloodthirsty when push came to shove for positions on the team. Guys did the same thing in football."

"Competition—healthy competition—is part of the curriculum at the academy," Allison said. "Mom wanted it that way. She felt that was the only way the students would push themselves to succeed."

"I'm not a big fan of 'no child shall be left behind' either," Rafe said. "If you're going to acknowledge the struggling student and build programs suited to him, you also need to acknowledge the achiever and build other programs accordingly. Competition is good when it's healthy and the playing field is level, but it's got to be fair at both ends. How many other relationships were damaged at that time?"

Allison was quiet for a moment. "I don't think this is pertinent."

"I do."

"I don't have time for this." Allison turned back to the computer.

Rafe remained steady. "You've let this thing go on for fifteen years, Allison. So has Shannon Connor."

"It is what it is."

"Yeah, I think so, too. And if it's what I think it is, it's pretty sick and twisted."

Allison looked at him, then sighed. "You're not going to let this go, are you?"

"Nope."

"Why?"

Rafe struggled with that one for a moment. A lot of why he wouldn't let it go was because over the past couple of weeks of keeping Shannon under surveillance he'd come to like her. "Because you let me meet her without knowing all the subtext on this relationship. It didn't color my view of Shannon Connor."

"That was my mistake, but I hadn't planned on you getting this deeply…involved." Allison said the last word meaningfully.

"She's attractive," Rafe admitted, knowing he had to own up to it. "I saw that straight off. But there's more to it than that. I like the way she acts around people."

"She's selfish."

"I haven't met a person yet who didn't have his or her own agenda."

"Meaning me, because I dumped this on you? Fine. I'll bear the guilt on that one."

"Not just you. Me too. When you asked me to take part in this, I did it for me. Not for you. I had my own agenda, too. I wanted to see if I still had what it took to work out in the field." Rafe shrugged. "I've got a little farther to go physically, but my instincts are still good."

Allison didn't argue with that.

"My instincts are telling me that something is wrong here," Rafe said.

"My instincts aren't."

"You're not as objective as you could be." As he watched the color fill Allison's face, Rafe was certain he'd gone too far. She was going to blow—and then she was going to toss him out on his ear.

Chapter 17

"If you don't hear me out," Rafe said, "you're going to have to have security remove me from the building. And I'll make it hard on them."

Allison studied him and tried to make herself be calm. It was hard. Shannon Connor had been a sore point for a long time.

But that's exactly what he's saying, isn't it?

Instead of responding, Allison got up from the chair and paced the room. She could still remember her mom coming to her room and asking about the theft charges against Josie Lockworth.

Allison hadn't been able to accept that her mom could believe even for a second that she would do such a thing. But she had. And that had hurt Allison in ways she hadn't even been able to imagine back then.

Things had gotten even worse when she thought about some of the things she'd done to Rainy Miller later. In the end, her mom had been right to suspect her. She took a deep breath and let it out as she paced. Then she turned back to Rafe.

"This can't be about high school," Allison declared.

"Arachne's part in this, no. Definitely not. But the logjam created by you, Shannon, Tory Patton and possibly some of the other women that came out of that?" Rafe shrugged. "Maybe. None of us really leaves high school completely behind. Biggest social crippler there is."

"Shannon is the bad guy in this," Allison said. "I want Shannon to be the bad guy in this."

"Fine," Rafe said roughly. "Make me believe it."

"How?"

"Tell me what she got out of the relationship with Arachne. Or whoever's been feeding her the information she's been getting."

"Look at her career. She's skyrocketed at ABS."

"So?"

"Without those stories, she wouldn't ever have gotten the star potential she did."

"Maybe. I've watched her, Allison. She's a good journalist. She gets people to open up and talk to her. She listens. She's not afraid to tackle hard stories or big names."

"She gets those opportunities because she rides roughshod over people."

"People who've screwed up or are hiding something criminal, sure." Rafe remained stubborn. "You and I track them down and either take them out of power...or—if it comes to it—we kill them. A lot of people would say we're the bad guys."

Allison cursed. He was right. Worse, he knew he was right. But worst of all was that *she* knew he was right.

"The payoff is missing," Rafe said. "If Shannon is working— *was* working—with Arachne, where's the payoff?"

"Her career."

"Not good enough. She could have had a good career anyway.

She might have settled for a lesser career. Or she could have been doing something else."

"There's no money," Allison said.

"You didn't find any. And you looked. I saw the financials you put together on her. You and I both know that money is easy to follow."

"If there's enough of it."

"You know I'm right. I can read between the lines in your reports. You've been asking the same questions there. You just haven't wanted to deal with it."

Allison sighed. "I know."

Rafe was silent. One hand was massaging his knee.

"Okay," Allison said, forcing herself to be analytical. It was hard to do that when the subject was Shannon Connor. "Let's say that Shannon Connor isn't—"

"Wasn't," Rafe said with a smile.

"—*wasn't* Arachne's partner."

"Arachne, from your notes, didn't seem to be the type to take on partners."

"What does that make her?"

Rafe's smile was grim. "What do you call something you use to accomplish something you want to do?"

Allison reflected for a moment. "A tool?"

"That's pretty much what I'd call it. You said that Arachne was a master manipulator."

"She was," Allison agreed.

"Then what's the best tool she could use against your mother and the Athena Academy? And I'm admitting, given the stories Shannon's been covering, that the academy was a definite target."

"Shannon," Allison said. "Because it's possible people could see that she was the one failure of Athena Academy. And they could see the attacks she made against the school's setup, funding and overall mission statement. Even if she didn't make her story against the academy stick, she could be a reminder that it didn't always work."

"Because it didn't work in her case."

"No." Allison sipped a breath. "It didn't."

"Arachne used Shannon against you, Allison," Rafe said.

"It's possible," Allison said grudgingly. Then she shook her head angrily. "It's probable."

"Yeah."

"But she's still not a good person. Look at the way she drugged you and left you there to be killed."

"We boxed her," Rafe stated quietly. "We let her step into that confrontation with Vincent Drago so we could learn her secrets."

"You mean *I* did."

Rafe nodded. "I do. And once we fixed it so she had nowhere to go, once she knew she was trapped, how do you think she felt?"

Allison didn't answer.

"How would you have dealt with it?" Rafe asked softly.

"I would have escaped by whatever means I could," Allison said.

"Yeah. So would I. So why are we faulting Shannon for doing what she did? Somebody—" Rafe nodded at the computer monitor with the spider symbol on it "—gave her the chance and she took it. You and I would have done the same thing."

Allison stared at the computer monitor. "Whoever sent that is evil."

"I think so, too. But Shannon doesn't know that."

"She should."

"Shannon thinks we're the enemy. And there's that old saying—The enemy of my enemy is my friend."

"She doesn't know I'm involved."

"I've been thinking about that, too. When she handed me that water in the hotel room, she told me, 'Hydrate or die.' She asked me if that was what we military types said."

Allison caught the inference almost at once. "You didn't tell her you were a soldier."

"No. She's done a lot of military interviews in Iraq and Berzhaan lately. She's been around military guys. She could have heard that there, but what made her say that to me?"

"She could have simply figured you were a soldier."

"Or someone could have told her."

"While you were in the hotel room?" Allison shook her head. "I was monitoring her phone. I didn't show any activity."

"The taps you had on the hotel's security system were hacked. Whoever you're working against, they're as talented as you are."

Allison wanted to argue that out of pride, but she couldn't. It would have been a waste of breath.

"Her friend told her," Rafe said. "She worked the hotel room as soon as you booked it."

"I put that into play at the same time I ordered the car for you." Allison thought about the time frame. "There was a window…if whoever did this moved quickly enough."

"There could have been someone else shadowing Shannon. You said Drago was supposed to kill her."

"Yes."

"Whoever set that up would have had someone on hand to make sure it happened. That would put a team down in the D.C. area."

"All it would have taken was one person."

"One person would have been hard to spot," Rafe agreed.

"It also means the Drago countermove was designed to bring me out of hiding." Allison suddenly felt incredibly stupid.

"And me," Rafe added.

"We've been played."

"Yeah. Pretty well. You gotta respect that. Drago nearly kills Shannon and I show up just to take her into custody."

"We're the bad guys." Allison understood everything then.

"Once your name is mentioned—and I'm pretty sure it was—then Shannon realizes she's got no way out of the trap she's in. The D.C. police want her. We have her. But there has to be one other thing her mysterious source offers her to get her to trust her enough to possibly poison me."

"You think she worried about that?" As soon as she asked the question, Allison knew she was being too cynical.

"She put a pillow under my head after I went down," Rafe said. "Do you think she would have done that if she wasn't concerned about whether I lived?"

"No." Allison breathed out in disgust. "I hate getting played."

"Then you do what you do best," Rafe said. "Get it sorted out. Find this guy's weak spot, and let's track him down."

"I thought you were out of this."

"That's when I was busy feeling sorry for myself for reading Shannon wrong."

"Even if what you're saying is right, it doesn't make her a good person."

"Hell, Allison," Rafe said quietly, "*good* people don't do what you and I do."

Rafe drank another cup of coffee while he watched Allison work. He didn't know what she was doing and wouldn't have understood it if she'd tried to explain it. Computers weren't his forte.

People were.

That's why learning he had gotten Shannon Connor so wrong had thrown him for a loop. After North Korea, after the physical disability he'd dealt with—*Are still dealing with,* he told himself—he needed to know that he could trust his instincts.

He'd read Shannon as self-centered. A lot of people were when it came to relationships and careers. But Shannon had had reason not to trust anyone outside herself. She'd felt as though she had adversaries at every corner and she'd had something to prove. She'd had no choice but to be self-centered.

Rafe understood that. When he'd first joined the Rangers, he'd worked through the same feelings. Given the family history she'd had, which wasn't far removed from his, she'd had no choice but to try to excel.

Shannon had been forced to discover her own worth. Only she'd gotten double-whammied. Her family hadn't cared that much about her, and she'd gotten kicked out of the Athena Academy.

All things considered, it was a wonder Shannon had turned out to be any kind of person at all.

Back aching, knee throbbing, Rafe tried to find a comfortable position and failed. He glanced at his watch. It was almost six in the morning.

He couldn't believe Allison was still at it.

He wanted to know where Shannon was. He held out hope that she was all right. There was no reason for her not to have been one of the victims when the four men came to the hotel room.

"There's one thing we're missing," Rafe said.

"What?"

"Why Shannon's informer wanted her pushed into a point of no return. It would have been easier to just kill her."

"Maybe Drago was supposed to."

Rafe shook his head. "You know better than that. You want someone dead, you hire someone unknown to them, have them walk up to them, shoot them and walk away. Easy as buying a paper."

Allison looked at him. "There's only one sure bait this person could have used on Shannon."

"Yeah. A story. But it couldn't be just any story."

"It has to be something about Athena Academy."

"Yeah. What secrets does that school have?"

Allison hesitated just a fraction of a second too long. "There aren't any."

Okay, Rafe thought, *we're not completely trusting yet.*

But that was okay. He hadn't told Allison how he felt about Shannon, either. If he had, she would have already put him out of the op.

A short time later, Allison leaned back. "I found out how Shannon left."

Chapter 18

Rafe watched as Allison flicked through the overlapping camera views inside the hotel to track Shannon Connor's departure from the building. She hadn't been in a hurry. She didn't act like someone who had just left behind a man she'd poisoned. She also didn't act as if she knew a hit team was on its way.

She'd talked on the phone as she went.

As he watched, Rafe's chest grew tight. Shannon had been missing for hours. He knew how easily people could fall off the radar and become lost. It had happened to him.

"We're going to have to get a phone dump on her cell," Rafe said. He knew that would take a while. The courts wouldn't be open till eight.

"I've already been through her cell phone records," Allison replied. "I used the Homeland Security blanket."

"Who was she talking to?"

"The number was out of Los Angeles. I tracked it to a movie rental place."

Rafe checked the time/date stamp in the lower right corner of the monitor. "Two-seventeen in the morning in Washington D.C. is eleven-seventeen at night in L.A."

"The store was open," Allison said. "But verifying whether the person who made the call to Shannon was on-site is a different matter."

"I doubt a movie rental clerk would have made that call."

"So do I."

On the monitor, Shannon walked to a car and, after a moment, got inside.

"Were you able to trace the crack into the hotel's surveillance systems?" Rafe asked.

"Not yet. I'm still working on it." Allison tapped the keyboard.

The sequence of Shannon at the car door repeated in slow motion. Her hand pulled at the door release, but it didn't open.

"The door was locked," Rafe said.

Still in slo-mo, Shannon reached for the door release again. This time it opened.

"Did you see a key?" Allison asked.

"No."

A small smile curved Allison's lips. "That's because whoever Shannon's source is, she's also able to crack into telematics systems."

"Don't know what that is."

"Neanderthal," Allison said. "It's onboard car services."

"Not a big fan. I like older cars." Rafe stared at the screen as Shannon drove out of the parking spot. "Can you get a copy of that license plate?"

"I'm trying."

The car was tagged on front and back, but somehow the camera angles worked against them. As they watched over and over, the car pulled through the parking area and out onto the street. Within a minute it disappeared.

Then, just as Rafe was about to give up in frustration, the car turned for just an instant and the camera caught the plate.

Allison froze the playback, captured the image, then blew it up. When the number was legible, she accessed another computer screen.

Okay, Rafe thought, *give me something I can use.*

"The car was a rental," Allison said as she flipped through computer screens. "A lot of rental cars come equipped with vehicle-tracking systems packed with GPS technology. We got lucky. This one did."

Rafe watched the screen as a map of the city spread out. Then a single red dot flared to life.

"I'm going to speed up the cycle," Allison said, "but you have to remember that she could have gotten out anywhere along the way."

"This has been too direct," Rafe said. "Whoever her contact is, somebody had an agenda in mind. She wouldn't have stopped till she got to where she was going. The risk was whether or not Shannon got out of the city fast enough. That's why a stolen car wasn't used. If the police pulled it over, Shannon could have gone straight to lockdown."

"He or she probably also didn't think I'd streamed the video feeds into a hard-drive dump of my own." Allison clicked keys. "I'm thorough. Once I get my head up and can look around."

"She stopped there."

On-screen, the car was once more in motion.

"Where is that?" Rafe asked.

Allison ran the cursor over the route and a block of text lit up. "Dulles International."

The hope that Rafe had been harboring in his heart that Shannon would be all right dwindled somewhat.

"Hold on. I should be able to access the airport cameras."

The NSA, Rafe knew, had blank checks where a lot of government buildings and public transit hubs were concerned.

Allison accessed the airport cam menu, then pulled up the cameras she wanted to check.

Rafe waited tensely. Minutes passed as Allison matched the time/date stamps of the car's brief stop at the airport. When she had them in sync, she rolled the footage slowly.

"There," Rafe said, spotting Shannon Connor as she got out of the car and talked briefly with an Asian man.

"I've got her."

On the screen, a square blue graphic formed around Shannon's head. Allison had to start and stop several times while she learned the flow of the cameras inside the terminal.

Minutes later, Shannon checked in at the Air China desk.

Rafe cursed. Although he'd known from the team that had come to the hotel to kill him and from the man Shannon had met that they were probably looking for an Asian connection, he wasn't happy about having confirmation.

"We're not going to get a lot of help at that end," Rafe grumbled.

"No. But the computer relays I traced came out of Shanghai. This fits with what we already knew."

"Where's the plane landing?"

Allison consulted a computer screen. "First stop is Beijing. Seventeen hours from now."

"Do we have anyone there who can watch for her in case she gets off there?"

"We do." Allison made a quick call, talked briefly, made and sent a follow-up e-mail that had Shannon's image and information and turned her attention back to the monitor. "Beijing is covered. The flight's final destination is Hong Kong."

"Do you have—"

"Yes," Allison said. "I do."

"One of these days," Rafe said, "I'm going to have to get a look at this Rolodex of yours."

"If you ever saw my Rolodex," Allison said, "I'd have to kill you."

Rafe thought she was only half kidding.

Less than thirty minutes later, Rafe was packed and ready to go. He stood beside the military Hummer assigned to take him to Dulles.

The sun had dawned in the east and beat back the night from the city. A gentle wind slid through streets already choked with traffic.

"You don't have to do this."

Rafe turned to look at Allison. He gave her a crooked grin. "Who else could you possibly send that Shannon's going to trust?"

"You don't know that she's going to trust you." Allison stood there with red-rimmed eyes and her arms folded.

"No, but at least she knows me."

"She thinks you're the enemy."

"I can't just walk away from this thing either, Allison."

"China is a dangerous place right now," Allison said. "We don't have a really good spy swap program. And the NSA can't own you on this. If you get caught over there, this may be North Korea all over again."

For a moment nausea twisted and churned inside Rafe's stomach. He knew that. He didn't need her to tell him. The whole time he'd packed clothes that she'd sent out for him, he'd thought of nothing but that.

He didn't want to be captured. He didn't want his freedom stripped from him again. With everything he'd lost the first time, he didn't know if he could survive that.

"I won't be able to help you," Allison said.

"I know. But Shannon's over there and she thinks she's doing the right thing. She doesn't know she's being used and set up." Rafe paused. "You brought me into this thing because you knew I'd stick. And I accepted because I needed to know I would. Well, I am. I think maybe I'm the only one who's surprised here."

"All right." Allison stepped forward and gave him a hug. "Be careful out there, Rafe. And don't trust her any more than you have to. You can't save someone who doesn't want to be saved."

"I know. But I can't leave her to hang. I've got to try to bring her home." That was his job. That was what he'd signed on to do with the Rangers, and that was part of what he'd done while working with the NSA.

If he gave up that part of himself, if he let fear of all those long, torturous months in that North Korean prison stop him, then he'd never escaped.

He turned and stepped into the Hummer. He didn't look back. Instead he focused on what lay ahead of him. That was the only way he could get the job done.

Chapter 19

At Hong Kong International Airport, Shannon finally got through the long line to Customs in Terminal 1 after waiting as patiently as she could to be processed. She pulled her carry-on behind her and tried to reflect on what she'd learned about genetics research.

She'd covered the topic several times before. It was one of those interests that occasionally burned white-hot, then ebbed but never truly went away. Too many people believed that genetics research would ultimately end up creating soulless creatures, Frankenstein's monsters, a slave race or a line of enhanced men and women that might take over the rest of humanity. Or be their saviors.

Either way, there was a lot of emotion involved on all sides. Science was at the threshold of one of the greatest mysteries ever, and efforts to see what was there were being hamstrung.

Shannon hadn't thought about genetic tampering too much because it had always seemed like science fiction to her. But all the information she'd read about Dr. Aldritch Peters and Lab 33 had been real. And it had been amazing.

In addition to the information Kwan-Sook had given her, Shannon had also searched for the man on the Internet. She'd gotten thousands of hits.

The problem was that there was so much information it was hard to decipher what was pertinent—or even the truth. Some of the genetics pages she'd landed on had praised Peters's research as some of the most forward thinking of his time and said he should have been allowed to continue his work.

Other Web sites blasted the geneticist as being more interested in the pure science of the possible than in the ramifications such ability would engender.

It was all exciting, and Shannon had no doubt that she would turn it into an equally fascinating story. The bonus was getting to lambaste the Athena Academy, Allison Gracelyn and all those others who had looked down their noses at her for so long.

The iPhone rang. She hadn't noticed it at first. She was seriously jet-lagged from over twenty hours of nonstop flight. The quick layover in Beijing had been nothing more than a bump in the road.

"Shannon," she answered. Then hoped that no one paid too much attention to her. The ID she was traveling with listed her under another name.

"Where are you?" Randall Bellamy demanded. He was her main producer. He'd grumbled about giving her a couple days off to deal with the business in Washington, D.C.

Shannon looked around at the crowded terminal. "I'm in Hong Kong."

"What?" All the wind in Bellamy's sails seemed to leave at once. "Tell me you're joking."

"Not. Joking." Shannon kept walking and skirted people slower than she was.

"What are you doing in Hong Kong?"

"Chasing the story of my life," she replied. And if it didn't turn out that way, she was going to be really upset.

That got Bellamy's attention. "What story?"

No matter how upset he was, he was still a newsman.

"Genetic experimentation on humans."

"Why are you wasting your time with that? Unless you can show people a two-headed goat or one hundred and one Dalmatians all cloned from one dog, viewers aren't going to care. Did you know you're still wanted for questioning by the D.C. cops?"

"It would be kind of hard to forget that, don't you think?"

"What are you going to do about it?"

"Nothing. They'll sort that out there. I didn't have anything to do with that." Shannon was certain Allison and Rafe would have to make that problem go away if they were going to have any peace in their lives.

In fact, the story about Vincent Drago and the four men killed at the hotel had already fallen off the radar.

"You were identified there. I've seen YouTube videos of you running through the streets with some guy with a gun after you. Some of those clips even show the car that ran the guy down just before it looked like he was going to shoot you."

YouTube, Shannon thought. *That would be one area that Allison couldn't control.*

"Would you listen to yourself?" Shannon asked. "I'd think those are perfectly good reasons for me not to be there."

"They were trying to kill you in D.C.," the producer pleaded. "The fans in New York still love you."

"There are people there," Shannon said in an icy tone, "who are not fans."

"The point is," Bellamy said in exasperation, "that the whole *world* has footage of ABS's star news reporter running for her life while being chased by an armed madman, then saved by a guy who brought a car to a gunfight—but *we* don't!"

Star news reporter sounds good. Shannon smiled to herself.

"The next time I've got getting chased by a madman on my schedule, I'll make sure I've got a cameraman scheduled," she said.

"This is the first time I've gotten through to you in the last twenty-four hours."

"I've been busy." *And I've been avoiding this call because I knew this was exactly what I was going to get.*

"Busy?" Bellamy cursed.

"Did I mention the illegal genetics experimentation?"

"In Hong Kong?"

"The experimentation was done in Phoenix, Arizona. Senator Marion Gracelyn knew about it."

Bellamy cursed, then got hold of himself. "Shannon," he said in a voice that sounded forced and artificially calm. "Do you realize how many stories you've tried to do about the Athena Academy and Marion Gracelyn?"

"More than the network has let me run."

Bellamy was quiet for a moment. "This feud you've had going with Tory Patton is approaching irrational."

"That's because you don't take it personally enough." Shannon looked around and found the signage advertising ground transportation.

"This story isn't something we want to do."

Shannon felt a little threatened by that. Her world lurched. But she felt a spark of anger and she nourished it. This was her vindication against Marion Gracelyn, Allison and Athena. She wasn't going to be deprived of it.

"This story is *exactly* what we should want to do," she said calmly. "It's smart. It's sexy. And it's cutting-edge. More than that, it's got so much controversy surrounding it that people can't help but take notice."

"You need to come back, Shannon."

Shannon went down the steps and looked out at the skyline

of Hong Kong. She'd been to the city before, but it was always breathtaking.

Hong Kong International Airport had been built on land reclaimed from the sea and had opened for business in 1998. The locals knew it as Chek Lep Kok Airport, named after the island it was built on. A hotbed of activity, the airport was the main passenger and cargo hub of the area. It operated twenty-four hours a day. Every time Shannon had been there, the airport had been noisy and crowded.

"I need to do this story," Shannon stated firmly.

Bellamy paused. "Corporate is talking about suspending your pay until you get back here."

That angered Shannon even more. Threats didn't sit well with her. "Tell corporate I've got vacation time coming."

She'd worked years without taking vacation or sick days. Trying to beat Tory Patton had been demanding. It was hard for Shannon not to be in front of a camera. That was the only time she was making points in the competition.

"They're not going to be happy with that," he warned.

"I'm not happy now."

"You're putting your job on the line, Shannon. I have to tell you that."

"All right." Shannon couldn't believe she said that so calmly. Her job meant everything to her. It was the only thing she had that was truly hers.

"Don't tell me that you—"

"There are YouTube video clips of me out there running for my life," Shannon interrupted. "That was part of this. Those people tried to kill me. An agent of the National Security Agency took me hostage tonight. I'm tracking a geneticist who is believed by some to be the second coming of science, who ended up getting shut down by the federal government—with all his research being locked down. And you think this is a career buster?"

Bellamy didn't say anything. She knew she had him thinking.

"Personally," Shannon said, "I think if I bring this story in, I'll be able to write my own ticket for anywhere I want to go." She took a deep, shaky breath. "You tell corporate that. And you remind them that I've been a team player all these years. If they want to change that and not respect that relationship, then I'll keep that in mind."

"Shannon." Bellamy's voice softened. "Don't be hasty. Let me talk to corporate and lay this out for them. You know that I've always valued your work."

Sucking up so does not become you, Shannon thought. She wanted to tell him that. She was sorely tempted. But those words could be a stumbling block later.

"Give me a day or two," Shannon said. "Long enough to run down the leads I've got. If something comes of this, you'll be the first to know."

"All right. This story sounds really big."

Amazing how quickly the tune can change when you get on board. Of course, if this blew up in her face, things at the network would be difficult for a while. But her life hadn't been anything without adversity.

"Miss Connor?"

Startled by the man that seemingly appeared out of nowhere at her side, Shannon said, "I've got to go." She closed the phone before Bellamy could protest. She looked at the man. "Do I know you?"

The man was Asian, only a few inches taller than she was. He wore a black suit, slim-line black gloves and wraparound sunglasses that reminded Shannon instantly of Rafe Santorini. That was disturbing because she didn't want to think about Rafe. There were too many questions and too many uncertainties she had about the man. She still didn't know what had become of him. Three men, none of them Rafe, had turned up dead outside the hotel room they'd shared.

Almost shared, she reminded herself. They hadn't spent the night there. On the flight over, she'd found herself thinking about how he'd looked partially obscured in the steam from the bath. And how he'd picked her up and carried her when she'd hurt her foot. Despite his damaged knee, he'd managed her easily.

"No, Miss Connor. I am Inspector Liu of the Hong Kong Police Department." The man smiled, but it looked artificial.

"Do you have any identification, Inspector Liu?" Shannon asked.

"Of course." Liu reached inside his jacket and brought out an ID case.

The information was in English and Chinese. The picture was a good one and proved that Inspector Liu did, indeed, have eyes.

"What can I do for you, Inspector?"

Liu returned the case to his jacket. "I would like to ask you a few questions."

"All right." Shannon stood and waited.

Liu looked confused. "Perhaps this isn't an appropriate place."

"I'm comfortable."

"I thought we could speak somewhere less public."

"Not unless you have a warrant or a writ." Shannon's warning radar was screaming at her.

Liu gave her a cold look. "Things in China aren't done as things are in your country."

"If I've made a mistake," Shannon said, "then we should get someone from the State Department to explain that mistake to me."

"If you wish. Do you think someone from the State Department could explain how you entered this country under a false name?"

Chapter 20

Shannon's confidence drained. The illegal identification she carried damned her. Only then did she realize that the man had addressed her as *Miss Connor,* not the assumed name she'd traveled under.

"Maybe we could talk in private," she said.

"Good." Liu took her arm and walked her toward the curb and the waiting line of taxis and bicycle rickshaws that would take arrivals to the ferries to the mainland. His grip was tight enough to make Shannon feel more captured than escorted.

Liu moved quickly through the crowd toward a sleek black Isuzu with tinted glass all the way around. It didn't really look like a police department vehicle. The sedan was too upscale.

"You're not with the police," Shannon said.

"Don't be difficult," Liu grated.

Shannon dug in her heels hard enough to bring the man

around. For the briefest moment the pistol tucked under his left arm showed under the jacket.

"What if I stop here and scream?" Shannon tried to free her elbow, but the man had a death grip on her.

"Then you'll attract a lot of attention before you die." His face was hard.

"If I go with you, you won't kill me?"

"No."

The lie slid easily off the man's tongue, but Shannon still recognized it for what it was.

"Come with me," the man said. "Or things will go very badly for you."

Shannon relented and walked with him. They closed on the car, and she knew if she got inside the car she wouldn't have a chance.

Walking beside the man, Shannon got the cadence of the man's steps. Then, when his back foot lifted to step forward, she kicked it behind his other calf. It was an old trick from grade school, just a prank that kids pulled on each other. But it was unexpected.

Liu's foot caught behind his leg and he fell. He was quick, though, because he caught himself on his free hand and one knee. Crouched on the ground, he glared up at her.

That was a mistake. Shannon set herself and drove a front snapkick into his face.

The kick drove the man backward, but he didn't release his grip.

Shannon spun into him, twisting her wrist toward his thumb to break the hold. She lifted her right leg over her head then brought it down in an ax kick aimed at his head. The man managed to move his head, but he caught the kick on his shoulder. Something snapped.

Shannon was free. The first lesson taught in any martial art was to escape when escape was possible. She turned and tried to flee through the crowd, but there were too many people around.

Without warning, those people dropped to the ground and cried out in terror.

Afraid of what she was going to see, Shannon turned and saw the man push himself up from the ground. He had a pistol in his fist and wore a look of rage. He took deliberate aim.

Shannon dived to one side and rolled. She pushed herself up again, expecting to feel a bullet slam into her at any moment. When she heard the two quick reports, she felt certain she'd been hit and was surprised there was no pain.

From the corner of her eye, she saw Liu look down at the crimson suddenly staining his shirt in two spots right over his heart. His knees buckled and he went down.

Out in the line of cars behind the black sedan, an Asian woman held a pistol in a two-handed shooter's grip. She was petite and young, dressed in a simple gray woman's business suit. Despite having just shot a man in public, she didn't look panicked.

"Shannon," the woman called. "Shannon Connor. Come with me. I can help you."

Shannon didn't think so. That woman shouldn't have known her name either.

The driver of the black sedan shoved the door open and got out with a pistol in his fist. He started firing at once at the young woman.

Shannon turned and ran through the cowering pedestrians. She thought about stealing one of the rickshaws, and just as she was about to attempt it, she saw a young driver taking cover behind a car. He held a sign with someone's name on it.

Desperate, Shannon ran for him. She seized the sign and hoped he spoke English. Gunfire continued to ring out behind her.

Holding the sign up, Shannon said, "This is me, okay?"

The young driver nodded and looked panic-stricken. "Okay."

"We want to get out of here, right?"

"Okay."

Shannon grabbed the young man's arm and hauled him to his feet. She opened the car door and shoved him inside. "You drive."

"Okay. I drive." He fumbled for the keys in the ignition.

Shannon opened the rear door and threw herself inside. When she looked back, she spotted the young woman still engaged in the gun battle. Then the sedan's driver spun and went down.

Turning back to the driver, Shannon slapped the seat. "You go, okay?"

"Okay." He put the car in gear and peeled away from the curb, merging almost effortlessly with the traffic.

Shannon lost sight of the woman with the gun immediately. Then she groaned when she realized she'd left the valise with the computer and her carry-on bag behind.

She didn't have clothes. Again.

"Where to?" the driver asked in a tense voice.

"The ferries. I need to get to the mainland."

"Okay." He changed lanes and took the next turn. "You not shoot me, okay?"

Shannon looked at him and couldn't believe that he'd asked that question. "Okay," she said.

The sound of a ringing phone dragged Rafe from the coma he'd fallen into almost from the moment of takeoff. He experienced a moment of disorientation. Then he found the phone and brought it to his face.

"Santorini."

"Shannon's in Hong Kong," Allison said without preamble.

Rafe sat up a little straighter. "Good to know."

"We're not the only ones who know. Someone tried to apprehend her there, then tried to kill her."

Rafe forced himself to remain calm. "She's all right?"

"She got away. But the woman I had who was going to tail her got involved in the gunfight and lost her."

"Is she all right?"

"Yes. She's good at what she does. If I'd thought this might happen, I'd have doubled up on the tail. I wanted to streamline it. Keep it simple and easy to hide."

"That was the right call," Rafe said, but inside he was cursing. "So we've lost her?"

"Not entirely. While Shannon was at the terminal, she got a phone call from one of her producers at the network. Since she changed phones, I haven't been able to trace her phone, but I put tracers on the phones of everyone I thought she might be in touch with."

"Can you find her?"

"Yes. Shannon evidently swapped out the SIM card and has been letting her answering service pick up her calls. The call she took showed she was at the airport. I've called, just to check to see if she would answer, but I got dumped into the answering service, too."

The anxiety inside Rafe elevated a little. "But you're sure she's all right?"

"Yes. My agent told me Shannon broke free of her abductor and managed to escape in a car."

Rafe felt a little proud, but he didn't say anything.

"It's not all good news," Allison said.

"She's got her old phone number," Rafe said. "She shouldn't have kept that."

"That's right. If her contact instructed Shannon to remove the SIM card and didn't have her change phones entirely, that was deliberate."

"It could have been an oversight."

"Judging from the caliber of computer work we're dealing with here, I'd have a hard time believing that."

"Maybe whoever contacted Shannon didn't want to spook her by asking her to cut herself off completely from her friends and work."

"And maybe we're supposed to be able to track her."

Rafe had already made that leap in logic, too, but he knew Allison would want him to think about it and not dismiss it out of hand. "You're saying this could be a trap?"

"Yes."

"Anybody ever tell you that you're a cynical person?"

"I don't listen to those people," Allison responded. "They don't know what they're talking about."

Rafe grinned.

"Let's look at something else," he suggested.

"What?"

"That whoever Shannon's contact is underestimated you. Maybe you weren't expected to tap the phones of all Shannon's friends. I know what you did isn't easy, but other people may think it's impossible."

"I don't think so."

"And whoever did this might know that Shannon would eventually talk to one of those people no matter what and know that it is easier to trace a landline than to triangulate a cell phone."

"Harder but not impossible." Allison paused. "Anyone trailing Shannon is going to be easy to pick out, Rafe. A moving target brings out a moving hunter. Whoever Shannon's contact is has control of this situation."

"Because that person knows where Shannon's going to be at any given time."

"Yes." Allison paused. "I have to be honest. This isn't making me happy."

A question surfaced in Rafe's mind and wouldn't go away.

"It doesn't make sense that Shannon's contact would try to abduct her. Not after establishing a false identity. So who tried to abduct Shannon at the airport?"

"I don't know," Allison admitted. "I'm still working on that."

"There's more going on here than Shannon and her contact," Rafe said. "Someone wants Shannon out of the way as much as her mysterious contact wants her in play."

"I know."

"So who's the second party?"

"I'm not sure. I traced those four men from the hotel. They're mercenaries. I found identities they'd been traveling under and managed to trace them back. They were in Kenya a few weeks ago. That's where they were hired."

"Kenya?" Rafe tried to wrap his brain around that. "How is Kenya connected to this?"

"That's where one of Arachne's three mysterious packages was sent."

"Did the survivor say who hired him?"

"I was given a name. It's a shell. Nothing real there. Probably deep enough to satisfy the mercenaries and—for that matter—most anyone who cared enough to look. I did more than look."

"Did you get a description?"

"A very beautiful black woman."

"Well," Rafe said with dry irritation, "that really narrows the field."

He glanced at his watch. Getting a flight on United Airlines had been difficult, but Allison had managed it. She'd also arranged for a team to meet him in Hong Kong. He was going to hit the ground there nine hours after Shannon did.

He hoped that gave him enough time.

"My operative also recovered Shannon's luggage from the airport," Allison said. "Shannon left a valise and a computer behind." She paused. "There was a lot of material loaded onto the computer."

"Does it help?"

"To find Shannon? No. But it lets me know what this is about."

Rafe waited.

"Have you heard of Aldritch Peters?" Shannon asked.

Rafe thought for a moment, then said, "No." Before North Korea, he'd been out of the country a lot.

"He was a geneticist. There's a lot about him that I have to tell you. Something I probably should have already told you."

"All right."

"And I will. Just not yet. But I will tell you this—one of the most influential geneticists who worked with Peters is currently in Hong Kong. His name is Dr. Chow Bao. I think that's who Shannon is there to see."

Chapter 21

After getting off the ferry, Shannon took a rickshaw to the Sha Tin district and entered the huge Citylink Plaza mall above the rail station. She wanted to be around a large group of people, and the mall was one of her favorite shopping destinations in Hong Kong.

Not that it will help, she told herself sourly. *You can't be around many more people than at the airport.*

She wandered through the mall's shopping center where the clothing and cosmetics were. Kwan-Sook had included cash in the valise. Shannon had transferred it to her purse. There'd even been credit cards issued in the name of the false identity she was using.

A boutique caught her eye, and she went to it to study the showcase. The dresses on the mannequins were Chinese as well as Western.

The iPhone rang and she scooped it out of her purse. A quick check revealed the same three-one-oh area code she'd seen before. However, before she answered the phone, she looked around to see if anyone was showing undue interest in her.

"Hello?" Shannon was angry enough to go on the offensive at once, but given what had happened at the airport, there was no guarantee something hadn't happened to Kwan-Sook.

And if something had happened to her, Shannon didn't know what she was going to do about it.

"Are you all right?" Kwan-Sook asked.

"Yes. What happened back at the airport?"

"It appears that the identity I assigned you has been found out."

"By whom?"

"By the person I told you I was concerned about."

Shannon pulled herself back against the wall by the shop so she could watch the pedestrian traffic. "Who is that person?"

Kwan-Sook hesitated. "I'm not at liberty to say at this time."

"That guy tried to kill me."

"I know. I apologize for that."

"Terrific," Shannon said. "You can have that engraved on my headstone."

"Shannon," Kwan-Sook said in a soothing voice, "doesn't the mere fact that an attempt was made on your life tell you that this story is important?"

That was true. Shannon made herself breathe and push her outrage aside.

"I'm doing the best I can," Kwan-Sook said. "Allison Gracelyn continues to make things more difficult, as well."

"She doesn't know where I am."

"She may. I have been lax in some of my own security. And, not to take away from it, she is very good with computers."

"Great. You guys can have brunch and form a mutual admiration society."

Kwan-Sook was quiet for a moment.

In the background Shannon distinctly heard electronic beeping that reminded her of a hospital. Had she heard that before? She thought back and tried to remember.

"You'll have to be careful," Kwan-Sook said finally.

"I'm being careful." Shannon sipped a breath. "How long before I meet the person you wanted me to talk with?"

"A matter of a few hours."

"Why not now?"

"He's very reticent."

"Trust issues?" Shannon asked.

"Attempts have been made on his life, as well."

"What does he know about Aldrich Peters's work?"

"I can't go into that. Please wait till a more appropriate time."

"Why can't you tell me?"

"I don't want that information to fall into the hands of others."

Translation, Shannon thought sourly as paranoia bit into her, *she doesn't know if she can keep you safe.*

"I'll make this happen as soon as I can," Kwan-Sook said. "But Dr. Chow knows about the attempt on your life this morning. You can appreciate his reluctance."

Actually, Shannon could. If attempts had been made on the geneticist's life, she didn't really want to be around him until his security was intact either.

"All right. What am I supposed to do until then?"

"I arranged for rooms for you. If you'll allow me another hour, I can have them ready."

"Not a problem," Shannon said. "I need to do some shopping. All my clothes—and the computer—got left at the airport."

For the first time, Kwan-Sook's voice took on a hard edge. "You *left* the computer?"

"Did I mention the part where I was ducking and running for my life as bullets flew a few inches over my head?"

"Forgive me. That information was sensitive."

"That information," Shannon said, "could take a bullet better than I could."

"You're right. I'll make sure you have things there that you may need."

"Thank you. But if it's all right to spend this money—"

"Of course. I'll make sure there is more by the time you reach your room."

"It might help if I can call you for a change," Shannon said.

"At this point, that's not possible."

"Why?"

"When we meet, I'll explain everything. Be careful."

Before Shannon could protest and point out that she *had* been the careful one, the line clicked dead. She took a deep breath and put her phone away.

Then she went shopping because it was the only sane thing to do.

Why is it, Shannon asked herself, *that when you shop for underwear you think of a man seeing you in it?*

She prowled through the sexy, silky sheerness of fantasy in one of the intimate-apparel shops. She loved how the material felt against her fingertips and she thought about how it would feel against her skin.

Why can't you just shop for underwear and think about seeing yourself in it and be happy?

But her mind kept wandering, and she didn't like where it wandered to. Was Rafe Santorini the kind of guy who liked a woman in next-to-nothingness? Or in shimmering falls of color and satin that hinted at all the curves it was supposed to?

It bothered her that she didn't know. She could usually tell a man's preference within five minutes of meeting him.

Strong and silent Rafe, with his mysterious scars and harsh attitude, was an enigma. He was the kind of man who would protect a woman even when he was hurting. And he was the kind of man who could turn vicious in a heartbeat if he had to.

So which would he prefer?

More than that, Shannon asked herself, *why do you care? You're not ever going to see him again. And if you did, it would only be because he was there to arrest you or run over you with his car.*

But as she rounded a corner she saw a white embroidered eyelet babydoll that looked absolutely divine. She put her hand under the material and could see her fingernails perfectly. In fact, she bet she could probably read through the material. A pair of solid white panties accompanied it.

The babydoll was the perfect blend of naughty and nice that she felt would drive someone like Rafe Santorini crazy. Shannon knew she had an all-over tan that would make the white material work, and the honey-gold of her hair would be subtle and striking at the same time.

Rafe Santorini would never survive the meltdown he'd get just from seeing her in that.

But he'd never get the chance.

Shannon felt a little disappointed at that. If he hadn't been such a jerk—and a friend of Allison's—it would have been nice to see what kind of guy would wear those scars and be willing to carry an injured woman for blocks. Those kinds of guys, Shannon knew, didn't come along very often.

She bought the lingerie on impulse. Sometimes that was the best way to buy things so no guilt was front-loaded.

Standing on the balcony of the small apartment Kwan-Sook had arranged for her in Sai Kung Town in Hong Kong's New Territories, Shannon looked out over the ocean and drank in the beauty.

Before it had become a retreat for Hong Kong residents and

tourists who could afford it, Sai Kung Peninsula had been home to fishing villages. Fishing boats and the junks that were the remnants of the once-mighty Tanaka fleet lay at anchorage or sailed in the harbor.

Shannon breathed in the salt air and felt safer than she had all day. This part of Hong Kong operated with a frenzy and a pressure that drove the rest of the city.

However, a storm was building on the horizon out over the sea. It was monsoon season, after all. Shannon chose not to view the blossoming mass of clouds as an omen of bad things to come.

It was just weather. Weather happened.

All right, that's enough goofing off. Reluctantly Shannon turned from the view and reentered the apartment. It was small and simply furnished, but the furnishings were traditional Chinese, so it was almost dressy.

The bed took up a lot of space, but there was a small entertainment area created by furniture placement and a curtain of beads. Her new clothing, again in bags and boxes, had beaten her to the apartment, which spoke Kwan-Sook's obvious efficiency.

There was a new computer, fully loaded with the same files she'd had on the other one. It didn't have the notes she'd made or the Web site links she'd saved, but Shannon felt comfortable with the grasp she had on the material.

A bouquet of fresh-cut flowers stood bright and colorful on the table. There had also been a picnic basket of fresh fruit, cheeses, crackers, breads, jams and jellies and chocolate. The refrigerator was filled with juices, herbal teas and wine. The pantry held canned and dry goods. All of it was welcome, but it was enough to feed a small family for several days.

The iPhone rang and Shannon answered it.

"I trust the accommodations are acceptable?" Kwan-Sook asked.

"Very." Shannon took a papaya juice bottle from the refrigerator. "You didn't have to do this."

"This way you won't have to go out. I think you will be safer."

"Probably." Shannon thought she heard beeping in the background again. She tried to isolate it, but she didn't hear it again.

"I have arranged a meeting with Dr. Chow for eight o'clock tonight," Kwan-Sook said.

"Where?" Shannon took a pad and pen from the desk.

"Do you know where the Ten Hau Temple is there in Sai Kung?"

"Yes. I've been here—and there—before." The Tin Hau Temple was dedicated to the goddess Matsu, who was respected as a mother-ancestor of China. She was also revered by sailors and fishermen because they believed she protected them and anyone else who was upon the ocean.

"There is a restaurant not far from there that features private rooms for private dinners. I have arranged for one of those rooms. Dr. Chow will meet you there at eight o'clock."

"All right."

"We will talk again after you have met with him."

"Wait," Shannon said.

"Yes?"

"When will I get to meet you?"

Kwan-Sook hesitated. "Soon. More than that, I can't say. Good luck." The line went dead.

Shannon gazed back through the balcony doors. The wind had picked up enough to whip the curtains on either side of the doorway. The temperature had dropped at least a handful of degrees while she'd been on the phone.

According to her watch, it was only shortly after one o'clock. She had time for a nap before she made the meeting.

That only made her think of the lingerie she'd bought. As

soon as she was thinking about lingerie and bed, she was thinking about Rafe Santorini.

And that was a totally frustrating train of thought in more ways than one.

Knowing she'd never be able to sleep at the moment, she retreated to the refrigerator long enough to make a smoked-salmon-and-cream-cheese sandwich. Then she headed to the computer.

Since Rafe Santorini wasn't going to stay off her mind, it was time to find out all his secrets.

Chapter 22

"A lot of the stuff about this guy is buried pretty deep," Gary said. "That's why it took so long to find it. Usually I'm better at this."

"That's all right." Shannon took small bites of her sandwich as she cruised through the files Gary had put together. There was a lot of information. Evidently Rafe Santorini wasn't one to let the grass grow.

Shannon understood that completely.

"When it comes to tough guys, Shannon, this guy's the real deal." Gary's assessment held awe and respect. Those weren't normally in his lexicon for anyone. "He did the Rangers—"

"We've been through that. Have you learned anything new?" Shannon was impatient to find out what made the man tick.

"I did deep research on him because I figured you'd want it."

"I do."

"I even went tiptoeing into places I shouldn't have, and spooky things happened."

That caught Shannon's attention, and she looked away from the pictures Gary had found of Rafe Santorini's various high-profile military engagements. There were pictures of deserts, jungles and bombed-out urban areas. In his eight years of sol-diering Rafe Santorini had been in a lot of hot spots.

"What spooky things?" she asked.

"When I do that kind of digging, I never do it from anywhere close to my home twenty. I went slumming in Brooklyn. Hit a couple Wi-Fi places and used throwaway accounts."

"Save the computer mumbo-jumbo for someone that will understand and appreciate it."

"Somebody in the government's watching Rafe Santorini's files."

Shannon thought of Allison. That wasn't surprising.

"I got a hinky feeling—"

"'Hinky'?"

"Yeah. That's another word for—"

"I know what it means. You're just too young to say it."

"Whatever. Anyway, I got a bad vibe about the whole deal when I kept getting hung up on simple page shifts, so I closed up my computer and blazed. A few minutes after I left the bar where I'd been hanging and doing my thing, this hot looking chick—"

"'Chick'?"

"Sorry. Woman."

Shannon hadn't been offended by the term. It was just that every time she looked around, there were women involved. All of them appeared to be specially skilled. That was what the Athena Academy had been about.

This is all an Athena operation, she thought. *Just the way they were in Kestonia, Puerto Isla and Cape Town. What is going on?*

That made her feel good. If she was asking questions, she knew her audience would be. Only, when they got to asking questions, she'd be able to answer them.

"This woman goes into the bar," Gary went on, "and starts showing my picture around. *My picture!* Dude, I so could not believe that."

Shannon could. The word *conspiracy* locked into her brain. Genetically modified women were coming out of the Athena Academy.

She thought about that, wondering if that was too big a leap to make. Then she realized Gary was talking again.

"I'd really suggest you stay away from Mr. Hero Guy," Gary said. "I mean, not only does just digging into his name through the Net seem to trigger the wrath of the Internet gods, but he had a screwed-up childhood."

"All of us did." Shannon couldn't help thinking about her own dysfunctional family. She'd escaped. Not everyone did.

But Rafe had escaped, too. He'd gone into the military.

"All of us didn't try to kill our father," Gary said.

The support personnel Allison had set up were sharp. They met with Rafe at the airport without a hitch. They were also Asian, which meant they would blend in where he didn't.

"Captain Santorini," a young woman said when she fell into step with him.

Rafe looked at her. "I'm out of the military and I don't know you." He never broke stride, forcing her to keep up. The last few hours of the flight, it had been all he could do to stay in his seat.

"I'm your contact, sir. Allison sent me."

When he glanced at the woman, though she was a full head shorter than he was, Rafe saw that she had no problem keeping pace. He wasn't ready to just assume the first person who approached him was his contact. Whoever was helping Shannon Connor also had access to people.

"Then you'd have a code word," he told her.

The young woman smiled. Her hair was cut square with her shoulders. She was beautiful and deceptively thin. But her stride was perfect, powerful and cadenced. She could have been a dancer.

"Yes, sir. I would. *Hardhead.* She said you shouldn't take it personally."

"I won't."

"But that I should also keep it in mind while I'm dealing with you."

Despite the situation and his anxiety over Shannon, Rafe had to grin. When he spoke again, it was in Cantonese. "What's your name?"

Another smile curved the young woman's lips. "Fang Xiaoming. You speak the language pretty well."

"'The' language? Not 'our' language?"

"I am an American. English was my native language."

Rafe passed through the doors to the transportation area. "How do you know Allison?"

"We went to school together."

"I would have bet you were going to say that."

"My father is Chinese, but my mother is American. They choose to live here now, but I was invited to attend Athena Academy. It was a very prestigious honor."

"I guess it was. You guys seem to stick together."

Xiaoming nodded. "Loyalty is highly regarded among graduates. And often we find we have many similar interests."

"Like world peace?"

"We do what we can."

Rafe had been joking, but he saw that the young woman wasn't.

"Do you have a vehicle?" he asked.

Xiaoming pointed toward a compact SUV at the curb, then she led the way.

Rafe followed. His knee twinged slightly, but his interest

was focused on the young woman. He had to admit, Allison Gracelyn topped the charts when it came to interesting friends in interesting places.

"What are you talking about?" Shannon asked.

"I found a police report in the military file on Rafe Santorini that I wasn't expecting. Apparently when he was fifteen, he got into a fight with his father. Of course, at the time his dad had been wailing on his mom. All of them ended up in the hospital that night. According to the follow-up reports, Mom and Dad were heavy into extracurricular combat. Extreme parenting. They took turns beating on each other. Then every now and again—"

"They beat Rafe," Shannon whispered.

"Yeah. Pretty hard-core stuff. Everybody blamed everybody for the shared misery. Rafe was just a kid. He was made a ward of the court and placed in a juvenile shelter. And I have to tell you, boss lady, what Rafe Santorini didn't know about violence and fighting going in, he learned by the time he got out. I've been there a few times myself. Not fun."

Shannon stared at the hard, handsome face of the man on the computer monitor.

"Then there was the whole North Korea thing," Gary stated.

"What happened in North Korea?"

"Rafe Santorini was in North Korea on some mission—I'm guessing it was an assassination, but the report didn't spell everything out—and he got caught. The North Korean army kept him imprisoned for five months. The report I looked at said he'd been treated pretty bad. He's lucky they didn't kill him. A few months ago the State Department made some kind of arrangements to get him out."

Shannon looked at the man on her computer and realized that she really didn't know what he was capable of.

* * *

Fang Xiaoming headed up a six-man crew. There was one other woman. They were all Asian. From the way they moved and listened when he spoke, Rafe judged all of them to have military training.

They met in a small hotel in Sai Kung Town. That was as far as Allison had been able to pinpoint Shannon's location.

It drove Rafe crazy to think that he was so close but still unable to reach her. He kept himself calm by getting to know his team when they met in his room. With all six of them in there, the room was crowded.

Hua, the other woman, was a sniper and perhaps a handful of years older than Xiaoming. According to Xiaoming, Hua was a professional mercenary who had been taught by the British Special Air Service.

Xiyue was in his forties, a quiet, watchful man who was the electronics specialist. He also specialized in close-in grabs of assets and people.

Jintao and Zhenrong were both hand-to-hand experts, small-arms marksmen and demolitionists. Jintao chewed gum incessantly and listened to an iPod. Zhenrong wore manga T-shirts and long hair and would have looked at home on any college campus.

According to Xiaoming, she and her crew worked tracking down and preventing industrial espionage and corporate kidnapping of domestic and international businesses.

"The first thing you need to know," Rafe said, "is that the woman is not to be hurt."

"We don't do that kind of work," Xiyue said.

"That's what I was told," Rafe said. Allison's review of the team had been glowing. Evidently the NSA had used them before and been very satisfied. "But when push comes to shove and she *might* get hurt, we fade the heat and back off. I want us all on the same page with that."

They all agreed.

"There are at least two different teams playing this besides us," Rafe said. "They're at cross-purposes. Shannon Connor is trapped somewhere between them. We're here to get her out. Safely."

"I was told that she might not want to come," Hua said.

Rafe folded his arms. "Her last choice in the matter was to come here. She's in danger every minute she stays here and she's ill-informed about her decisions."

No one said anything.

"What do we have for equipment?"

"Anything you want," Xiaoming replied. "Weapons. Surveillance. Transport. Medical. We're a full-service entity. That's why Allison called me."

Outside, a long peal of thunder rolled across the sky. Then the clouds opened up and the deluge began.

Rafe glared at the window and saw the tree branches jerking in the high winds. Raindrops as big as the end of his little fingertip hammered the windowpanes.

"Does anyone know how long this is supposed to last?" he growled irritably.

"It's monsoon season," Xiaoming said. "It will last until it's done."

Rafe's phone rang. He peeled it off his belt and held it to his face. "Yes."

"I have her," Allison said. She sounded tired. "You're not far from her."

Rafe glanced at his watch out of habit. It was 7:26 p.m. He copied the address that Allison gave him as adrenaline spiked within him.

Chapter 23

Dressed for the night and the rain that blew nearly sideways, Rafe closed on the apartment building. The extra clothing was necessary in the galing winds and the rain, but it also helped hide the bulky Kevlar vest he wore and the pistol he carried at his hip. If he got caught with the weapon here on Chinese soil, he was going straight to prison.

If they didn't put him in a pine box.

Cheerful thoughts, aren't they? he chided himself. He slogged through the rain as he headed for the building's main entrance.

Xiaoming flanked him. She was so slight he would have thought she'd have been blown away in the wind, but somehow she seemed to walk through it without being touched.

Hua was stationed on one of the nearby buildings with a sniper rifle. Jintao and Zhenrong covered the apartment building's rear entrance. Xiyue drove the SUV and remained ready in case they needed to be exfiltrated.

All of them wore earwigs and remained in constant communication. Allison was also in the loop.

"Eyes," Rafe said in Cantonese as he walked through the doorway. Rain dripped off him and left a wet spot in the hallway.

"Yes," Hua responded.

"Anything?"

"No. I see no movement inside the room."

"She was just there twenty minutes ago," Allison said. "Maybe she's lying down."

"I see the bed clearly," Hua said. "She's not there."

"Maybe she's taking a bath."

The possibility reminded Rafe of the bubble-covered angel he'd seen in the tub at the hotel in Washington. Tension tightened his chest. He was thinking way too much about way too many things that weren't even supposed to be on his radar.

"She didn't come here to bathe," Rafe growled. He went up the stairs. According to Allison, Shannon was on the third floor in the south beachside apartment.

"Everything's going to be all right," Xiaoming said.

Rafe felt embarrassed that the young woman had even felt moved to tell him that. He wasn't acting completely professionally and he knew it. He hadn't made it all the way back from North Korea yet.

Or being around Shannon, always on the periphery and knowing she was in danger, had jacked his thinking.

He made himself breathe out. *Just chill. This is something you've done a hundred times.*

On the third-story landing they stepped out of the stairwell together. The hallway was empty.

"Back door," Rafe said.

"We're here," Jintao said.

"No sign of her," Zhenrong added.

Rafe went straight for her door because there was no reason

to beat around the bush. When he reached for the door, he discovered it was already open.

He looked back at Xiaoming as he drew his pistol. The young woman already had hers in hand. She nodded at him.

He pointed to himself, then pointed up. Then he pointed at her and pointed down.

Xiaoming nodded again.

"Door's open," Rafe whispered for Allison's benefit. "Eyes."

"I'm on the room," Hua said.

Rafe silently hoped the woman wasn't trigger-happy. He opened the door and went through. He stayed high while Xiaoming went low.

Covering each other as they went, Rafe and Xiaoming quickly scouted the room.

"She's not here," Rafe said in disgust. He holstered his weapon. "Control? Did you—"

"I heard you," Allison said. "All I know is that when she was last on the phone, she was in that room."

"Well, she's gone now."

The monsoon delivered rain in blinding sheets. For the most part, pedestrians and vehicles stayed off the streets. Restaurants and bars offered light and warmth against the night and the storm's darkness and chill.

Clad in a nylon jacket, Shannon peered out from under the hood and made her way to The Mizzen, the restaurant where Kwan-Sook had arranged the interview. The restaurant's interior had a distinct nautical theme and was definitely English in atmosphere.

She gave her name to the maître d', then provided the false identification when asked. Once the man was satisfied Shannon was who she actually wasn't, she followed him up to the second floor and the private dining room.

"Would you like a glass of wine?" the server asked.

Shannon briefly considered it, then declined. She wanted to be at her best. She asked for water.

Dr. Chow Bao was evidently late. But only by ten minutes.

"Please forgive me," he said in unaccented English when he arrived. He hung a drenched umbrella on a peg on the wall. "The weather is atrocious."

Shannon agreed.

The doctor was of medium height and a little paunchy. His black hair was longish and showing gray. He could have been anywhere from forty to sixty.

"You look like your picture," he said, peering at her more closely. "Very beautiful. You have good bone structure."

"Thank you." The attention only slightly bothered Shannon. Television required being stared at intently a lot.

"Have you had a chance to study the menu?" Chow asked as he sat on the other side of the small table.

"Not for very long."

"May I take the liberty of ordering for you? I know the cuisine here very well." Chow smiled a little.

"Of course," Shannon said.

Chow crooked a finger at the server, who'd been standing off to one side. He rattled off an order so fast that Shannon didn't know for sure what she was getting.

"You'll enjoy it," Chow assured her.

Shannon liked the idea of a man ordering her dinner, but it usually worked best if the man doing the ordering knew her well enough to do it.

The server went away.

"Now, since our time here is precious," Chow said, "perhaps we'd best get started."

"Of course." The man's directness surprised Shannon.

"I'm told you represent a consortium of investors who would like to put money into my research."

"Yes," Shannon replied. That was the cover Kwan-Sook had told her she'd arranged.

"Would you mind telling me who some of them are?"

"I can't go into names, Dr. Chow. I hope you understand."

Chow smiled. "Understanding is not too important. The million-dollar endowment I was given to have this interview with you was quite convincing."

Shannon was amazed. Kwan-Sook hadn't mentioned that. A million-dollar signing bonus would be a big enticement. Not for the first time, she wondered about her mysterious benefactor.

"I've read a lot of papers on Dr. Peters's work," Shannon said, steering the conversation in the direction she wanted it to go. "He seems to have divided the genetic-engineering camp."

Chow nodded and smiled like a genial grandfather. "Aldritch did. And he enjoyed the fact that what he was doing was a hot button for so many people. He liked having an audience and he liked starting controversy. Even more so when it was over something he'd started."

Shannon reached into her pocket and used the speed-dial function on her phone to call Gary. When they'd talked earlier, he'd agreed to tape the interview.

Chow, like most scientists and deep thinkers Shannon had met, rambled on at length about the genetics field and the probable outcome of what geneticists would one day learn and how they would be able to improve the quality of life. It all sounded wonderful on paper, but she knew Chow was deliberately not addressing some of the technical problems of those successes.

She let him keep talking till the arrival of dinner. It was a fifteen-minute diatribe that she'd heard before. She'd also heard the diatribes of the naysayers. It was an issue that divided a lot of people and one about which she wasn't sure how she felt.

Then she got down to the questions she'd come there to ask. It was time to nail the coffin shut on the Athena Academy once and for all.

Although he was seriously concerned about Shannon Connor's welfare, Rafe forced himself to move slowly and thoroughly. He and Xiaoming searched the apartment in tandem without saying a word.

Xiaoming yanked the chest of drawers open one at a time, starting with the bottom and working her way up. It was a technique an experienced investigator used. Rafe knew that because the NSA had trained him.

They didn't speak.

Rafe concentrated on the contents of the closet. He'd already linked the computer in the room to the satellite-driven Internet so that Allison could plunder its contents.

Then Xiaoming said, "This is interesting."

Rafe turned to her. "What?"

Xiaoming held up a wispy babydoll negligee. "You said she was here alone?"

"Yeah." Rafe stared at the garment and imagined that outfit on Shannon. His mouth was suddenly dry. He silently cursed himself for his reaction.

"Then she was meeting someone." Xiaoming studied the garment. "Someone I'd say she wanted to make an impression on."

Jealousy burned inside Rafe. He had to force it aside and only managed that by thinking of the attack on Shannon at the airport. Whoever the other party was that was tracking her wasn't pulling any punches.

You can't afford any distractions, he told himself. *If you get distracted, you can't help her.*

"What do you think?" Xiaoming looked at him.

Rafe wondered what Allison had told the woman and he wondered if Allison had sabotaged him to some degree. Maybe he was the stalking horse leading Allison's team to Shannon. Evidently there was a lot at stake that he didn't know about.

He had to make himself believe in Allison, but he knew that Allison was as motivated in her own way as he was. Possibly even more so.

"What do I think?" Rafe growled. "I think that if that flimsy excuse for underwear doesn't have a map and directions for finding Shannon Connor, it isn't a whole lot of help."

Xiaoming smiled, folded the negligee neatly and returned it to the drawer. She continued working.

"I have her again," Allison said over the earwig. "She's on her phone and staying in place."

Thunder boomed outside and made the balcony doors jump in their runners. Lightning streaked the sky as the wind howled.

"Where?" Rafe asked.

"Not far from your position. I'll lock you in as you go. Get moving."

But Rafe already was—and he was hoping he wouldn't be too late.

Chapter 24

"According to the files I was given," Shannon said, "Dr. Peters was convinced he could improve upon the basic human design."

"Yes. He was. He'd found a way to do it. I worked with him on the early permutations of the work. It was brilliant. Simply brilliant. He started working with egg harvesting long before anyone else did. Removing them from the uterus of the donor, fertilizing them and replacing them within surrogate mothers—all those things were done well ahead of many practitioners. Only Aldritch did all those people one better."

"He tampered with the genetic coding."

Chow grinned. "*Tampered?* No, he gave more promise to the idea of what it is to be human—or more than human—than anyone ever had before. People seeking to *correct* the DNA of diseased patients or eliminate particular illnesses or defects owe a lot to what Aldritch perfected." He shook his head. "He was just clearly ahead of his time. More to the point, he was working ahead of the moral compass points of the world at large. Anyone seriously working in this field is doing that."

"And he broke the law. He was conducting illegal genetic experiments at Lab 33."

Chow hesitated. "Yes. But the news that was released regarding that matter was skewed. People heard about the experimentation, but they didn't hear about his successes."

"What successes?"

"Imagine," Chow said more quietly and intensely, "if you can, what it would be like to be able to pay for extra abilities for your child."

"Like intelligence, strength and speed?"

"More than that, Miss Connor. Suppose you were able to graft on abilities that people have never before had."

"Like what?"

"The ability to heal more quickly. The ability to breathe underwater." Chow shook his head. "So many things that we take for granted in other creatures and simply think we can't do. The possibilities are staggering. Of course, one of the downfalls of his work was that the DNA resequencing could only be done with females. The Y chromosome just throws everything out of kilter. There are even some who believe the male of the species is gradually being bred out of the human race."

"Did you ever think Dr. Peters would succeed in those experiments?"

Chow laughed. "Think?" He shook his head. "Aldritch created some of those changes in the lab where I worked with him. I helped him implant the first three egg-babies he created in that lab. This was before he was allowed to use harvested human eggs at Lab 33."

"Why was the lab located next to the Athena Academy?" Shannon asked, though now she feared she knew the answer.

"Because of the girls, of course. Aldritch needed a steady

supply of eggs. He could get plenty of surrogates, but young donors—girls who didn't have the threat of sexual disease or genetic damage or even age—were hard to come by. Third World countries weren't the answer because most of those children aren't healthy enough."

Shannon thought she was going to be sick, but she hid those feelings behind a mask of self-control.

"You just don't always get a good genetic sampling in Third World countries," Chow went on. "No, the answer was to use American girls. The genetic diversity is stronger there, and the overall care is much better. Lab 33, located in the Phoenix area— which was then, and still is, largely unpolluted by today's accepted levels of toxicity—was *one* of the perfect places to find donors."

The cold, blunt way Chow stated his case offended Shannon on so many levels she almost couldn't react quickly enough to shut them down. She'd interviewed other people who had the same lack of qualms when it came to the lives of others. They weren't just politicians, either. They were economists, sports figures, celebrities and others. Even other journalists.

"When that location was made available to him," Chow said, "along with the girls' academy and government protection— though that turned out not to be as great as he'd been led to believe—Aldritch relocated his work immediately."

A cold chill washed through Shannon and suffused the rage and sickness she'd been experiencing. "Eggs were harvested from the girls at the school?"

"That was the plan, yes. I don't know if Aldritch actually did that, but I wouldn't have put it past him. The American military general, Eric Pace, was very much a part of the decision to move Lab 33. Until that time, Aldrich had only been able to work with a few human test subjects."

"The reports I read didn't mention that."

"It was horrid. Most of the babies that he worked with at the time aborted naturally. Only a few drew a breath of fresh air. Most of them didn't live long."

"You had a working relationship with Dr. Peters as he developed the process."

"I did."

"What broke that relationship?"

Chow put his knife and fork away. "The things that usually destroy good partnerships among scientists. Ego and money. Aldritch didn't care to share either." He spread his hands and shook his head. "I should have seen the writing on the wall when Aldritch forced me to dismiss my staff. Some of my people had been with me for years. It was a very sad occasion. I was left without the funding and access to resources I needed to continue my studies. You can't investigate the nature of life itself, like Dr. Frankenstein did in those ghastly movies. You need a proper lab and materials."

Shannon thought Chow sounded more broken up over losing the funding than losing his people.

"Aldritch also felt threatened," Chow said. "My own studies were approaching the level of his. I have to admit, I learned a lot from him. But I was also developing procedures that were mine. With the funding I get from your people, I'll be able to enhance everything Aldritch Peters was doing."

Shannon's phone vibrated against her thigh, signaling an incoming call. She debated answering the phone, then chose to at least check to see who was calling.

While Chow was going on at length about how he was hoping to graft DNA strands, Shannon pulled her phone out and checked caller ID.

It was the L.A. number Kwan-Sook was using.

Shannon slipped the phone from her slacks while Chow turned his attention to his wine.

"Hello?"

"You've got to get out of there," Kwan-Sook said breathlessly. The beeping in the background sounded more agitated. "They've found you."

"Who?"

"Allison Gracelyn and Rafe Santorini."

Shannon was stunned. "How?"

"I don't know yet. Dr. Chow has his phone turned off or he's forgotten it again. Get him out of there and—"

At that moment a ruby dot centered on Chow's forehead. He was smiling at Shannon, patiently waiting for her to turn her attention back to him.

Shannon knew what the red dot signified. She'd been around the military on different interviews. Laser spotting scopes were mounted on several kinds of weapons.

"Get down!" Shannon yelled as she tried to get up from her chair and go to Chow. It was only then that she realized she might have a similar ruby dot on the back of her head.

Chow's smile went away. Then the top of his head went away in a violent rush of blood and bone. Slowly, almost comically, he fell over backward in his chair.

Shannon threw herself to the floor and resisted the urge to curl up on the floor. She had to get out. Then she saw the ruby dot sliding across the floor toward her….

The harsh crack of a high-powered rifle drew Rafe up short. He'd been trotting down the street, knowing that most onlookers wouldn't question a man moving quickly through the driving rain.

Now he ran past the dark bulk of the Tin Hau Temple that was one of the centerpieces of the small town. A lightning flash tore through the shadows and revealed the red paint, dark as blood in the night, that colored the front of the temple.

Xiaoming paced him easily, and for a crazy minute Rafe wondered if he was holding her back. His knee throbbed, but the strength didn't fade. Some of the old fear came railing back at him, though. If it came apart on him—

Don't think about that, he ordered himself. *Hold it together yourself. Will it to stay together.*

He ran, blinking against the harsh slaps of the rain that tore at his face. His breath burned in his lungs and turned gray against the coolness of the storm.

"Where is she?" he asked.

"Ahead," Allison replied. "On the right."

Rafe looked and spotted the restaurant. Neon signs advertised beer and wine and that the business was open. A weathered sign held the name The Mizzen.

"Can you tell where she is inside?" Rafe asked.

"No." Allison cursed. "I just lost her. The phone connection ended."

The rifle cracked twice more.

"Eyes," Rafe said.

"Yes," Hua responded.

"Find that shooter."

The woman's voice was uninflected and unhurried, both good traits for a sniper. "I will."

Rafe reached the door at the same time Xiaoming did. They fell into place on either side of it. Both of them had their pistols out.

Another rifle shot punctuated the night.

A man crashed through the restaurant's doors.

Rafe stepped in front of the man and stopped him with a hard, flat hand to the chest.

"Don't shoot!" the man pleaded in English. "For God's sake, don't shoot!"

Knowing that the man was just a patron and scared out of his wits, Rafe fisted the man's shirt and pulled him forward to get him into motion again.

"Go!" Rafe ordered.

By then a veritable torrent of people cascaded from the restaurant, driving Rafe and Xiaoming backward.

Shannon rolled across the floor as two more bullets ploughed splinters from the wood surface. They missed her by inches. She came to a stop under the window the sniper was shooting through. Jagged pieces of glass tumbled down onto her, mixing with the rain that now drummed into the room, as well.

Only a few feet away, Dr. Chow Bao lay sprawled in death.

Get up! Get moving! Shannon screamed at herself, but she was frozen. Then she remembered to breathe. After that, she remembered the Athena Academy training she'd been given.

While at the school, students learned a lot of things, but most of all they learned how to survive. Although she had never and would never want to, Shannon knew how to live off the land and find water.

She also knew how to handle herself in high-pressure situations. And this was definitely high-pressure.

The door was ten feet away. The distance wasn't impossible. But all it took was one bullet.

Yells and screams from the dining room below invaded the room.

If you stay here, they're going to trap you. Taking another quick breath, Shannon pushed herself into motion and threw herself across the room. At the last minute she threw herself down into a baseball slide and shot through the door.

Two bullets chopped into the door frame only inches above her head.

The floor was slick enough that she slammed into the wall and knocked the breath from her lungs. She also hit her head. Black spots danced in her vision.

Another bullet stuck the wall and kicked splinters over her face. She threw herself forward, landed on the floor once, then pushed herself to her feet just in time to start running down the stairs.

The lower dining room was in total chaos. Diners were torn between running and hiding.

Three black-uniformed men with assault rifles came through the kitchen area. One of them pointed at Shannon. When red flared through her vision, she knew the laser sights of one of the weapons had swung across her eyes.

She ducked, and bullets tore into the wooden railing of the stairs.

Chapter 25

Finally, through the confusion of people abandoning the restaurant, Rafe spotted Shannon taking cover on the stairwell. A laser light flashed across her forehead. She flattened against the stairs as a hail of bullets struck the railing.

Spotting the three men in black uniforms on the other side of the dining room, Rafe raised his pistol in both hands and snap-fired, operating on instinct, training and experience.

His bullets knocked one of the men down before they even knew he was there. He shifted his aim to the second man, aiming for center mass and not trying to be selective about his target.

The man wheeled toward him and raked a spray of bullets around the room that vectored on Rafe's position. Despite the threat, Rafe stayed locked on target and kept firing. His bullets slammed into the man's chest.

The shooter locked up, then dropped.

Rafe shifted to the third man, fired once and missed and watched as the pistol slide blew back empty.

"Move," Xiaoming ordered.

Rafe rolled to the side and abandoned his position. Xiaoming stepped into it and framed her arms into a triangle as naturally as drawing a breath. When she fired, the shooter's head snapped back. Even at that distance, Rafe saw the small hole dotted perfectly between the man's eyes.

It was one of the coolest shots he'd ever seen in his life.

Xiaoming tracked the pistol across the dining room, but there were no more targets.

"Lucky?" Rafe asked as he reloaded his pistol. "Or are you that good?"

"I'm that good," Xiaoming replied without looking over her shoulder. "You did well."

"Nothing like that," Rafe said. "You've got point. We get Shannon first."

"All right. Ready?"

Rafe tripped the slide release and the pistol snapped back together. "Ready."

Xiaoming moved forward quickly. She kept her shoulders square, her knees bent and her seat dropped slightly to lower her center of gravity and provide a smoother gait.

She definitely knew what she was doing.

Rafe followed her toward the three men they'd dropped. The restaurant's patrons, lying on the floor, hastily scrambled out of the way.

Xiaoming reached down for one of the assault rifles and tossed it to Rafe. "Just like the video games," she said. "Weapon upgrade."

Rafe checked the rifle's action and magazine. When he nodded, Xiaoming picked up an assault rifle, as well. Then they divvied the magazines. Rafe shoved a fresh one into his weapon.

Then he turned his attention to Shannon.

Her eyes met his, then she fled back up the stairs.

That was where the sniper was.

"Eyes," Rafe bellowed as he charged toward the stairs.

"Yes," Hua said.

"Do you have that damned sniper in check yet?"

"No."

Rafe pushed himself harder and tried to ignore the burning pain strafing his knee.

Shannon knew she was trapped between a hard place and a rock. She didn't know the three men that Rafe Santorini and his companion had killed, but she had no doubt that Rafe was there for her.

She'd seen that much in his eyes.

Upstairs, she also knew she might be fair game for the sniper that had killed Dr. Chow Bao. Still, she had a plan.

She ran down the length of the hallway, not at all surprised when the sniper spotted her and started cracking shots in her direction. The second floor of the restaurant was lousy with windows.

The ruby laser strobed in all directions. Windows shattered and bullets ripped gouges in the walls.

Shannon ran for all she was worth for the balcony overlooking the east side of the restaurant. Rafe had come in the front. The men in black had come in the rear. She hoped to split the difference.

When she reached the balcony door, she flung it open. No one was outside, but she checked anyway. Whoever was out to get her, including Rafe, wasn't holding back.

A bullet cored through the door as she held it open. She felt the vibration and it jarred her into movement. She ran through the scattered tables and chairs and tried not to think about how far below the ground was.

Shots hammered a table beside her and knocked over a chair.

Shannon didn't break stride as she placed her hands on the railing and vaulted over. For a moment, in the pelting rain and the howling winds of the storm, she was disoriented. But all the gymnastics training she'd had at the academy and in the martial arts dojos afterward came back to her.

She went limp at the moment of contact and rolled through the landing to come up on her feet. Her hair was already wrecked, plastered to her head. She had to rake it out of her face. Even as she did, she saw the man step toward her with his assault rifle raised.

He aimed the rifle butt at her face and she almost escaped it. The metal plate partially caught her forehead and drove her backward.

Confident now, the man came at her. Dazed, Shannon gave ground before him. He lifted the rifle to take aim. There was nowhere to run.

With a howl of inarticulate fear and rage, Shannon rushed the man, pushed the rifle aside with her left hand, kneed him in the crotch with her right leg, raked his face with the nails of her right hand, then head-butted him in the face. His nose snapped under the impact.

Shannon ripped the rifle from the man's grip and swung it like a bat. The buttstock slammed into the side of the man's head. He tried to stay on his feet, but he stumbled with the effort. Shannon swung again. This time the rifle came apart in her hands.

The man fell at her feet.

And she saw two more black-uniformed men coming up quickly from the alley. She stood, chest heaving, and knew she wasn't going to make it out of the alley alive.

Liquid agony throbbed along Rafe's knee as he powered up the steps. It lightened somewhat when he reached the second floor.

At the landing he hesitated for just a moment, trying to figure out which way Shannon had gone.

"To your right," Hua said. "I took out the sniper." Her voice sounded pained.

Rafe raced to the right and heard Shannon yelling out beyond the balcony. At first he thought she'd tried to jump over the side and hurt herself in the fall. But when he reached the balcony railing, he was just in time to see her swing the rifle into her attacker.

Then movement to Rafe's left caught his eye. The two men materialized out of the darkness and raised their weapons.

In a split second Rafe weighed his chances of taking out both gunners. They wouldn't know he was there above them until it was too late. But he felt it would also be too late to save Shannon if he didn't kill them immediately.

He felt rather than saw Xiaoming closing in from behind him. It was all part of the battlefield awareness he'd developed over years of being in bad situations. He dropped the assault rifle as he threw himself over the balcony railing toward Shannon.

"Two men to your left," Rafe said as he dropped.

Although he'd known the move was going to send screaming agony through his knee, Rafe was unprepared for the sheer brain-frying pain that ripped through his consciousness. For a minute he was afraid he was going to pass out. What made it even worse was landing on his feet instead of rolling out of the drop.

But he landed and remained standing only a few feet in front of Shannon. He lurched forward one step, dragging the injured leg, then wrapped his arms around her before she could escape.

Behind him, the two shooters opened fire. Hammer blows struck him. Something clipped the side of his head and he fell forward as he blacked out.

Rafe's dead weight almost crushed Shannon. She tried to get her breath and couldn't. Beyond him, she watched as someone on top of the balcony fired down at the two men that had shot Rafe. Both men went down.

Shannon struggled, wishing she had enough air in her lungs to tell Rafe that he could get up now, that the danger was past. But she couldn't. When she noticed the still slackness of Rafe's body, she couldn't even vent the scream that filled the back of her throat.

She managed to leverage one of Rafe's shoulders up and slither free.

The figure above her dropped lithely over the balcony's side and landed as effortlessly as a cat. Lightning ripped the sky and revealed the woman's features as she reloaded the rifle she carried.

Panicked, scared and not wanting Rafe to be dead, Shannon tried to find the wounds in his back. If she could stop him from bleeding, he would have a chance.

"That," the woman with the rifle said, "has got to be one of the stupidest things I've ever seen a guy do."

"It's definitely in my personal top ten," a young Chinese man with long hair said as he joined them.

"Shut up and help me," Shannon yelled. "He may still be alive."

"Oh, he's still alive," the woman said. "He was wearing a vest."

Shannon brought up her hand and showed them the blood that covered it. "He wasn't wearing a vest on his head."

The woman tossed her rifle to the man and knelt down with Shannon. The woman took a penlight from her pocket and played it over Rafe. The right side of his head was a bloody mess.

"It's okay," the woman said. "He's still breathing. As long as he's breathing, he's going to be all right."

"Unless he's got brain damage," the man said.

The woman glared up at him. "You're not helping."

Self-consciously the man shrugged. "I'm just saying, is all."

"Transport," the woman said. "I need you. East side of the restaurant."

Feeling helpless, not knowing exactly how she was supposed to feel, Shannon looked around. Several faces were pushed up against the restaurant's windows.

She knew she should run. She didn't know what Rafe or these people with her now had orders to do. For all she knew, they were going to kill her at the first convenient opportunity.

"If you run," the woman said quietly, "we're going to have to come after you. If we come after you, we may not be able to help Captain Santorini. Do you understand?"

Shannon looked at the woman and nodded. Even if she could have gotten away, she found she couldn't just leave him there. That surprised her almost as much as having Rafe throw himself from the balcony and use himself as a human shield.

"I'm not going anywhere," Shannon said.

It looked as though Allison and Athena Academy had won after all. Whatever secrets they were protecting were going to stay hidden.

Chapter 26

Shannon sat with Rafe in the dark underground room where the people he'd been with had taken him. He lay in bed for two days and never regained consciousness. After the first couple of hours, one of the men had started an IV feed.

For the first day the people that had been with Rafe hadn't bothered to introduce themselves. They largely ignored her and didn't talk to her.

When the woman entered the room to change the IV bag, she saw that she'd arrived early. Without a word, she sat with her back against one of the cinder-block walls with the bag in her lap. She was quiet and controlled.

"Why are you keeping him here?" Shannon asked. "He needs a doctor."

The woman ignored her. A moment later the IV machine beeped and reminded Shannon of the sounds she'd heard during Kwan-Sook's calls.

The woman got up effortlessly and went to change the bag. When she was finished, she walked toward the door.

Shannon stepped in her way.

The woman regarded her. "You're not big enough to stand there."

"I want answers," Shannon said.

"You," the woman said, "are lucky to be allowed to stay in this room. If I hadn't seen Captain Santorini willing to sacrifice himself to save you, your presence here wouldn't have been allowed."

"I don't know why he did that."

"Neither do I."

"Look." Although she tried not to let it happen, Shannon's voice broke. "I...I just want to know that he's going to be all right."

"Why do you care?"

Shannon couldn't answer that. She just kept thinking about how Rafe had been raised and how he'd put his life on the line since he'd met her.

The woman started to leave.

Shannon didn't try to stop her. She couldn't have anyway. The rest of the group were in the next room. They made sure she had plenty to eat and drink and they let her go to the bathroom, but her movements were restricted.

The woman halted at the door and hesitated. "He's going to be all right. He's strong. He's healthy. He's just...resting."

"He needs to be in a hospital."

"He's in this country illegally, Miss Connor. As are you. China is not the United States. They're not as generous here. Given his background and who he really is, he could be shot as a spy. That's why we don't take him to the hospital."

"Can't Allison get him out of here?"

"I don't know anyone named—"

"Don't," Shannon interrupted. "*Don't* lie to me. I know Allison Gracelyn is NSA and I know that Rafe worked with her. I don't know what their interest is in me, but I know who they are."

The woman just looked at her.

"Please," Shannon said.

The woman nodded. "If Allison could get Captain Santorini out of here, she would. But transporting him while unconscious and wounded would raise questions we're not at this point ready to answer. Likewise, transporting him could be dangerous."

"I thought you said he was going to be all right."

"I believe he will be. But I don't know everything."

"All right. Thank you."

"You're welcome." The woman paused. "Try to get some rest."

Wordlessly Shannon returned to the straight-backed chair where she'd been sitting for the last two days. She sat and, after a while, took Rafe's hand once more in hers. The hard calluses on his fingers and hands gave her reassurance that he couldn't be permanently harmed. She held on to him, afraid that if she let go, he might not return.

The beeping of the IV bag woke Shannon and made her think of Kwan-Sook. She blinked blearily at the bed and hoped to find Rafe looking back at her.

He still slept.

"You're awake," the woman said as she hung a new bag. "Good. Allison wants to talk to you."

"Why?" Shannon asked.

"I don't know. You'll have to ask her."

The front room of the basement the group occupied wasn't much better than the one they'd put Rafe in. There was more furniture, a few chairs and cots. An entertainment/video game center with a stack of DVDs and games sat against one wall. A bookcase held a lot of tattered books in English and Cantonese.

The woman pointed Shannon to the notebook computer on a small metal secretarial desk. With the other members of the team in the room, private conversation was out of the question.

"Hello, Shannon," Allison said. Her image showed on the computer monitor.

At first Shannon had been reluctant about a face-to-face meeting with Allison when she'd seen the built-in video camera hookup on the computer. She hadn't been able to do much beyond shower in the small cubicle adjoining the basement area.

But when the monitor opened on a view of Allison, Shannon saw that the days had worn on her, as well.

"Hello, Allison," Shannon said. "I know we've had our problems in the past, but if there's anything you can do for Rafe, you need to do it."

"He's a friend of mine. If there was anything I could do, I would. We'll give it another couple of days and see where we are. He's strong. In North Korea—"

"He survived torture and imprisonment for months," Shannon said. "I know."

Allison smiled a little at that. "I thought I recognized your hacker friend's touch when he raided those files."

"He's a good guy," Shannon said. "He was just trying to help me out. Don't do anything to him."

"Actually," Allison said, "I was thinking of offering him a job."

Shannon laughed before she knew she was going to. "If you do, he'll be blown away. He's dreamed of being spy guy."

Allison laughed, too, and she looked grateful to have the distraction.

"Rafe Santorini is a fantastic guy, Shannon."

"I know."

"You don't find many like him."

"I know that, too."

"I heard what he did."

Shannon took a deep breath. "The general consensus is that it was a pretty dumb thing to do. Especially for me."

"Rafe believes in you," Allison said.

Despite her circumstances, Shannon took pride in that. But she knew the truth, too. "He doesn't even know me. We never met until the night Vincent Drago tried to kill me." And that seemed like a million years ago now.

"He knew you longer than that," Allison said. "I'd had him watching you for weeks before that night with Drago."

"Why? Because of everything that happened at Athena?" Some of Shannon's anger returned full force.

"No. Because I've been tracking the person who's been tipping you concerning the news stories you've been breaking."

"How did you find out about that?"

"Lately you've been everywhere we've been."

"We?"

Allison grimaced. "I'm tired. Just let it go at that. I can't talk about it."

"Just like you can't talk about Lab 33 and Aldritch Peters?"

"Just like that." Allison took a drink of the coffee at her elbow. "The person that's been giving you those tips isn't a good person."

"The people I brought down weren't good people," Shannon said.

"Not all of them, no. But some of them were just people who made mistakes. The person tipping you didn't give you that information to square the scales of justice. It was for profit, pure and simple."

"You have proof of that?" Shannon challenged.

"I do. When there's time, I could prove it to you."

"So you could prove I was wrong?"

"So I could prove you were taken advantage of," Allison said.

"I wasn't taken advantage of."

"Rafe was the one who made me start thinking about what might really have happened all those years ago at Athena."

Shannon folded her arms. "We don't need to talk about that."

"I think we do. This—*all* of this—started there and then." Allison looked at her. "You still say that I sent you the e-mails that told you to frame Josie Lockworth."

Shannon bridled at that. "You know you did. And I know you lied about it to save yourself. Your mom would have killed you."

"My mom," Allison said, "knew me better than I thought she did. She thought I had sent those e-mails you say you got."

"I *did* get them."

"We'll get back to that. The point is that I wasn't a very generous teenager. I had my issues. I wanted to beat Rainy Miller at everything. Rainy wasn't like that. She only wanted to do her best. Unfortunately for me, her best in those days was generally better than what I had to give." Allison paused. "Did you know she had a crush on my brother David? And that he had one on her?"

Shannon smiled at the memory. "Joe College with the incredible hook shot on the basketball court? Of course I did. A lot of us did. But with Rainy you could just see it was deeper than that."

"I know. But back then I sabotaged that relationship before it could get started. Rainy had ended up in some hard times and Mom had taken her in. I knew she had my mom and dad wrapped around her little finger—which I know now wasn't really the way it was—but I didn't want her to have David, too. So I broke them up before they had a chance to get started." Allison took a deep breath. "I only recently got to help fix that."

Looking at Allison, Shannon was surprised to find that she felt badly for her. "You were young, Allison. When you're young, you make mistakes."

"I know. I keep telling myself that. Maybe one of these days I'll believe it."

"Just like the mistake you made in sending me that e-mail to frame Josie. Admittedly, I shouldn't have done it, but that was *my* mistake. If you'd have just admitted—"

"Shannon," Allison interrupted. "I didn't send those e-mails. There was nothing for me to admit to."

Shannon closed her mouth. She couldn't believe after everything that had gone on, after what they'd just said to each other, that Allison was going to continue to deny what had happened.

Shannon's anger got the better of her. With all the strain of worrying about Rafe and being virtually held prisoner by people she didn't know, she was ready to explode.

"Before you reach critical mass," Allison said, "listen to me for just a moment. I think you were set up."

Chapter 27

Allison's statement caught Shannon so much by surprise that she temporarily forgot her anger. "You think *what?*"

"That you were set up. Look at what we're dealing with—a master computer cracker capable of getting the dirt on what seems like everybody. There were actually two people involved in this. I know who the first one was, but I don't know who the second one is."

Everything suddenly got confusing to Shannon. "What do you mean, *two people?*"

"What I'm going to tell you now is classified," Allison said. "I only this morning got permission from President Monihan to tell you and Rafe's team."

Shannon was suddenly conscious of everyone in the room paying attention to the conversation.

"Her name," Allison said, "was Jackie Cavanaugh."

As Shannon sat and listened to everything Allison said about the woman, she grew more and more amazed.

"You think this enemy of your mother's set me up?" Shannon asked. She felt dazed. Her head spun. Everything made sense. Sort of.

"I do," Allison said. "You'd have to study the woman's profile. I had an expert put together a forensic composite of Jackie Cavanaugh."

"Did Chesca Thorne do the profile?" Shannon asked.

Allison looked a little surprised. At first it seemed as though she wasn't going to answer, then she decided to keep everything out in the open. "Yes. How did you know?"

"I've been keeping tabs on her career at the FBI's Behavioral Science Unit and have thought about doing an interview with her. I knew she was an Athena graduate."

"Chesca did it. When I talked to her about you and everything that happened with Josie, she told me that long-range planning like this was something Cavanaugh was capable of. If Cavanaugh was going to try to bring down Mom's school—the one dream that Mom cherished above all others outside of her family—she needed someone from inside."

"Since that wasn't possible," Shannon said, feeling the pieces click into place, "she decided to create an inside person."

Allison nodded. "Cavanaugh knew about my rivalry with Rainy. She also picked up on the fact that I was more intense about it."

"So she wrote those e-mails to me and pretended to be you."

"Yes." Allison sighed. "There's no way to know for sure at this point. But it *feels* right." She paused. "For what it's worth, I apologize. And I'm sorry about what happened to you."

Shannon had to take a deep breath before she could speak. "Me, too." Before she knew it, tears brimmed in her eyes. She felt embarrassed. Then she saw that Allison was crying, too.

"When you get back," Allison said, "we're going to have a long talk."

Shannon nodded. "Okay. But in the meantime we've still got a job to do."

"We?" Allison looked at her.

"I talked to Dr. Chow about the three egg-babies that he helped Aldritch Peters create before he came to Lab 33."

"I know. I copied the conversation, as well."

"You did?" Shannon couldn't believe it.

"Sorry," Allison said. "It's this spy business."

Shannon laughed. "Then you've had the same thing I've had all this time and you haven't seen it."

Allison frowned. "Had what?"

"A way to find out about the egg-babies."

"How?" Allison looked confused.

"While he was talking to me, Dr. Chow mentioned that before Aldritch Peters canned him he'd fired all of his staff."

"His staff isn't going to know every—"

"Not his staff," Shannon agreed. "But I haven't met a doctor yet whose head nurse didn't know more about the office and the people they dealt with than the doctor."

A pleased smile spread across Allison's face. "I think you may have something."

"I know I do," Shannon said confidently. "It's just that here, in this country, I wouldn't know where to begin looking. I thought I was stymied. But that was before I had the resources of a spy."

"I'll see what I can find out."

"Allison."

Allison looked up.

"I want in on this," Shannon said. "It's my story."

A troubled look filled Allison's face. "This isn't going to be one that you can tell."

"I know." Shannon tried to tell herself that she could accept that. "But I'd still like to close it out. I'm a professional. I don't like to leave part of a story hanging."

After a moment Allison nodded. "Rafe is of the opinion that you could get a rock to tell you its story. If I find this woman, she may not want to talk."

"Find her," Shannon said. "I can get her to talk. Bet on it."

"Okay," Allison said. "If I find her, she's yours."

"When," Shannon said. *"When* you find her. Rafe said you could do anything."

"Wow," a thick voice said from the back of the room. "It sounds like I promise an awful lot while I'm shot near to death."

Startled and excited, Shannon turned in her seat.

Rafe Santorini, head bandaged and still looking groggy, stood in the doorway.

Shannon wanted to go to him, but then she didn't know what would happen. It could be very uncomfortable for both of them. But her heart sped up and she felt a tremendous weight lift off her.

"About time you woke up," she said.

Rafe smiled and looked a little uncertain. "I must have been really, really tired." He looked around. "I need to know what I missed—maybe even what day it is—and something hot to eat. I noticed I've been on a liquid diet for a while."

It took Allison four days to find Lin Ci'an, who had been Dr. Chow Bao's head nurse for twenty years until she'd been released from his service nearly thirty years ago. Allison had finally been able to find the woman through census and hospital records. As it turned out, Ci'an had never left the medical field. Getting those records, Allison had admitted, had been hard.

"Impossible would have taken a little longer," Allison had told Rafe.

Ci'an was a brown nut of a woman in her seventies. Despite

her age, she had no infirmities and her mind was incredibly clear and uncluttered. Her gaze was piercing and direct.

She was, Rafe knew to his bones, a survivor above all things.

Shannon contacted her in the clinic she worked at in Hong Kong. Dr. Chow had arranged a job for her when he'd let her go from the research lab.

Now she sat in the luxurious hotel suite Allison had booked for the "interview" Shannon was conducting. As it turned out, Ci'an was a fan of Western television and she had a particular ax to grind concerning the rights of women in China.

Rafe hadn't picked up on that at first, even when he'd heard Shannon talking with the woman. But Shannon had.

Seated at the desk, Rafe pretended to be the camera operator. They had a two-camera setup on the woman, giving the talk the feel of a real television interview. Allison watched, hooked in through the camera feed.

Shannon was incredibly patient. The woman obviously wouldn't talk about the times with Dr. Chow easily. She avoided them every time Shannon headed the conversation in that direction.

Rafe didn't think he would have been able to handle an interrogation that lasted that long. Shannon worked the woman carefully, getting into safe territory, bringing laughter, then tears, and heading once more back to Dr. Chow. Then retreat and do it all over again.

The cursor on the computer screen in front of Rafe suddenly sped across the screen.

She's incredible.

Rafe knew that Allison was talking about Shannon. He put his hands on the keyboard and pecked his way through a message.

Tell her that someday.

I've never seen her work like this before. When you see the news stories, they're chopped and cut. You don't realize how much time you have to spend to get a story.

Yeah, the same way you do reports and situation evals.

Shannon kept hammering away, politely and firmly.

You two have a lot in common.

I know.

The break came almost an hour later. Shannon knew it was there, just beyond her reach for the last forty minutes. The woman had a secret she wanted to give up. Shannon felt it, and it drove her crazy not to be able to reach it.

Then, in a brief moment of clarity, Shannon realized how to get to it.

"China as a country isn't very friendly to girl children," Shannon said. "Since I've been here I've heard stories of women who take their newborns home and feed them oleander poison. Others instantly give them up for adoption or sell them on the black market."

"Regrettably," Ci'an said, "that's all true." She was well-spoken for someone who was primarily self-taught. "With the government enforcing only one child per family, families want boys who will grow up and care for them. At present, the male population coming of marrying age outnumbers females in a four-to-three ratio."

"Doesn't sound like it's going to be fun to be in the dating circles here," Shannon said lightly. "Unless you're a woman."

"No," Ci'an said. "Not even the women will be happy. In China women aren't prized as individuals. They're brood stock and homemakers. Useful only for producing boy children and cleaning house."

"I've talked to a lot of women who, like you, have jobs," Shannon pointed out.

"We still remain the exception to the rule. Most women have terrible lives."

"Wouldn't it be good if there was a way to make China take pride in and see the worth of its women?"

"It would, but I fear that day will never come."

"When I was talking to Dr. Chow before his unfortunate death," Shannon said, "he was talking to me about some research he was doing that would enhance the standing of women. Through genetic manipulation."

According to the news, Dr. Chow had been the victim of an unsuccessful robbery. Allison had tried to track the dead men, but the Hong Kong police had no tangible leads that she could find in their files.

Ci'an shook her head. "I don't want to speak badly of the dead, but Dr. Chow's research was no good. I saw those three girls that were made in Dr. Peters's laboratory. All of them were cursed."

Shannon tried not to let her excitement show. The time was now, but she had to be careful how she progressed. If she pushed too hard, she'd lose the woman.

She started to speak, then decided against it. Silence was sometimes an interviewer's best friend. People grew nervous when it got quiet, and that was especially true when they were on television.

"Those babies," Ci'an said in a hoarse voice a long moment later, "were all monsters. *Abominations.* Two of them killed their own mothers. I saw it happen, and there was nothing anyone could do about it."

Chapter 28

"As Dr. Chow's head nurse, I was present at the birth of all those children," Ci'an continued. "The first was born in Shanghai, and I—" She faltered then. Tears filled her eyes.

Slowly Shannon leaned forward and put her hand on the old woman's shoulder. Sometimes a single touch was better than a million words.

After a few minutes, Ci'an got control of herself. "Forgive me."

"It's all right." Shannon released her and leaned back.

"All of this," Ci'an whispered, "has been hard. Dealing with it then and talking about it all these years later. I've been silent about all the bad things that happened for so very long."

"Sometimes," Shannon said, "it helps to talk about things." She deliberately didn't try to tell the woman that talking about this, *now,* would help. That would have been too direct. What the woman had shouldered for so long took a more subtle approach because it had become so much a part of her.

"Dr. Chow persuaded me to join him with the very argument you mentioned," Ci'an said. "He said that only being able to change the genes of women indicated how special we were." She shook her head sadly. "I was no young woman then. I wasn't a fool. I just wanted to believe what he said."

"We all want to believe we are special at some point," Shannon told her.

Ci'an reached for Shannon's hand and took it in her own. Her palm was hard from years of manual labor in the hospitals.

"I recruited the girl who was killed by the giant baby," she whispered. "She was the daughter of my sister. My niece. My sister knew she shouldn't have kept a daughter, but she did. Her husband was too softhearted to insist that my sister do her duty and get rid of her."

The woman's pain and guilt radiated through Shannon. She couldn't save herself from it. Her eyes filled with tears just as the woman's did.

"I thought I would do them a favor," Ci'an said. "I talked my niece into volunteering for the experiment. I helped them negotiate enough money for my niece to attend college in America and make something of herself." Her voice broke. "And it was done. Everything went well, except that the baby got really big from the very beginning. My niece…she was such a small girl. But we thought there would be no complications."

Shannon held on to the woman's hands, anchoring her to the room instead of that time years ago.

"But there were. When I told Dr. Chow of the difficulties my niece was having with the pregnancy and that it needed to be aborted, he had her brought in. Then they strapped her to a bed and watched. My niece screamed in pain for days as the baby grew inside her like some rotting fruit."

Shannon cursed, but she didn't break eye contact with the woman. That would have broken the spell.

"They wouldn't give her anything for the pain," Ci'an continued. "They didn't want to taint the pregnancy. So my niece screamed until the baby grew so large that it suffocated her and burst her heart."

Shannon shuddered. She noted that Rafe sat at the desk mesmerized. *And I can't do this story,* Shannon reminded herself.

"Once my niece was dead," Ci'an said, "they had no choice but to take the baby. They did. When they delivered the baby, she weighed almost thirty pounds."

"Why was she so big?"

"Because of the things that Dr. Chow and Dr. Peters did to her genes. The child continued to grow at an alarming rate, but her bones were brittle. When she tried to walk or even pull herself along, she suffered multiple fractures. The doctors had to find a way to immobilize her at all times. She was made a prisoner of her own body. I was told she was incredibly intelligent, though. A genius."

"Were all of them like that?"

"No. The second was born to a girl in India. The surrogate mother died, as well. At first no one knew why. Her water broke, and she went into toxic shock. She was dead within seconds. The surgical team that delivered the baby died, too."

"Why?"

"Because the child's skin secreted poison. No one knew this till later."

"What about the third child?"

"That was the only birth that seemed not to be marked with tragedy. But only weeks after the delivery, someone killed the surrogate."

"Do you know where these children are now?"

"If there is justice in the world, they are all dead."

The vehemence in the woman's voice shocked Shannon.

"I don't know where they are," Ci'an said. "Their wretched mother took them."

"I thought their mothers were dead."

"The surrogates only. Remember—the eggs were harvested from a single woman. It was she who funded this program as Dr. Peters was getting ready to move to America. He wanted one last attempt to make as much money as he could. I was told the woman paid millions to have her children carried by others. They took her eggs and, according to her request, each was fertilized by a different father."

Rafe held up a manila folder. Seated as he was, the old woman couldn't see him.

"Did you meet the woman?" Shannon asked.

"Yes. On a number of occasions."

Shannon freed one of her hands and reached for the manila folder on the floor beside her. "I have pictures of a woman here. Can you tell me if this was the mother?"

Ci'an took the manila folder and opened it. She gazed at the pictures for only a moment before nodding.

"This is her."

All of the pictures were of Jackie Cavanaugh at different ages.

Finally, it was over. Shannon put on a smile and thanked Ci'an for her time. She and Rafe escorted the old woman downstairs and put her into a cab.

"Damn," Shannon whispered as the cab drove away.

"Yeah," Rafe agreed. He knew neither of them had the words for what they'd just heard.

"Kwan-Sook couldn't have figured you'd have found out about Jackie Cavanaugh," Allison said. She sat in front of her computer console and studied lines of code pouring across her screens. They represented the huge search that was going on through China's banking systems.

"We don't even know if Kwan-Sook is her name," Shannon said sourly.

"It really doesn't matter." Allison typed in another line of code to narrow the search. She was beginning to detect a pattern, and that was definitely good. "Kwan-Sook beats calling her Madame X."

On the computer screen, Shannon grinned. "Madame X sounds more sexy for journalism."

"We're not doing journalism," Allison reminded her gently.

"I know. That hurts, because this is a great story."

"A lot of people would get damaged by this story if it were allowed to go public."

"I agree. And I understand why you want this closed out."

"Not just me," Allison said. "President Monihan does, too."

"The biggest thing would be the harm it would do to the school."

"We narrowly avoided that last time. If this came out—"

"It would look like a cover-up."

"Yeah."

"Athena does too much good to be shut down," Shannon said.

"Glad to hear you say that. Considering the way you've felt about the school in the past."

"Not the school. Just some of the people."

"Point taken."

"Don't count on the competition between Tory and me going away. That was there even before the thing with Josie."

Allison grinned. "I know. I remember."

"What are you doing now?"

"I," Allison declared with authority, "am tracing Dr. Chow's bank accounts in the Caribbean."

"He had accounts there?"

"Yes. And before your meeting with him, the combined amounts swelled to over a million dollars."

"That's what he said Kwan-Sook paid him to meet with me."

"That's right."

"I thought information about those accounts was limited."

"It is. But I refuse to be limited."

Shannon looked straight at her through the computer camera link. "You're tracking the money that was put into those accounts."

Allison nodded. "It's proving harder than it should, but I'm patient. Kwan-Sook used a number of different accounts from different shell corporations. But she hasn't invented any tricks that I haven't seen."

"What do we need to do?" That was Rafe from somewhere in the background.

"If you want to leave," Allison said, "I—"

"No," he said. "I told you I'd stick for the duration. I meant that. You want to speak to this woman."

"I do," Allison said. "One of those packets Cavanaugh fired off headed in this direction. I want to know what they were." She typed in more code, furthering the search field. "Until I find out anything concrete, all you can do is wait and make sure you're rested for when that time comes."

"All right."

"And it *will* come, Rafe. Whoever this woman is, she owes me for what she's been doing."

"Let me know."

Allison said she would. Then she broke the connection and focused all her energies on the search for the money Dr. Chow Bao had gotten for meeting with Shannon.

The answers were there. All she had to do was sift away everything that wasn't an answer.

Shannon lay awake in bed and listened to the whirlpool bath working. The sound wasn't keeping her awake. That noise was low and moderate, not intrusive at all. It was thoughts of Rafe Santorini sitting in the tub that haunted her.

After they'd basically been put on hold by Allison, there hadn't been much to do. Both had agreed that returning to the basement where Xiaoming and her crew had let him recuperate didn't sound pleasant. Rafe had also been reluctant to let her stay on her own, so they'd gotten the suite.

Xiaoming and the others had rooms at other nearby hotels. That way they weren't all together in case Kwan-Sook or the other person involved in the attack on Dr. Chow proved to be more adept at finding them.

Although they'd tried, Rafe and Shannon hadn't had much to say to each other. There was a subtext going on beneath the surface of their words that kept demanding attention. Only neither of them would address it.

Shannon knew what her problem was. Being around that much male was distracting. When she'd been watching over Rafe while he was in a coma, she hadn't once thought of him in a sexual manner. She'd just wanted him to be all right.

But now that he was up and around, now that she had gotten Ci'an to talk and linked Jackie Cavanaugh to the egg-babies and the genetic experimentation at Lab 33 and was feeling good about herself, she was definitely aware of Rafe hitting her sexual radar. Big-time.

You need to just chill and relax, she told herself.

However, relaxation seemed to be something she couldn't do. She kept thinking of Rafe in the tub. She knew he was running the whirlpool because of his leg. He'd gotten around on it well throughout the day, but she knew he'd probably damaged it dropping off the balcony to become a human shield to save her.

She still couldn't believe he'd done that. No one she knew would have done anything like that.

He'd been watching her today, too. She'd caught him doing it. And when she did, he'd gotten embarrassed and looked away. That made it even harder to have a normal conversation. As if there was anything normal about what they were doing there.

They were risking their freedom, if not their lives, by staying. But Shannon didn't want to leave any more than Rafe and the others did. Kwan-Sook—if that was her name—owed her.

Jackie Cavanaugh owed her, too, for crossing her up at Athena, but it was too late to collect on that debt.

However, the sins of the mother—if that's what she was— could be delivered upon the child.

Abruptly, the whirlpool stopped.

Shannon listened as Rafe got up and returned to the living room area. He'd already pulled out the queen-size bed from the couch.

A moment later the television came on.

Evidently he couldn't sleep either.

With a sigh, Shannon got out of bed, thinking maybe a glass of wine would help her sleep. She wore a long T-shirt over panties. She missed the negligee she'd bought, but she hadn't felt like shopping while they'd been busy the last few days.

Chapter 29

In the living area, Rafe sat on the couch/bed clad in a pair of gray gym shorts that looked pale against his bronzed flesh. He had a pistol beside him. Both his hands were busy massaging his knee. It was visibly swollen, but he hadn't complained.

Shannon was willing to bet not many people heard complaints from him.

His eyes raked her from head to toe, pausing at her breasts and along her thighs. Shannon suddenly felt the heat of his gaze. He looked away quickly.

"How bad is your knee?" she asked.

"Not too bad," he replied. "I still have to work to keep it loose. The surgeon told me I'll eventually get most of the articulation back. It's just going to take time."

"I'm going to get a glass of wine. Do you want anything?"

"I think I saw a beer in there."

Shannon padded to the refrigerator. After she poured a glass of wine, she asked, "Do you want the beer in a glass?"

"No. Thanks."

She took the beer to him and saw that he was watching the news on television.

"Mind if I join you?" she asked.

"Sure." Rafe looked up at her with worry in his eyes. "Are you all right? That thing today was pretty ugly."

"I'm fine." Shannon sat. "Just wound up. Finding out a big piece of the last fifteen years of your life has been based on a lie is kind of…disturbing."

"Yeah. But you get through it. Everything in life changes you one way or another."

Shannon thought about the childhood she knew he'd had. His strong fingers worked the scar tissue surrounding his knee. She set the wineglass to one side.

"Here. Let me do that." She reached over and took his leg.

"It's all right," he protested. "I can handle this."

"Hey," she said quietly, "you jumped off a building and got shot to save my life. A knee massage is the least I can do for you." She didn't release his knee.

Reluctantly he let her pull his leg into her lap. She kneaded his flesh, feeling the taut muscles and the hard scar tissue beneath her fingertips. She also felt the heat of his flesh.

This is such *a bad idea,* she told herself. But she was too stubborn to stop. She was conscious of how quiet and still he'd gotten, and he didn't feel relaxed at all.

"I think that's good," he said.

She looked up at him and saw how uncomfortable he was. She also noticed that her touch had had an effect on him that the gym shorts didn't quite disguise.

"Still feels like there's a lot of tension," she said, staring into his eyes. "But maybe that's just me."

Rafe had to clear his throat to speak. "Really. It feels better. You just worked a miracle."

Unable to stop herself, she trailed her fingers up the inside of his thigh to the edge of the shorts. He trembled under her touch.

"Don't," he whispered.

Shannon smiled at him. "Don't what?" Her fingers snaked upward again, and this time she slid them under the edge of the shorts.

"I've never much cared for a tease," he said.

"I'm not teasing," she whispered.

He hesitated for just a moment, then he reached for her, gripping her by the shoulders and hauling her up to him as he leaned back against the couch.

Shannon straddled him, feeling his hardness against her flesh as she scooted upward. He groaned and his hips bucked slightly. He pulled her close, wrapping her in his strong arms. Then his lips were on hers.

She kissed him back, and her need was so great that she ground down to meet him as his hips rose. He felt so hard, so *good,* that her head seemed to spin and turn inside out.

He broke the kiss and looked up at her. "I've wanted you from the moment I first saw you almost three weeks ago. If this isn't what you want to do, you'd better stop now."

"I don't want to stop," Shannon whispered. "I bought a negligee a few days ago that I intended to tempt you with. If you ever caught up with me again."

"I saw it." Rafe rolled beneath her, sliding his length along her channel. "I thought you'd just bought it to wear."

"Not just to wear," she replied huskily. "I had you in mind."

"Good." He put his hands on her hips and pulled her even more tightly against him. He moved and drove himself against her.

Her liquid heat had already dampened her panties. She felt

herself swelling with need, wrapping his engorged flesh through the material. He bumped against her just right, and the rocking motion was already threatening to push her over the edge.

"Are you sure this is what you want?" he asked. Fire danced in his eyes.

"Yes."

With one hand, he reached down and tore the panties away. He lifted the T-shirt, then lifted her to graze his flesh against her. She was so slick that he slid through her puffy lips easily. But he didn't penetrate.

"We don't have anything," he said.

"Wait." Dizzy with passion, Shannon went to the minibar. Inside, with the snacks and bottled water, she'd seen an intimacy kit. She took out a condom and returned to Rafe. She held it up with pride. "I love staying at a hotel that thinks of everything."

Rafe started to get up.

Shannon put a hand in the center of his chest and pushed him down. Then she tore the condom package open and sheathed him with hardly any trouble at all.

This time when she threw a leg across his hips, she took him in one hand and gently guided him into her. He was hard and thick and possibly the greatest thing she'd ever felt.

He started to move, but she winced in pain.

"Wait just a minute," she whispered. "It's been a long time. I need to get…more comfortable." She rocked on him slightly, taking him slowly and steadily deeper. He held back, but she could feel his desire trembling in his body.

A moment later she had settled comfortably all the way onto him. She lifted and fell onto him, telling herself she was going to take her time—and take his breath away.

Instead, taking his cue from her, he gripped her hips and drove himself into her. Weakly she fell forward across him. His lips claimed hers and her senses exploded.

Once she'd come back to herself, she looked down and found him smiling. "That was just a fluke," she said. "I have more control than that."

"We'll see," he said.

"Ego much?" she asked. But that was the last thing she could say for a time as the world seemed to come apart around her again. His lips suckled her breasts and turned them hot and heavy.

Before she could recover, before she could once more take charge, he pushed her from him, sliding out of her. She started to protest as he laid her facedown on the bed. Before she could move, he threw a leg over her hips and slid into her from behind.

The full weight of him across her hips and back drove her crazy with desire. She rolled as best as she was able to drive her rear into him and take him deeper with each stroke. She was so wet that he had no trouble powering in and out, faster and faster.

He gripped her wrists in his hands and wrapped them under her, propped himself on his elbows to keep some of his weight off her, then held her in a tight embrace as he drove himself even deeper than he had before.

She cried out, and that embarrassed her because she didn't do that. But it felt so good she couldn't stop. He got harder and stronger inside her. She knew he was out of control now, too, could hear it in the rasp of his breath and the frantic way he moved to keep them joined.

Then he rocked forward and strained against her buttocks a final time. She crested once more, joining him in a nuclear-powered, mind-wiping climax.

After a few moments, he rolled over on his side. But he hooked her hip with his hand and rolled her over with him so he never slid free. She liked him for that. She wanted him inside her.

He kissed her shoulder blades as he held her, his hands still gripping her wrists as he hugged her strongly enough to make her feel small in his embrace.

"Wow," she said a few minutes later.

"Yeah," he said.

Then he got another condom from the mini-bar.

They made love throughout the night, sleeping for a while, then wordlessly joining again, learning more and more about what the other wanted and needed. It was the most amazing thing Shannon had ever experienced.

When she woke the next morning, she was still wrapped in his embrace, facing him this time. Looking up, she discovered that he was awake and looking down at her.

"Hi," he said.

"Good morning," she mumbled.

"It's past morning."

Shannon squinted at the balcony window and saw that the sun had been up for hours. "Oh." She looked back at him. "Have you been up long?"

"No." His eyes were serious.

"What's wrong?"

He looked at her for a moment. "I didn't plan this."

"If anyone's guilty of that, it's me." Shannon felt a little embarrassed. She pulled the sheet to her and started to get up.

"Wait," Rafe said. "I didn't mean I didn't enjoy this. I did."

"I'm glad to know that." Shannon felt hurt and confused.

Rafe reached up and brushed her hair out of her face. "I'm not very good at this."

Shannon just looked at him, dreading what he was going to say. He was going to politely brush her off. She told herself she could deal with that. That it wouldn't matter.

"I don't do things like this," Rafe said. "Unless this is going to go somewhere, I can't do it again." His voice thickened. "I like you way too much already. If you're only looking for a distraction…"

A smile spread across her face and her worries vanished. "You, Rafe Santorini, are not a distraction. You're very probably the most amazing man I've ever met."

He grinned a little self-consciously. "Maybe you're a little too impressionable."

"Maybe," she agreed. "Want to impress me again?"

He reached for her and pulled her into him.

Just after one that afternoon, while they were sharing breakfast brought up by room service, Allison called on Rafe's phone.

"I found her." Allison sounded tired. "I know where she is."

Chapter 30

Rafe stood in the prow of the speedboat they'd rented for the infiltration of the island where Allison believed Kwan-Sook was holed up. He used light-amplifying binoculars—Xiaoming and her team *were* definitely well-equipped—to scout the irregular coastline.

"Yangshan is the newest port being developed in Shanghai," Allison said over the earwigs they all wore. "Construction on it started in 2001 and it won't be finished until 2012."

"So there's a lot of building going on constantly in the meantime," Rafe said.

"Exactly."

"It provides perfect cover for someone who wishes to hide," Xiaoming added.

"Yes," Allison said. "And if you want to do upgrades to your favorite base of villainy. I tracked the money that was given to Dr. Chow to several companies. After *hours* of intensive scrutiny,

I tracked those companies back to a single corporate entity. White Dragon Enterprises. As it turns out, WDE owns a handful of development companies currently working on Yangshan Port projects. I've reviewed those projects and discovered properties that WDE owns under other names. One stood out in particular."

Rafe focused the binoculars on the coastline. Even at eleven at night many of the ships' berths were occupied and busy. Cargo cranes stood tall and imposing as they worked under bright lights.

"Black Swan Construction," he said.

"Yes," Allison said.

"Why that one?" Shannon asked. Like the others, she was dressed in black for the night. She also wore a Kevlar vest and carried a pistol on her hip.

Rafe had been reluctant to let her come along. Maybe she was trained to use small arms and a rifle, but training was a lot different from being in the field.

More than that, he hated the idea of losing her after he'd found her.

"Black Swan Construction did a lot of dredging to clear the port for deep-water operation. This is the only port in Shanghai capable of handling off-loading of container ships. But it was also the perfect smokescreen for underwater construction."

"You're sure there's an underwater complex under that construction yard?" Rafe asked.

"Yes. There has to be. Based on the electricity usage in that section of the city, I'd say it's pretty large."

"Why has no one else found this place?" Xiaoming asked.

"Because no one else has been looking where I've been looking," Allison said. "This is what I do." She paused. "If I'm wrong, we'll look elsewhere. But I don't think I am."

"What about the satellite?"

"It'll be in position by the time you get in place."

Allison was also providing satellite surveillance on the op and monitoring the video equipment they wore. She would be their extra eyes.

"All right." Rafe took a deep breath. "Let's go see what we can see."

Shannon felt awkward aboard the speedboat. She wasn't used to the heaviness of all the gear, and the Kevlar vest felt like a straitjacket. She was also the only one who didn't have something to do aboard the boat. She sat in the back as Rafe powered them toward the docks.

You really *shouldn't be here,* she told herself again. *Athena-trained or not, you're not used to operating at this level.*

But she hadn't been able to stay away. The story was here. Maybe Allison had all kinds of data to back that up, but Shannon felt it in her bones.

Minutes later Rafe powered the boat into a slip at an engine repair shop a quarter mile from the construction site. The shop was closed, and a high security fence surrounded the grounds.

Shannon clambered out with the others and they made their way along the walkways lining the docks. They all wore long jackets like most of the other workers at the sites. The monsoon season had hung on and the night was filled with spitting rain and the promise of more storms.

No one in the group spoke. Although she was dying to talk and break some of the tension she felt, Shannon remained silent, as well.

As it turned out, Kwan-Sook was expecting company. Extra guards were posted around the construction yard's perimeter. There were also guardhouses, after a fashion.

Rafe spotted the men in the tall earthmovers and he didn't

miss the fact that they were positioned so they had overlapping fields of fire.

"She's scared of someone," Xiaoming said.

"Why do you say that?" Shannon asked.

"Because she has so many guards posted," Rafe said as he watched through his binoculars.

"You can't post this many guards on a regular basis and hope not to get noticed," Xiaoming stated. "She has more posted tonight than she normally does. You can believe that."

"How many do you count?" Rafe asked.

Xiaoming hesitated a moment. "Stationary and roving? Fourteen."

"Can we take fourteen?"

"We can take a few of them before the others are alerted. We could probably take them all, but not before the ones that are sure to be below are alerted."

"That's what I was thinking, too," Rafe admitted.

"Isn't there some kind of air shaft or back door to the under-ground room?" Shannon asked.

Rafe and Xiaoming looked at her.

"I mean," Shannon said, "there always is in the movies."

"If this was a movie," Xiaoming said, "perhaps we could count on that. In real life we do it another way."

"Disguises?" Shannon asked. "Because I thought of that and figured that wouldn't work at all."

"Actually," Rafe said, "it's going to be simpler than that." He pulled back into the darkness.

"These guys aren't loyal minions like they have in the movies," Rafe said. "They're rent-a-thugs. Professionals or semi-professionals. As long as everything is easy, as long as they hold superior numbers or superior position—"

"Or they truly believe in their cause," Xiaoming put in.

"And we have no reason to think they do," Rafe said. "Then—when confronted with someone who has superior numbers, fire-power or position—they'll fade the heat."

"What do you mean?" Shannon asked.

"They're trained to fight," Xiaoming said. "But they're also trained to surrender. We just have to convince them to surrender."

"Or die," Hua said as she assembled the sniper rifle she'd carried in an equipment bag. She smiled. "I can be very convincing."

Shannon believed the woman.

Rafe stepped out of the darkness and came up behind the man he'd targeted. The guards weren't as well trained as he was. That made a difference.

When he reached the man, Rafe slid an arm around his neck in a choke hold, then screwed the barrel of his pistol into the side of the man's head. The man froze at once. Under the conditions, it was the only intelligent thing to do.

Rafe spoke Cantonese so the man would understand him. "If you do anything—*anything*—you're a dead man. Nod if you agree."

The man hesitated, then nodded.

"Now here's what I want you to do," Rafe said. "Use your radio. Talk to your men. Tell them to withdraw from the area."

The man tried, for just an instant, to be tough. "You're going to be in a lot of trouble."

"You won't be around to see how it all works out," Rafe promised.

The man grabbed the handi-talker on his shoulder. He spoke quickly.

"They're not convinced," Xiaoming said over the earwig. "The guards are moving in on your position."

"Convince them," Rafe said. Then he turned his attention to the man he held. "Tell your men that one of them is about to die."

The man didn't respond.

"Now!" Rafe ordered.

In a broken, scared voice, the man did as he was told.

"They're still coming," Xiaoming said.

"Which one?" Rafe asked, intending the question for Hua.

"The man in the earthmover in the southeast corner," Hua said.

"Tell them your buddy in the southeast corner is dead," Rafe said.

The man did.

In that instant, the man in the earthmover tried to bail. But even as he moved, his head snapped back and he sat—for a moment—in the control cabin. Then he began the long, silent fall to the earth.

"They've stopped," Xiaoming said. "Now they're withdrawing."

"There's an entrance to the underground area," Rafe said. "Where do I find it?"

"In the warehouse. There's a cargo lift. It goes down if you have a key card. Then you can step off into the tunnels there."

"Do you have a key card?"

"No."

"Don't worry about the key card," Allison said. "I can get around that."

Rafe frisked the man he held, removing his weapons and finding his identification. He held it up to the man. "If you come back with friends, if someone shows up that I think is connected to you, if the police come, you're going to die."

Fear showed in the man's eyes.

"Do you believe me?" Rafe asked.

"Yes," the man whispered. "Yes, I believe you."

Rafe released him. "Then go away."

The man fled.

Rafe held his position until his team was ready. Then they went forward.

Anxiety threaded through every fiber of Shannon's being. She had to remind herself not to breathe shallowly and to keep her lungs filled with fresh oxygen. She followed Rafe, only a few steps behind him when they reached the warehouse.

He hesitated outside the door marked Personnel and held an electronic device to the lock. A moment later the lock snicked back.

Allison, Shannon realized. *Man, she must really love the cool spy toys.* Back at the academy, Allison had always loved the cutting-edge computer hardware and software.

No one was inside the warehouse.

They made their way through stacks of building supplies to the cargo lift.

Rafe held the electronic box to the card reader. A moment later the lift sank into the floor. Rafe, Xiaoming and the others stood on the side and pointed their weapons down into the lighted hallway beneath.

The hallway was empty.

"Okay," Rafe said. "One at a time."

They dropped into the hallway and waited until everyone was together again. There was only one door at the end of the hallway.

Rafe used the electronic box and they went forward with their weapons ready. He carried a silenced submachine pistol in his hands and moved in a slightly sideways gait.

Shannon's heart pounded. She went empty-handed. Rafe had told her not to draw her weapon until she knew she had to use it. Now she knew why. As keyed-up as she was, she might have accidentally discharged it and shot one of her teammates. She liked to think she wouldn't have made that mistake, but she was honest enough with herself to realize she didn't know.

When she heard the familiar beeping ahead of her, Shannon knew they were close to their quarry. And she also now knew what the sound was.

A door blocked the way. Without warning, locks within the door slammed shut.

"We're blown," Rafe said. "Get us through that door."

Jintao stepped forward and slapped a shaped plastic explosives charge to the door.

Shannon stood and watched until Rafe grabbed her by the front of the Kevlar vest and yanked her into the wall.

"Now," Jintao said softly and pressed the detonator in his hand.

Sound and fury exploded to violent life in the hallway. But it was controlled enough that only the door was blown to pieces. Before those pieces had time to fall to the floor, Rafe had the submachine gun in his hands and was moving through it.

Chapter 31

Shannon followed Xiaoming through the shattered door. Smoke filled the hallway from the blast, but there wasn't as much of it as she'd expected. In the movies there was always a cloud.

She stopped thinking about that, stopped thinking at all when she saw what lay inside the room.

A gargantuan woman lay in a specially constructed hospital bed in the center of the room. She had to be at least nine feet tall and weigh at least a thousand pounds. She was a quivering pool of blubber.

Fear and outrage warred for control of her misshapen features. Her hair was pulled back.

All around her and on the ceiling were dozens of computer monitors. Each monitor pulsed data and images. Shannon saw that some were news feeds, but others appeared to be views into public buildings and private homes.

The huge woman had cables attached to her head. No, that

was wrong, Shannon saw. The cables were actually implanted *inside* her head.

For a moment Shannon thought she was going to be sick.

The sight evidently had an effect on Rafe and the others, as well. They all stood speechless with their weapons drawn.

"Shannon," the huge woman said.

"Kwan-Sook," Shannon whispered.

"Yes." The massive head didn't move, but the frightened eyes did. "Are you here to kill me?"

Drawn by the woman's helplessness, Shannon walked toward the bed. Rafe tried to stop her, but she pushed his hand away. This was a story. A *hell* of a story. And she had to know it.

"We're not here to kill you," Shannon said softly. "We came so that we could understand."

"There's nothing to understand," Kwan-Sook said. "I am what my mother made me."

"Your mother was Jackie Cavanaugh."

Kwan-Sook hesitated, then said, "Yes."

"Aldritch Peters altered your genetic makeup."

"Yes. My mother learned of his research. Since Marion Gracelyn destroyed the child that she carried, my mother wanted to have children. But she wanted them to be special."

"What…" Shannon faltered. "What did they do to you?"

"My intellect was enhanced. My IQ doesn't even register." Kwan-Sook took a breath and the sound of the hospital equipment beeped around her. "But I was trapped in this body. For a while they experimented on me, trying to find some way to counteract the weakness in my bones. But they couldn't."

Shannon sipped her breath and tried to turn off the feelings of sympathy that swirled within her.

"I think in the end even my mother would have let them kill me. But I was smarter than they were. I used my access to computers to create businesses for myself. I knew I needed money if I was going to protect myself. I hired a team of mercenaries to break me out of my prison when I was sixteen. They killed anyone who tried to stop them. And then, for the first time in my life, I was free."

Shannon listened, stunned. "You could have found someone to help you."

"No. No one could help me. I could only help myself." Kwan-Sook's eyes locked on Shannon's. "So I helped myself. When Allison Gracelyn and her agents killed my mother, I became Allison's enemy, as well." Her eyes took on a bright sheen. "Even if she didn't love me the way she was supposed to, Jackie Cavanaugh was my mother."

"But your mother knew about you," Shannon said. "When she died, she sent you a package."

"She knew about me, but she didn't love me. In my whole life I only saw her in the flesh a handful of times." Kwan-Sook paused. "I know she was repulsed by me. Everyone is."

"Ask her what was in the package," Allison prompted through the earwig.

"Your mother cared about you or she wouldn't have sent you that package," Shannon said, changing the presentation of the question.

"She sent that to me so I could get revenge for her death." Kwan-Sook opened her mouth carefully and laughed. Her teeth were broken stumps in her head. "We were born to be her revenge. The package contained a third of all the information she'd collected—all the blackmail victims and secrets—over the years." She looked at Shannon. "That's how I knew about you."

"Me?"

"My mother was very clever," Kwan-Sook said. "She broke into the Athena Academy's computers and discovered you and Allison Gracelyn were driven to beat the other girls. My mother pretended to be Allison and sent you e-mails to frame one of the others."

"Josie Lockworth," Shannon said.

"Yes." Kwan-Sook did the obscene laugh again. "Is that not the most clever thing you've ever heard?"

Shannon didn't say anything.

"And then you were reborn," Kwan-Sook said, "as the academy's only failure and the greatest enemy they could ever hope to have."

Shannon shook her head. It was all so sick and twisted.

"Now what are you going to do with me?" Kwan-Sook asked. "If you try to move me from this place, you could break every bone in my body. You might even kill me. Is that what you want?"

"No," Shannon said.

"Why? Because you pity me?"

Shannon didn't bother to deny the charge. She did pity the woman. Not just her physical state but the way Jackie Cavanaugh had brought her into the world and then didn't bother to give her a mother's love. She realized how close she and Rafe had come to being just like the hideous creature lying on that hospital bed.

"I don't want your pity," Kwan-Sook stated angrily. "Save it for someone who is weak. I have millions of dollars. If you're not willing to kill me, my lawyers will eventually get me out of prison and make all charges go away." Her eyes brightened. "You're here in China illegally. As spies. I think you'll all be shot before I even have to go to court." She laughed again.

She's insane, Shannon realized. But Kwan-Sook was a functioning madwoman. She was dangerous.

"In fact, how do you know I haven't already sent for the Shanghai police?" Kwan-Sook asked.

Abruptly, all of the dozens of computer monitors changed to exactly one scene. They all showed Allison Gracelyn seated at her desk. She looked tired and worn, but she also looked indomitable.

"I know," Allison said in a harsh voice. "I'm inside your head now, and you can't do a thing unless I let you."

Shannon felt a surge of pride as she looked at her friend. And she was surprised to discover that she thought of Allison as exactly that: her friend.

Kwan-Sook opened her horrid mouth and screamed. Without warning, something metallic and inhumanly quick darted from beneath the bed.

It was an appendage of some sort. Shannon had read about experimental robot arms that would be under the control of paraplegics. But none of those were as sleek and efficient as what streaked for her.

Or as deadly.

She saw the barb at the end of it and knew that it was a weapon. Instinctively she swept her right arm across her body in a blocking maneuver. Her forearm knocked the metal whiplike arm off course. It streaked across her shoulder, cutting into the flesh, then struck the wall behind her.

By that time, Rafe and Xiaoming had their weapons up and firing. Bullets chopped into the gargantuan body and soaked the sheets with blood.

The arm had embedded in the wall behind Shannon. It gave a couple fitful tries to pull free, then went slack.

The hospital machines all filled the room with a steady warning chirp.

No one came to help.

"Are you okay?" Rafe was at Shannon's side, examining her wound.

"I'm fine." Shannon couldn't take her eyes from the corpse lying on the massive bed.

"Something's wrong," Allison said. Her voice came from the earwigs as well as the room's speakers. She worked her keyboard frantically. "Someone else is in the computer. They've hacked in from outside."

The computer monitors went blank.

"Where's the hack coming from?" Rafe demanded. He jogged out of the room.

"Upstairs," Allison replied.

Rafe ran, and Shannon was at his heels.

By the time they reached the cargo lift, a group of armed men was waiting on them. They lifted their weapons and fired down into the hallway as the lift rose.

Rafe tried to stop. Shannon saw him dig in, but the weakened knee went out from under him, stranding him in the path of the bullets.

Instantly Shannon launched herself at his back, throwing her arms around him. They went down together, sliding in a tangle of arms beneath the cargo lift, which was already up a couple feet and rising.

Bullets slapped the hallway floor where Rafe had been. The lift shielded them from the gunners just as Shannon had hoped.

Xiaoming pulled a grenade from her combat vest. "Grenade!" she yelled as she threw it onto the rising lift.

Shannon wrapped her arms around Rafe. The grenade exploded and the noise sounded impossibly loud in the enclosed space.

Rafe broke out of her grip and pulled a knife from his boot. He slashed the hydraulic lines attached to the lift. Thick viscous fluid poured out, but the lift quit rising.

"Someone is capturing Kwan-Sook's files," Allison said. "I can't get them. I'm blocked."

"We're still moving," Rafe said. He sheathed his knife and picked up the submachine pistol. He looked at Shannon, then kissed her. In the next minute he was gone, hauling himself onto the lift.

Shannon followed, but Xiaoming and Hua blew past her. Jintao paused on the lift and offered his hand. She took it and he pulled her up.

* * *

"I've got a lock on the download," Allison said. "It's in the main building."

Rafe got his bearings, remembering the blueprints Allison had given them. He ran, but his leg throbbed mercilessly and threw his gait off. It worked all right in front-to-back motion, but he knew any lateral movement was going to be nearly impossible.

Xiaoming was at his side and matched his pace.

A trio of gunners stood at the doorway to the main building. Rafe brought up the submachine pistol and squeezed off three-round bursts as Xiaoming did the same. He felt at least two rounds hit the Kevlar and another plow through his side.

But the three men went down.

Inside the main building, Rafe slowed his pace and went to the left. Xiaoming went to the right. They created an overlapped field of fire as they went more deeply into the building.

"At the back of the building," Allison said.

They kept going, moving quickly. Two more gunners held positions, but they went down, as well.

Then they reached the back office and saw the woman standing at the computer terminal. She was tall and beautiful, with café-au-lait skin and short-cropped black hair that framed her face. She wore counterterrorist BDUs and carried pistols at her hip and under her shoulder.

"Hello, Captain Santorini," the woman said.

"Step away from the computer," Rafe ordered.

The woman lifted her left hand and showed the grenade she was holding. Her thumb flicked and the pin fell to the floor with an audible ping.

"Oops," the woman said and smiled to show even white teeth. "I'd advise you not to shoot unless you want us all to go *boom*."

"We might survive," Xiaoming said. "I guarantee that I'll

shoot you between the eyes. You'll expire before that three-second fuse does."

The woman looked back at the computer. "I've been following you people for days," she said conversationally. "I was beginning to wonder if you were ever going to find my dear sister."

Rafe held the submachine pistol steady. "Kwan-Sook was your sister?"

"Was?" The woman smiled. "So she's dead, is she?"

Rafe didn't say anything.

"It's just as well. I wasn't going to let her live anyway. She was far too dangerous. Even to me." The woman smiled.

"So which one are you?" Rafe asked, thinking if he opened a dialogue, it would buy them a little time.

"I'm Echo," the woman said. She raised her voice. "Did you hear me, Allison? It's going to be a name you'll hear again and again."

None of these women are sane, Rafe thought.

"Well," Echo said. "Looks like my download is all done. Time to go." She tossed the grenade at them.

Xiaoming was quicker on the trigger than Rafe was, but he fired, too, already starting the three-second count.

One...

But instead of going down with her face blasted into ruin, the woman smiled again. Somehow, even at the short distance, Rafe knew that he and Xiaoming had missed her.

Or had they?

As he watched, another of Xiaoming's bullets stopped in midair right in front of Echo's face. Then it fell to the ground. Echo leaped up and caught a rope that trailed through an opening in the ceiling.

Two...

Rafe went to ground, wrapping a hand over his head.

The grenade went off. Thankfully it was a high-explosive grenade instead of an antipersonnel one.

Dazed and deafened, Rafe got to his feet with difficulty. He ran to the computer terminal with the submachine pistol and gazed up through the hole. As he watched, the woman climbed up a rope ladder to a helicopter that was already flying away.

"It's too late," Rafe said. "She's getting away."

"I see her," Allison said. "I see her, and there's not a damn thing I can do about it."

Rafe lowered his weapon. There wasn't anything any of them could do. The game, whatever it was that Allison was doing, wasn't over.

"Get your team out of there," Allison instructed. "Get safe."

Rafe turned and limped out of the building. Shannon met him, then slid up under his arm and helped him walk to the waiting speedboat. She squeezed him and he hugged her back.

Epilogue

Shannon walked through the receding tide along the North Carolina beach. Although Jacksonville wasn't Rafe's home, he'd wanted to redo his rehab there.

She'd missed him when she'd had to return to New York and make sure she still had a job at ABS. Corporate had been angry at first, but while she and Rafe had been forced to wait for Allison to arrange passage for them back to the United States, she'd filmed several pieces about Chinese women and their pursuit of equality not only for themselves but for the baby girls that were habitually put to death there.

When she'd shown the pieces at ABS, there hadn't been a dry eye in the room. It was, Shannon had had to admit, some of the best work she'd ever done.

But that was because she was in a good place in her life. So much of the old hurt and confusion was gone.

More than that, she was in love in a way she'd never known before.

Rafe had left her alone to fight her own battles with the production company. She'd loved him even more for that because she knew it was in his nature to champion the battles of others.

Instead he'd concentrated on getting healthy.

And he'd sent her flowers at work every day.

None of them had had a card, but she knew they were from him. They couldn't be from anyone else.

He hadn't been at the cabin when she'd arrived. It was her fault for arriving early, but when the flight had opened up, she couldn't resist. She gazed out at the rolling waves of the Atlantic Ocean and felt more complete than she had in a long time.

She was even talking to Allison on a regular basis. And, through Allison, she was starting to talk to others who had graduated from Athena Academy. She'd even had a good talk with Christine Evans.

It was like returning to a family she thought she'd lost.

She smiled at the setting sun. Life couldn't get any better.

"Hey."

Recognizing the voice behind her, she turned to find Rafe standing there.

He looked tanned and fit. He wore only swim trunks. He carried his scars proudly. They were part of him, and she knew he'd paid a price for them. They'd all contributed to making him who he was.

And she loved who he was.

"You're early," he said.

"Are you complaining?"

He shook his head and smiled. "No. Just don't like the idea of not being here if you needed me."

"I'm fine." Shannon nodded out at the ocean. "There's a lot of peace here. I can see why you enjoy it."

"If I stayed in New York, we could probably see each other every night."

"No," Shannon said. "You're more complete out here right now than you would be there."

He took her hand. "You can hear yourself think," he said. "I've had a lot of thinking to do."

"Oh? Did you hurt yourself?"

"Not yet." He grinned at her. "The phone works. You could have called, let me know you'd be a couple hours early."

"I wanted to surprise you."

"You don't surprise me," he told her. "You make me happy."

"A woman likes to be mysterious."

"Okay. You make me mysteriously happy. Or you mysteriously make me happy. Take it however you want it." He put his hands on her sides and drew her close.

"I got your flowers," she said.

"You did."

"Every day."

"Every day?" He shook his head. "I didn't send flowers every day. I didn't send them Tuesday."

"Maybe I didn't get flowers Tuesday."

He smiled at her. "Then I'll have to have a word with the florist, because I left strict orders."

"The flowers were wonderful," Shannon said. "No card. That made them mysterious."

"Well, your mysterious ways left me inspired."

"Nice try." Shannon ran a finger along his lips. She felt his body responding against hers and she liked that he could lose control that easily around her. "The flowers made everyone in the office talk."

"I know. That's why I sent them. You give a woman flowers, she knows she's loved. You send them to her work, she knows everyone knows she's loved."

"You're a very smart man."

"I try," he whispered as he bent down and kissed her.

In that kiss, Shannon realized that he wasn't the only one who had little control over personal responses.

"Well," she said huskily, "do you want to go back to the cabin or leave interesting impressions here in the sand?"

* * * * *

Don't miss the next exciting Athena Force Adventure,
Untouchable by Stephanie Doyle.
Available June 2008.
Turn the page for a sneak preview.

Chapter 1

"Lilith! You must come quickly. Lilith!"

The sound of her name penetrated her sleep. She focused on the language that was being used. English. Not Hindi. One of the nuns rather than a villager. Slowly she opened her eyes and turned her head toward the noise. The heavy tarp that served as the door to her hut was pulled back. Sister Joseph filled the space.

"They are asking for you on the hill. You must hurry."

The plump older woman stepped inside, and instantly Lilith pushed herself farther back on her sleeping mat. "Do not get too close. I am not dressed."

The sister obeyed and turned away. Lilith got out of bed and began to assemble what had become her unique habit. First a cotton slip. Then a long bolt of silk she pulled over her head that covered her from neck to foot, shoulder to wrist. Ties secured the material to her body, making the uniform less cumbersome. At times she was sure she was mistaken for a mummy.

Finally she reached for the gloves that sat on her writing table, the only other piece of furniture in the small hut other than her sleeping mat. As she slid the gloves up her arms, Lilith felt the material cling to her skin. It was a sensual feeling that she allowed herself to enjoy for only a second.

"The brothers have need of your…medicine," Sister Joseph told her with her back still turned to her. The brothers were Buddhist monks rather than Christian Brothers, but the nuns who lived in the village situated below the monastery treated them with as much reverence.

"They have a visitor among them. Looking for retreat, I think. I believe a leg wound has festered."

"Leprosy?" Lilith asked. "Has he become infected by one of the villagers?"

"No." Sister Joseph shook her head. "He hasn't been exposed to anyone long enough. Unless he contracted it somewhere else. Listen to us," she said sheepishly. "A man comes in with a wound and we automatically assume it is one of the rarest and hardest to contract diseases in the world. We're growing paranoid, I think."

"But this is our world," Lilith reminded her. "It is what we see every day. It is natural to make assumptions. I will go to the brothers. I'll see what can be done."

The woman backed out of the hut and Lilith followed her at a distance. It was still night but nearing morning. Animals in the forest just beyond the village sent signals to their comrades to start the day. They were familiar sounds but still exotic to Lilith's ears even after all this time.

She followed the path that led from her camp up a steep hill that was flattened at the top. A hundred years ago devout monks had come together to build a monastery as a tribute to Buddha. Today it served the same purpose.

Deep in the region of Arunachal Pradesh, near the China

border, this tract of forest was almost forgotten to the rest of India. As were her human inhabitants. It's why the monks had claimed this space in their search for solitude. It's why the lepers had been banished here, ejected from society.

It's why Lilith called it home.

The trail steepened noticeably, but Lilith didn't falter, her legs well used to the path. Although she chose to live among the Christian nuns who had come to care for the lepers, it was with the monks with whom she continued her spiritual education. Poor Sister Joseph tried so faithfully to convert Lilith. But while she enjoyed the stories of the man known as Jesus, for in many ways he was also an outcast from his people, there was something about the monks' teachings that appealed to her.

Maybe because she was surrounded by so much death, the idea of coming back to life to try again appealed to her. Obviously there was more to the religion, and Lilith embraced all facets of it. But it was the idea of returning as something different, someone different, that appealed to her.

Not that she ever planned to tell Sister Joseph. The woman would be crushed if she knew there was no hope for conversion. Still, despite their varying religious beliefs, the monks and the nuns had no problem coexisting. If neither subscribed to the other's beliefs, they still respected the sacrifice each had made for their faith.

As she climbed higher, the air thinned. Lilith could see the structure in the dark. The monastery was built of stone and mud bricks. An impressive site, it rose three stories and had over a hundred different rooms linked by long corridors. It was a square design with an orchid garden in the center of it that Lilith knew the monks referred to as "the inner sanctum."

At the main entrance Lilith pulled down hard on a rope several times to announce her presence. The bell clang could be heard throughout the compound.

Eventually it opened, and beyond the door she recognized Tenzig, one of the younger brothers. His head was shaved and he was wrapped in the traditional saffron-colored robe that declared his spiritual path. His expression was, as ever, serene. He stepped back to allow Lilith to enter, clearly not surprised by her arrival but not in any particular rush. They spoke in the hushed tones of his language as he directed her through the labyrinth of hallways.

"Tell me again, why I am here?" Not that she didn't trust Sister Joseph's version of events, but she found herself needing the distraction of conversation. There was always risk involved when her medicine was needed. It always made her nervous. She could feel her heart racing just thinking about what needed to be done.

"A visitor came to us. Looking for peace. He walked with a limp. Now the fever has taken him and we fear the only recourse is to remove the leg. He needs to…sleep…before we can do this. You understand?"

"Sister Peter has seen him?"

"She is already with him. We went to her first."

Sister Peter had recently arrived from the United States. A medical school dropout who had been called by her faith to take a different path, she had proven herself an invaluable asset among the monks, the nuns and the villagers very quickly. If Sister Peter was concerned the leg would have to come off, then the situation was as grave as Tenzig said.

"You can't take him to a town? Find a real doctor?" Lilith could only imagine the shock the man would suffer to be put to sleep against his will only to wake to find a leg missing.

"There is no time and it is too far to travel even by automobile. Also, we think he would not want to leave this place. We think he would not want the exposure that his wound might cause in a village large enough to have a hospital."

Lilith nodded. Many who came to the monastery who claimed to be searching for peace were actually looking to get lost. This man, it seemed, was no exception. A criminal, maybe. Dangerous, possibly. Perhaps she would serve a greater good by giving him more than a numbing sleep. It would be so easy. A simple touch.

If only death weren't so very disgusting to her.

They stopped beside a door and Tenzig knocked gently. He was commanded to enter. Inside the room Lilith saw another brother, Punab, sitting side by side with Sister Peter as the two of them tended to the man on the bed.

The patient was naked but for a cloth that had been draped over his hips, no doubt in deference to the sister's sensibilities. His hair was thick and ink-black. Damp, too, from either the fever or the cold compresses being applied.

His chest was broad and covered with the same inky black hair as on his head and well defined with muscle. His legs, too, looked thick. Strong. It was as if he exuded strength despite the flush of fever on his cheeks. There was a heaviness to the man though he wasn't fat. A solidness that his entire body conveyed. Even in his hands and his feet.

Lilith wondered how much his body matched his spirit. If they were at all close, she predicted he would be stubborn. It would not be easy to kill this man.

Cole's Red-Hot Pursuit

Cole Westmoreland is a man who gets what he wants. And he wants independent and sultry Patrina Forman! She resists him—until a Montana blizzard traps them together. For three delicious nights, Cole indulges Patrina with his brand of seduction. When the sun comes out, Cole and Patrina are left to wonder—will this be the end of the passion that storms between them?

Look for

COLE'S RED-HOT PURSUIT

by USA TODAY bestselling author

BRENDA JACKSON

Available in June 2008 wherever you buy books.

Always Powerful, Passionate and Provocative.

Romantic
SUSPENSE

Sparked by Danger,
Fueled by Passion.

Seduction Summer:
Seduction in the sand…and a killer on the beach.

Silhouette Romantic Suspense invites you to the hottest
summer yet with three connected stories from some
of our steamiest storytellers! Get ready for…

Killer Temptation
by **Nina Bruhns;**
a millionaire this tempting is worth a little danger.

Killer Passion
by **Sheri WhiteFeather;**
an FBI profiler's forbidden passion incites a
killer's rage,

and

Killer Affair
by **Cindy Dees;**
this affair with a mystery man is to die for.

Look for

KILLER TEMPTATION by Nina Bruhns in June 2008
KILLER PASSION by Sheri WhiteFeather in July 2008
and
KILLER AFFAIR by Cindy Dees in August 2008.

Available wherever you buy books!

Visit Silhouette Books at www.eHarlequin.com   SRS27586

REQUEST YOUR FREE BOOKS!

2 FREE NOVELS PLUS 2 FREE GIFTS!

HARLEQUIN®

INTRIGUE®

Breathtaking Romantic Suspense

YES! Please send me 2 FREE Harlequin Intrigue® novels and my 2 FREE gifts (gifts are worth about $10). After receiving them, if I don't wish to receive any more books, I can return the shipping statement marked "cancel." If I don't cancel, I will receive 6 brand-new novels every month and be billed just $4.24 per book in the U.S. or $4.99 per book in Canada, plus 25¢ shipping and handling per book and applicable taxes, if any*. That's a savings of close to 15% off the cover price! I understand that accepting the 2 free books and gifts places me under no obligation to buy anything. I can always return a shipment and cancel at any time. Even if I never buy another book from Harlequin, the two free books and gifts are mine to keep forever.

182 HDN EEZ7   382 HDN EEZK

Name	(PLEASE PRINT)	
Address		Apt. #
City	State/Prov.	Zip/Postal Code

Signature (if under 18, a parent or guardian must sign)

Mail to the **Harlequin Reader Service:**
IN U.S.A.: P.O. Box 1867, Buffalo, NY 14240-1867
IN CANADA: P.O. Box 609, Fort Erie, Ontario L2A 5X3

Not valid to current subscribers of Harlequin Intrigue books.

Want to try two free books from another line?
Call 1-800-873-8635 or visit www.morefreebooks.com.

* Terms and prices subject to change without notice. N.Y. residents add applicable sales tax. Canadian residents will be charged applicable provincial taxes and GST. This offer is limited to one order per household. All orders subject to approval. Credit or debit balances in a customer's account(s) may be offset by any other outstanding balance owed by or to the customer. Please allow 4 to 6 weeks for delivery. Offer available while quantities last.

Your Privacy: Harlequin is committed to protecting your privacy. Our Privacy Policy is available online at www.eHarlequin.com or upon request from the Reader Service. From time to time we make our lists of customers available to reputable third parties who may have a product or service of interest to you. If you would prefer we not share your name and address, please check here. ☐

ATHENA FORCE

Heart-pounding romance and thrilling adventure.

A new 12 book continuity begins this August with *Line of Sight* by Rachel Caine.

The Good Thief by Judith Leon
Charade by Kate Donovan
Vendetta by Meredith Fletcher
Stacked Deck by Terry Watkins
Moving Target by Lori A. May
Breathless by Sharron McClellan
Without a Trace by Sandra K. Moore
Flashpoint by Connie Hall
Beneath the Surface by Meredith Fletcher
Untouchable by Stephanie Doyle
Disclosure by Nancy Holder

Available wherever you buy books.